Wind in the Stone

Wind in the Stone

~

Andre Norton

AVON • EOS

Copyright © 1999 by Andre Norton
Interior design by Kellan Peck
ISBN: 0-380-97602-1

AVON EOS TRADEMARK REG. U.S. PAT. OFF. AND IN OTHER COUNTRIES, MARCA REGISTRADA,
HECHO EN U.S.A.

Printed in the U.S.A.

FIRST EDITION

With deepest appreciation to Rose Wolf, without whose ability to read scribbled revisions and translate them into smooth prose this book would never have come to be; and to Jennifer Brehl, an editor whose aid in a stressful time meant so very much.

Wind in the Stone

Part I

1

AMONG THESE HIGH AND NARROW MOUNTAIN VALLEYS, THE PAST winter had been a cruel one. Supplies carefully harvested and gathered during the short summer had shrunk. There were tightly pulled in belts and children who sometimes whimpered in their sleep, sucking with cracked lips on the edge of thin blankets during frost-filled nights. Even the carefully selected breeding stock for the next season had been twice more culled and slaughtered. It seemed as if the world was passing into a punishing grip of cold.

Now there was sluggish stirring suggesting the belated coming of spring. The first trader's caravan of the season had set out, though other merchants had shaken their heads at such recklessness.

Not only the traders ventured so: a handful of other travelers always joined such trains, either paying a few coins or offering to help with the animals. No one wanted to risk the early spring trails alone—all too often, deadly rockfalls occurred.

So it was with the young man who had drifted slowly to the end of the train of pack ponies. He was mounted on a horse so bony that its joints seemed to crack with every step it took. Now he edged himself and that sorry steed into the shadow of a rock spur as the others plodded by. Though it was still only mid-morning, men and beasts alike looked as if they'd been on the trail for hours.

The rider did not turn his head to view the trail back, but his attitude was that of one listening; and he was muttering almost at a whisper—a gabble of sounds that bore little resemblance to human speech. He pulled his riding cloak tighter against the probing finger of a sharp breeze, though he had lived long enough in the heart of the heights to accept the dreary cold.

Of course, he had been well housed. His thin lips curved in a smile that was half sneer, for, behind him there still showed the towers and walls of Valarian, the Place of Learning, where he had been a novice—whether or no in good standing—until a day ago.

That sprawl of buildings, which had been added to until it choked a valley and the mountains refused it any expansion, was so old that its core might have been wrought from the very bones of the earth. Among all the scholars, who blinked in their study cubicles like distempered, disturbed owls, there was probably not one who was interested enough in the past so lost in time—the era when the first stones of the first wall had been fitted together.

In years agone, the Place of Learning had housed many more seekers of knowledge than the shrunken number who used the nearly deserted halls today. There were names out of legend connected with it; but nowadays those gathered there were like the froth floating on a jack of ale—bubbles that never sank below the surface.

Each scholar had long since settled into a chosen area of study. His or her learning might be deep and authoritative, yet the subject would be nearly meaningless to a neighbor. Had anything really useful come out of there, even in the generation immediately past?

The rider's head snapped to the left as he caught a faint sound from the rocks. His lips pursed, and he loosed a chitter that sounded much like the complaint of a rockrat finding its

home territory invaded. Listening, he waited; however, there
was no movement in the brush, no misshapen shadow flitting from one rock cover to the next. Irasmus, fourth son of
a border warden by his third wife, smiled again. He dug
his heel into the mount's tough hide, and the horse shambled on.

He had come this way—how many years ago? Season
ran into season in the Place of Learning; they spoke there
of eons rather than days, months, or years. His mother who
had sent him to Valarian after seeing him engaged in one
of his secretive games in their neglected garden. He had
expected punishment; but instead, when he had followed
her obediently to her bower, his real life had begun.

Mind talents were largely a matter for bards and ballad
makers now; once, however, those fortunate enough to have
such had ruled without putting hand to sword hilt. On that
long-past afternoon, the shy youth had been encouraged to
try things that had never occurred to him.

Irasmus's mother had been a scrawny, gaunt-faced female very sparing of words, yet one who could, with a single glance, set a servant—or a child—quaking. He never
remembered her showing any approbation of his efforts to
please her; and his failures were made doubly sour by her
set face, just as the weapon trials with his brothers in the
arms yard had gained nothing but jeers from them and his
father. Still, he had known he possessed innate skills; and
some of the trials his mother had set him did end in triumph. In that hour, Irasmus had also understood that such
gifts were a private thing, not to be discussed openly. He
was not to astound his brothers by performing some of the
odd tricks that appeared to come naturally to him, nor let
his bear-strong father guess he had any more talents than
the woefully few he had shown so far.

Being the youngest, the slightest of body, and—apparently—the least-competent member of a fighting clan, the
boy had early learned to efface himself as much as possible.
He had approached happiness for the first time in his life

when his mother had informed him that he was to go into exile from his unloved and unloving home. Then the future had been up to him, to make his way in the outer world.

These days, there were few students applying to the Place of Learning. If children were born with the right mind power they were not encouraged to enhance a native gift by any manner of study. Irasmus owed a great deal to his mother—she had sent him to Valarian.

Being used to practicing unobtrusive spying on members of the barony from which he had come, the new scholar soon learned the advantage of becoming two persons in his new surroundings. One was the soft-spoken, nearly ineffectual youngster who was hardly able to carry through the simplest experiment without a senior at hand to make sure that he did not loose something he could not control. But his other self became an avid explorer, not only of the permitted portions of the ancient pile of buildings but particularly of those parts, mainly lying deep underground, where the dangerous or even forbidden knowledge had been hidden to molder away.

The boy had met his first wandering wraith in those corridors and had stood up to it valiantly, controlling his fear with iron will. It was fairly easy to discover that the ancient seals on half-seen portals could be broken. What lay within engaged his curiosity and desire to know more, rather than frightening him with evidences of ancient horrors left to warn off invaders.

Under tutorship, Irasmus had steeled himself not to show any signs of his growing mastery. His first concrete plan had been laid after he discovered that it was possible to draw secretly upon the talents, or even vestiges of talents, others possessed and to use the stolen power to strengthen his own.

The fledgling mage considered that he was succeeding very well. However, unfortunately for all his feigned dullness, the time soon approached when he had to pass the first of the tests which would either make him an inmate of the Place of Learning for the rest of his natural life or betray him utterly for what he was. He was still unsure of what power he could control.

It was then that he redoubled his secret searching. What he chanced upon had brought him out into the world this day, equipped as few men had been since the long-ago war between the Dark of Chaos and the Covenant of Light, that was supposed to tie the hands and tangle the thoughts of any who would break it. His discovery had also given him enough arrogant self-confidence to believe he had sufficient learning to further an ambition, vague at first but now grown brighter than the sun on the rock wall in the morning.

One last visit to a certain corridor, a speaking of words, the burning of certain herbs, and a well-practiced bit of ritual had made Irasmus sure he was now invincible.

It had been easy enough, then, to let the success of that attempt to tap the forbidden give him the courage to go before Yost and admit, with mock humility, that he was not the stuff of which a scholar was made. Nor had the arch-mage objected to his withdrawal from the school.

Now Irasmus had no wish to return to the barony where he had been born. The few scores he had once nursed in his mind to be settled there were trivial when placed against what he could now accomplish. He was riding on a path he had studied well ahead of time, and he knew exactly where he was going.

At night, when the traders gathered around the camp-fires, Irasmus hunkered down to listen. The talk he overheard confirmed his plan of action.

There was one last matter to be accomplished before he could part company with the caravan. In assuming power, he had also assumed responsibilities, and he could not put off much longer what must be done. Should he act tonight, he wondered, or were they still too close to the Place of Learning that he dared not take the next step?

By listening, he had learned of the way ahead. Tomorrow in the late afternoon they would come to a place where an ancient trail branched. That, he decided, was his goal for the present.

Habits of mind acquired early in the Place of Learning now led Irasmus to close his thoughts tightly on his plans for the future. The new mage might sneer at the petty preoccupations of those who presided over the hoary hall of lore, but he was also aware that they had wards and guards beyond telling; and he was certain he was not yet beyond those long ago set to ensure against any escape of things of the shadows or invasions of the Dark.

The symbol under which the former student had spent his past days developing mind and body was that of a scale. There was a mighty one of burnished metal set in the main hall at Valarian. The top arm supported chains from which depended to hold level, shallow pans. One shone brightly enough to light the hall, while the other held an inky pool that swallowed up any light which might so much as touch its surface. So did the masters hold ever before them the balance of the world. This device also had its wards, and it was rumored to give forth an alarm if its two pans did not continue to hang always in even balance.

Though—Irasmus was near open laughter now, his expectations bubbling within him—when had the Dark ever threatened in these later years? Those who had devised that artifact were long since gone. Could their lost knowledge be counted upon to give warning? He himself—poor, small, and still nearly negligible as he was—was proof that a crack in the ancient shields gaped and could be put to good use by any stouthearted enough to dare.

Now he called up a mental picture of a very old map and scanned it as he urged his horse on. The beast snorted, rolled its eyes, and sweated, as if it were possessed by fear— as well it might be, though its time had not yet come.

Yes, the mage's delving had given him the proper stage for the beginning of his conquest: Styrmir, a wide valley, rich even after the bad weather of this past cold season. Its stupid land grubbers were complaisant and actually held themselves aloof from any use of the talent: still, they came from a people who had once been possessed in such ability. That these earth-lovers had foolishly chosen to allow their gifts to lie uncultivated would be their downfall.

Much had been said at the Place of Learning of the Covenant; and its words were still solemnly intoned every tenth day in meetings that were now only empty formalities. There had been an ancient war, resulting in the devastation of half the world—or perhaps more. Traders did not travel far, even in these days; and there were strange and mighty ruins rumored to exist in places now so difficult to reach that no one wasted time trying to find them. Some great lord of the Dark—Irasmus now inclined his head slightly to right and left as if giving deference where it was due— had led a bloody wash of terror and death across more lands than one. However, he did not succeed in his purpose, since the forces of Light had arisen in close alliance to do battle.

There were conflicting accounts of what had ensued at the final confrontation, but most of the legends told of a windstorm of such awesome proportions that the very mountains had yielded slides of rock to its fury—a description that was undoubtedly a countryman's metaphor for some extreme release of power.

Unfortunately, though the Dark had been defeated, this destructive wrath had also smitten the redoubts of the Light. Those surviving leaders of the Light had sworn an oath that such a weapon would never be used again. The world, rent and torn, had settled back into what must at first have been sheer fatigue, which then dwindled through the years into an indifference and at last a half forgetting.

Again, Irasmus heard a squeak from the boulders that fringed the trail. The dank smell of horse sweat was heavy on the air, and his mount trembled under him. The sorcerer scowled. The creatures skulking out there were his, bought by him to be used as he would. Let them continue this kind of protest, and he would mete out punishment! His hand

went to his belt and what was sheathed there. Not a
sword—in fact, anything wrought of iron could well defeat
the purpose for which the artifact had been made—but a
wand, something he had not dared to gird on until he was
some distance from the Place of Learning.

"*Ssssaaaa*—" The sound he uttered was a warning hiss.
Now there was another taint beside the strong horse scent
in the air here between the two heights where the very
clouds hung dankly heavy.

Irasmus wrinkled his nose and drew forth from the front
of his shabby doublet a small bag which, when squeezed
tightly, gave off a spice scent. Raising it to his nose he
sniffed deeply. He only needed to put up with his otherworldly recruits for a short time; once in Styrmir, he would
have servants of another kind in plenty.

Styrmir—and the tower of Ronunce. There could not be
much left of that fortress after all these years; however, it
had been a stronghold for the valley lordling. Irasmus intended it to be refurbished to form his own headquarters. It
was well known that sites that had been used for trials of
strength, where emotions had been fired to great heights,
held locked within them the remnants of much energy and
needed only one who knew how to harvest such. There was
a tale or two of Ronunce; and Irasmus had tried to hunt
those out without arousing the suspicion of the archivist.
Unfortunately, for all his calm and placid exterior, Mage
Gifford seemed to possess some wards his pupil had never
been able to identify, and he had been wary enough to
evade Gifford's notice.

Irasmus chewed his lower lip and frowned. It seemed
all too easy. By his planning, the people of Styrmir were
asking to be delivered into his hands like fowls to a cook
whose pot was heating. After whatever had struck at the
end of that long-ago war, their dun Elders had taken an
oath to set aside any use of the talent from that time forth.
None of the valley's youths had ever come to the Place of

Learning. They seemed one with their land—heavy and awaiting harvest.

Harvest, yes—the sorcerer's momentary annoyance was forgotten—the harvesting would be his and his alone. The idea reminded him of the coming action. The caravan was perhaps three quarters of a day's ride from the Pass of the Hawk, which was now the only doorway into Styrmir. Yes, why wait until the morrow? Let these clods bed down early for the night, as they had been doing. His own venture could well begin!

2

In Styrmir, Sulerna of Firthdun straightened up from the washboard in order to, as Grandmam always said, "take the crick" out of her back. The strong odor of the soap made her sneeze, her hands were red and wrinkled, and she was inclined to believe that only magic such as spiced up the old tales could actually drive the grime out of men's work smocks. But Grandmam had a saying for that also: "Put a good hard elbow bend into it, girl, and keep at it!"

The taller of the bushes in first leaf around her had already been draped with the fruits of her "elbow bending," and she hoped the breeze was doing its best to roughly dry them. However, there were still two heaped baskets of dirty clothes awaiting her attention, and Jacklyn was dawdling somewhere. He should have been back with filled water buckets some time ago.

The young woman could not blame her young nephew too much. The winter had been a hard one, and these first days of real spring urged one out and away from the dun, to roam greening fields, sniff the scents of bloom in the orchard, drift awhile to let the sun sink into long-chilled skin and, as Mam would say, just "fritter away time."

Firthdun was one of the oldest, as well as the largest

and best kept, of the Styrmir valley holdings. The Elders, during their infrequent conferences, always honored Grandsire with the first speaking on any problem, though such discussions dealt mainly with matters connected with the land and its tending and thus were the common knowledge to them all.

Sulerna raised a soapy hand, gave it a quick wipe on her wide apron, brushed the sweaty hair out of her eyes, and retied the string which was supposed to hold her hair in place.

Then—

It had come as the softest of touches such as might have been delivered by a fingertip as impalpable as smoke. The girl's hand flew to her cheek over the spot.

The Wind!

Sulerna was as sure she had felt its wandering touch as if she possessed the very ancient powers and could see the heart of that force which could both save and smite. But the Wind had gone long ago, and many felt themselves the poorer for that.

Those of Firthdun held more tightly to the old faith and belief than most of their neighbors. However, only Widow Larlarn, who had turned her small nearby holding into a nursery for healing herbs, joined now with the dun kin at certain times to listen to the reading from a wood-backed book so old its hard surface was cracked and gouged by time.

No, those of Firthdun never scoffed at the old tales. How could they? Once the Wind had visited here, even as in the grove at full moon each month the womenfolk gathered to do homage to the Caller, She who was the only mistress the Wind had companied with when it had been free of the bonds laid upon it by the Covenant.

A sudden surge of a strange life-not-life coursed through the young dunswoman as she stood, still shielding her cheek where it had been touched. For a moment or two, all living beings about her, even the bird soaring high above as well as the earth under her muddy clogs—everything that was vibrant with life had been a part of her or, rather, she of it.

"Well, this be the last of it—thank the moon!"

Another girl, a wide and high-heaped washing basket tightly clasped in her hold, came up beside Sulerna. Dumping the basket onto the ground, she woofed forth a noise combining equal parts of relief and exasperation.

"One would think"—the newcomer had stooped to pick up a smock, which she held an arm's length away and frowned at—"that they slid around on their bellies out in the fields. I swear your brother Elias can stand there while dirt wraps itself around him!"

Sulerna paid no attention to her sister-in-law's complaint. She held her head high, turning it slowly from side to side. Surely there would be no more than just that one touch!

"*Aaagreee!*" It was neither a true word nor a whistle she uttered but a sound not akin to the world she knew.

"Sulerna!" The other young woman stared at her openmouthed, then laid a hand on her shoulder and gave her an impatient shake. "What would you do? Have them all down upon you for kin judging?"

Few threats were more dire, but the new-wakened one showed only a joyous face in answer. "Ethera, I swear by the moon, I felt it—the Wind! It touched me here—" She put a finger back on her cheek. "The Wind, Ethera—think of it! What if the old wards be broke, and it comes to us again? It will bring us the whole of the world, even as the old tales tell. . . ."

"Sulerna—" Now both Ethera's hands were on her shoulders, and the bemused Sulerna was being shaken in their strong grip. "The Wind is gone; that is all old babble from the past. Let Grandmam hear you spouting such nonsense—!"

The light faded from Sulerna's face. "Haraska is a dreamer," she said with the beginning of a sullen note in her voice.

"And how many times since you were first frocked and

set on your feet has Haraska true-dreamed?" Ethera demanded. "There are none to spin dreams now. The mountains are bare, and even the traders come our way no more
than once a season or so. You know that the forest is
warded. All heed the Covenant—even the Wind!"

The dunsgirl turned to her scrub board in fury. Everything the other said was true, and she knew it well. Still—
she wanted once more to touch her cheek. Instead, she got
her hands resolutely busy in the soapy water again.

No branch swung, no leaf rustled in that dark rim of
trees that was the final end of the known world as far as
those of Styrmir were concerned. The Forest loomed like a
dark curtain, and there was nothing on the other side of
which the inhabitants of the valley knew enough to draw
them.

But the Forest held its own world. Life and death were
known to it; but, more than that, here blew the Wind, uniting all. It bore messages of import for each kind of being it
reached. Seeds stirred in the ground under its probing; animals mated, produced their young, and fared forth to live.
And there were also the Great Ones, who made no attempt
to rule within the tree bounds but were all sworn to the
service of Her Who Could Call.

Mighty among the Forest's children were the Sasqua.
These were not of the human kind. In fact, so unlike were
they that men or women meeting them might at first feel
terror, unless the Wind had made it plain there was nothing
to fear from those tall, furred bodies whose muscular
strength was apparent in their every move.

There was no power in the Forest greater than the Sasqua except the Wind, and they were also a part of that. They
owed no allegiance to any save Her of legend who could—
and had—called the Wind, but they visited Her shrine only
when Her silent summons went forth.

This morning, a number of them were down by one of
the Forest streams, harvesting a fresh-grown reed that they

had discovered long ago was of usefulness manyfold. Not only were its roots sweet to the taste, but the reeds themselves, when rolled back and forth between the huge hairy hands of the Sasqua until the fibers were pulped, could be woven into nets for the taking of fish and the carrying of tubers and fruits.

Hansa squatted beside a pile of the stuff she had pulled and now and then sent a wistful glance at her neighbor, whose guttural laughter was quick to bubble forth and who had one cubling at breast and another playing beside her, striving to pull apart one of the tough reed stems. Grapea always had strong cubs, and she could take pride in remembering them even after they had struck out on their own. Hansa wrapped her arms about herself and squeezed. She had not had her first bearing season yet, but she hoped with all her heart that, when a little one came, it would be like Grapea's get.

Hansa fell to twisting reeds, hardly knowing what she was doing; rather, her mind was full of the joys of a cubling to be and what it would mean to share a night nest with a small being.

At that moment, the Wind sang in her ear, and the Sasqua female sat gape mouthed at its touch. Cubling to come, yes, but more—something so strange that Hansa could not sort it out before that fleeting message had vanished. She was to be given—she could not be sure what but a gift of great importance. However, this was not a thing to be spoken of among her kind; and there was a time between the present and its arrival which she could not reckon.

Up on the mountain trail, it had begun to rain; and the handlers of the pack animals cursed bitterly. It was too easy here for the footing to turn to slippery mud; and there were places not far ahead now where the trail dwindled to a mere thread, to be followed by only a very surefooted man or animal.

Well, thought Irasmus, trying to make his cloak cover

him as much as possible, the weather had given him his answer. Tonight he would make his move. That stout fellow there, tugging at the hackamore of a reluctant pony, would not have much longer to damn the day, these reluctant animals, or his own mistaken choice of employment.

The pack train had coiled down into a fairly level cup where a spring fed a pond. Pretus, the caravan master, gave the signal to camp, and his men were happy enough to obey. Irasmus had held his horse to a much slower pace and had stopped well behind the now-rising tents.

The mage gave once more that cricking, rockrat cry and was not surprised to hear it answered from almost immediately behind him. Rain was not favored by his present servants, and their tempers had not improved during the last half hour's travel. He swung out of the saddle and allowed his horse to back into a crevice between two rocks. The beast certainly wanted no meeting with those now flitting out of cover, and he did not blame it.

The creatures were a motley lot, with only one thing in common—excessive ugliness of body and feature. Green-yellow skin, much disfigured by warts and pits, certainly gave them no countenance a man would enjoy facing. Their eyes shone with a peculiar red-gold fire in the fast-falling dusk; and their slavering mouths gaped, showing discolored fangs. They boasted no hair on their elongated heads, which were mainly lumps, now slick with rain.

Though their joints sometimes protruded at what seemed almost impossible angles, the beings scuttled forward rapidly. In size, if they stood upright (their usual stance was a stoop), they could match Irasmus in height. Their clothing was rudimentary—either bits of hide crudely laced together or cloth that looked as if it had reached the state of rot that would lead it to fall speedily from an energetic body. From them arose a thick miasma of foul odor.

Their leader, Karsh, shambled forward. Spittle shot forth from his wide mouth along with his words as he addressed his would-be master.

"Hungry!" The nightmare raised one huge and long-taloned paw and slashed it through the air not far from the young man, who showed no sign of any emotion but complete disdain. "Eat," Karsh added.

"As you shall," Irasmus replied. "But these have weapons—"

Karsh's mouth sprayed froth even farther, and he held up his clawed hand yet higher. "So also we!"

"But not," the sorcerer returned calmly, "iron ones."

Karsh's jaws came together with a snap. "Gobbes kill from shadows. No time those"—he indicated the busy camp below—"have for weapons drawing."

Irasmus shrugged. "Warning; take it for what it is worth. But listen well, for you are bound to me by blood, and my orders shall be obeyed. I will go down to the camp. We will wait until they build their cook fire. What they have to cook will not altogether agree with the eaters." He did not know how much of what he said could be understood by the outworld creature, but he drew as sharp a mental picture as he could of men clutching their throats and reeling back from the fire. "It is for you," he continued, "to take out the sentries and so make sure there is no alarm."

Those bulbous eyes the color of swamp slime stared at him for a long moment. The mage waited but refused to believe that all would not happen as he had ordered. He had deliberately called these things into his service, and the spell that held them was a potent one none of them could break. The gobbes were very low-grade demons, and any powers they might try to raise could not stand against what he had learned.

Karsh apparently accepted the situation. "We do," he gabbled.

Two under the creature's command slipped back into the shadows, and Irasmus did not doubt they were about to do as they had been ordered—to remove expeditiously and noiselessly any watchers Master Pretus had assigned to guard.

Remounting, the sorcerer began the slow ride down into the valley. This time he did draw his wand from its sheath and held it ready. The confusion at the camp was his aid, for no one paid any attention to him. He did not add his mount to the horse line but fastened it some distance away before he walked among the others.

Gaszeb, the cook—if making the sorry concoctions the travelers had been forced to stomach could be called "cooking"—had already set up the stout rod that held his all-purpose pot over the fire and was busy tossing into it, with more or less accurate aim, handfuls of the dried lizard flesh that were all the meat left after the winter.

When Irasmus approached, the cook had turned to grab at a too-limp sack that held some undoubtedly now-moldy barley to be added to the mess beginning to bubble in the pot. A single glance around assured the mage that he was under no observation, and his wand moved, its tip aimed at the pot. A thin thread of dull red snaked into the stew, and for a moment he moved the thread back and forth as if from a distance stirring the kettle.

"So, young sir." Irasmus instantly whipped the wand into hiding as Master Pretus came closer. "Slim fare for active men. Better if we could eat like the beasts and so find us grazing! We be still three days from Ostermur, and that is a port, so they have foodstuffs from overseas to make up for this we gag down now."

"The trail runs straight to Ostermur?" Irasmus asked as if he had never seen a map.

"There be a side path down to Styrmir, but after such a winter the folk of that valley will have nothing worth trading for. Ostermur is more promising."

"Come along! Come along!" Gaszeb waved a great ladle to direct their attention to the pot as a young boy trooped over balancing a tower of bowls. Most of the men had already finished their immediate tasks and were able to line up for a well-filled bowl. Irasmus himself accepted one but did not raise it to his lips, making signs that he wished it to cool first.

A moment or so later, the sorcerer was not disappointed by the results of his own addition to the meal. With a whoop of pain and rage, one of the horse handlers spewed out— unfortunately across the feet of the man next to him—the mouthful he had taken. And he was not the last to be so stricken.

The saboteur emptied his portion quietly onto the ground. That action might have been a signal, for out of the night there came, sending both men and animals screaming in pain and terror, such an attack as their world had not seen for a thousand years or more. The gobbes were hungry; and the feast, to their minds, was ready. Shrieks of torment were stilled. Those who attempted to run were dragged down and suffered the fate of their comrades. The reek of blood was as strong as the stench of fear and pain. And the sounds—

The Wind might have been forbidden to course the outer world but, during the years since its binding by the Covenant, it had ventured forth a little, curious, seeking what it had once had— communication with all. What it gathered now, its innermost heart shrank from in horror. Then, very distantly, anger awoke, and power was shaken out of slumber.

3

IT HAD BEEN A NIGHT OF STORM, LIGHTNING LASHED AROUND THE ancient towers and walls; yet all wards had held. Only, just after dawn, there had been one occurrence which for he who had witnessed it had seemed ominous.

Unable to sleep, his drowsy thoughts presenting him in broken images such pictures as he never had any intention of drawing, Harwice had arisen when the sky was hardly more than gray.

As always after he had dressed, the artist mage sought the table on which he had left the sketches done yesterday. A new cover was needed for one of the Covenant missals, and he had been trying one design after another, attempting to find or achieve a motif that carried more meaning than these scrawls which had been his latest efforts.

Now the seer stopped short, and the candlestick he held shook a little so that the flame danced. The light was feeble, but it was enough to make plain what lay there: a depiction of the huge scale which was the ward and the heart of the Covenant.

But . . .

The table must have been jarred. Harwice put out a hand now to test its steadiness, but it stood solid and unmoving even when he increased his grip and shoved. Yet somehow, during the fury of the night just past, one of his small paint pots had been overset; and a dribble of murky red, like clotted blood, had fallen directly onto his sketch, blotting out the standard of the scale and leaving only the pans loose from any support and ready to spill all they had.

A warning—an omen—a matter he must speak about in open council? Sometime during this day, the dream painter would at least share this incident with Gifford, who had forgotten more about omens than any one man could ever hope to learn.

However, when he went searching for the archivist, Gifford was not, as customarily, in his stuffy room, a spider in a web of books. It appeared that he had been summoned elsewhere; Harwice's strange experience would have to wait for the telling.

The chamber was very old. Time itself had welded one great collection of wall blocks to another until they stood, and would stand, intact through the passing years which were no longer counted here. Yet there was color to temper the somberness of the room: richly brocaded cushions on the chairs and panels of fabric that rippled like wind-touched pools on the walls.

Archivist Gifford, who had just entered this room to make a report, paused before one of those panels and, as if his gaze had commanded obedience, the ripples gathered and began to form shapes. These sharpened and separated until it was as if the mage looked out a window down a long stretch of countryside that wore the bright-green livery of spring, with flowering bush and tree to set the season's seal firmly upon it.

"Styrmir?"

The single-word question from someone entering after him broke the spell. That expanse of land, rich in peace and plenty, disappeared, its colorful components dispersing to match the shaded bands on the other hangings. The archivist, who had been watching, turned to face the speaker.

Both scholars wore breeches and doublets of muted purple with loose robes the hue of sword-blade steel. The plainness of those garments was broken by a twisting of embroidered runes, which differed in tint and design on each of the two men. The men varied slightly in size also, the newcomer, with his thick crest of white hair, topping his fellow by several inches. Gifford was more full of body and face, with a splotch of ink on one cheek where a writing finger had been absentmindedly wiped. His hair was much more sparse and was held down by a round cap, as if the thinness of that natural covering brought a chill to his nearly bare scalp.

"One can remember even through the veil of years," Gifford said slowly. "Do you never regret the Withdrawing, Yost? Happiness and peace are reckoned to be the innermost desire of all our kind. Those of Styrmir have held that belief for centuries, and they raise no temples to any gods while the winds blow free."

Archmage Yost seated himself in one of the chairs that stood with its back to the banners on the walls. His features were sharply chiseled, and he had none of the lines of laughter, such as his companion displayed, bracketing his eyes beneath their bushy overhangs of white bristles.

"We did not meet"—his tone was close to a snap—"to exchange platitudes about our inner strivings, Gifford. What do you have to tell me, in truth?"

"This." Gifford raised his left hand and opened fingers which had been clenched in a tight fist to keep what they held safe. He did not glance down at the thing he bore but rather proffered it to Yost.

On the ink-stained palm rested a seal bearing marks from so far in the past that either man, for all his deep learning, would have had trouble extracting from them an intelligible meaning. This was all the more true as the seal had been broken, and its jagged edges were crumbling a little as the protecting flesh was withdrawn.

"Where?" The question came in a single word but one uttered with the force of a war captain's order.

"At the lowest level, midway among the sealed chambers. And this was not done recently, Yost. As you know, we inspect all seals in order, and have since, by the vote of the entire brotherhood, they were first set. I was last in that passage to check six tens of days ago—just before the testing."

The sparks that appeared to form the pupils of the archmage's eyes grew brighter. His thin lips tightened into a straight line before he said colorlessly, "The testing. And before that—a departure."

Gifford let the seal fall to the surface of a table nearby. "Surely we of the Old Knowledge should be able to judge one of our own kind who has taken the Path of Dark—?"

Yost shook his head. "Not of our kind; white does not brother with black. He is one who early learned to hide his true self and be to all men what each believed him to be, which means he was— and is—far more than we reckoned."

"Never has there been such treachery before," the archivist said heavily. "What would lead him to this path? Surely the selectors of the youth would not have sent us any who could not touch the True Flame without hurt!"

"On a journey, a man may choose to change paths. There is this about power: it grows from native talent. But with some—remember the days of the Covenant—it can change a man as a smith shapes iron upon an anvil."

"His later studies," Gifford persisted. "How was it he was able to hide for so long where he searched? Did none suspect?"

Again a head shake. "We have grown slack, woefully slack over the years. Sentries forget to faithfully pace boundaries when there is no dispute concerning them. What lies behind that seal?" He nodded at the disc on the table.

"Speculations—largely those of Arbobis."

"Speculations? Well, then he may have skimmed off a degree of knowledge presently denied us, yes. But he would not have dared to put such discoveries into practice here! Arbobis . . .'' The archmage's eyes flared again. He tensed in his seat, and his tongue swept over his pale lips. ''You have the records, brother—see what you can learn from them. Arbobis was one far too entwined with the search for the forbidden. However, any of his finished spells would be far too intricate to be within the reach of young Irasmus, no matter how eager.''

''That one is clever, though not as much as he believes,'' Gifford assented. ''But where has he gone, and what lies in his mind to do with what he has stolen?''

Yost was out of his chair with an agility that sent his outer cloak into a swirl.

''He went meekly enough with that trader's caravan, seeming downcast that he now carries only the right to say he has studied here but attained no mage standing. Yet have we not wrought well in the past? There is the sweeping of the mind as one goes through Claw Pass. Unless—'' The archmage strode to the table and thumped its surface until half the broken seal spun to the floor, ''—unless we have forgotten something we should have remembered, and that eater of forbidden fruit found the key to it. If so''—the sharp features were bleak—''what has our carelessness unleashed upon the world?''

Irasmus—had certainly never impressed any of the inner circle of mages enough that any could bring him readily to mind. He was a thin young man with a taste for drab-colored clothing. From time to time he had played with the melding of scents; which experimentation had earned him nothing but chaffing from the two others who had entered here as students at the same time. Still, his manners had always been above the slightest reproach—too much so at times, thought Gifford, grimacing at the memory. However, the youth had also presented the outward appearance of one who did not follow any study to great depth but rather flittered across surfaces, though he had been very ready with questions.

The archivist pursed his lips. Looking back, he winced. Some of those inquiries had been respectfully directed toward him, and he could not honestly be sure just how discreet he had been in their answering. The lad had seemed so little suited to residence here that the impatience of his tutors may well have been of secret value to him.

Now the old mage hurried along the deepest hall of the record house, his way lit by one of the sparkling balls that any occupant of Valarian could summon without thinking. For all Gifford's love of ancient lore—its reading being his true inborn talent—this section of his own domain had always cast a shadow upon him when he was forced to enter it.

All knowledge had two sides: one to help and one to harm. Neither could work, save for a man or woman trained to its use. But it was also true that a person born with even a nearly insignificant talent should instinctively shrink from the Dark Path, for he or she would be far too aware of the perils of loosing what could not be readily bound again. That long-ago time of the Covenant, when the Dark had been barely defeated and which had ended in an unspeakable period of chaos during which the whole world had shuddered—that grim history was too well known to any who delved into the Place of Learning.

Yet here and now, in the Hall of the Nine Doors, where the fireball awoke sparks from the protection seals, was much more of evil than a man of the loremaster's own time could conceive had once existed.

Gifford stopped before the door he sought. Though he has hastened to report his discovery to Yost, he had not left the portal unguarded—two bars of green light crisscrossed the unlocked entryway. He could dismiss those more easily than he had summoned them, but then he must needs step inside, to face—what?

The archivist unbuttoned the throat closure of his tunic

and drew out an irregular crystal that instantly caught the rays of the fiery sphere and turned them into a blaze. All thoughts or deeds dedicated to the use of power caused energy to gather within such amulets through the years, and every one fed the talisman's initial hunger. He had worn this crystal through three lifetimes of ordinary mortals, and he hoped now that what it had amassed through his own past actions would be enough to form a shield. The archmage knew where he had gone and would learn instantly if his brother were attacked by a thrust from the Dark; still, Gifford might lose his life in trying to do his duty, though he could not lose that which was in his core to evil.

A quick movement of his fingers, and the bars across the entrance disappeared. The archivist felt more than just the usual dank chill of the passage as he passed through the doorway and stepped into long-forbidden territory.

The light bobbed and wavered back and forth, but it did not pass the threshold. Gifford would have been completely in the dark if it had not been for his crystal, though its glow was now greatly dimmed.

As in any of the storage compartments of the place, the walls here were lined with shelves that seemed to shimmer a little. As with all such repositories, whether of good or ill, the spell of preservation remained.

The record keeper's attention was directed to the thick dust of years that carpeted the floor, which bore signs of recent disturbance. The mage stood quietly by the door tracing those tracks. There were certainly a number of them, and, while one or two trails led to side shelves, the majority pointed straight ahead.

The chamber was longer than he had expected, and one of the hardest things he had ever forced himself to face made Gifford add his own prints to the betraying spoor and follow its maker.

There came a whiff as if some unseen monstrosity had puffed out a putrid gust of breath. For putrid it was—so foul that the mage nearly choked, grasping quickly at the crystal to hold it to his nose for relief. Even the light of that amulet flickered; and when it gained full power again, held a dirty reddish tinge. Its wielder had once more to summon up all the courage a quiet scholar could accumulate in a sheltered life to go on.

He had reached the very end of the room, and here the dust on the floor had been overlaid by a dried skim of ichor. Gifford had no desire to look at what lay at stiff angles there; the creature had come to such a death as its kind knew, and not easily. Also, without having to go any closer, he could identify the corpse—not by name (such entities never served within these walls) but by species. It was a gobbe—born of tainted earth and an ancient, now near-forgotten will. So unnatural a being had no place in any dwelling used by humankind. Unless—

But the thing was *dead*. If it had been summoned to serve, surely it would not have ended thus. The loremaster pressed his crystal to lips suddenly gone dry and repeated within his mind a pattern of words no longer used by any race in his world.

There rose a shimmer, akin to that which curtained the shelves; within it followed the movement of slightly less-opaque substances. Gifford did not need to strain to identify the shadow he had summoned out of the past, which stood spear straight and motionless by the wall. He was only too sure he could give a name to that half-seen stranger: Irasmus.

The murk, which had gradually dulled even his talisman, was hard to pierce for clear sight. At length he touched the crystal against his forehead just above and between his eyes.

There was a sudden intensity in the dead and polluted air of this place. The mage recognized the forerunner of power, and he was forced to abandon his earlier belief that he had come upon the reckless dabbling of some overambitious amateur; Irasmus had known exactly what he had been about.

The outline of a hand arose, in it a rod that glowed with the deadly rotten-red light the crystal had picked up. Now there was no longer a body on the floor; instead, the shadow figure of Irasmus was drawing precise and well-calculated symbols in the dust, in the air above, and then in the dust once again. Over the vision's shoulder, the archivist could see one of the shelves. Its protective veiling had vanished, revealing an empty space where there must have once been stored the books or tube rolls that were now piled into an awkward tower that stood nearly knee-high to the illusory youth.

Thus, and thus—and thus! The loremaster knew he could not alter what had already happened here, perhaps days ago; he could only bear witness to these actions from the past.

A whirlpool of dust was rising from the floor, and out of that shambled—a gobbe. It was nearly the height of a tall man, but had the misshapen body, warty skin, and green-stained fangs peculiar to its kind. One taloned paw gripped a war axe, and a light of greedy anticipation shone in its red-lit eyes. The diet preferred by such spawn of evil was no secret, nor could it ever be forgotten that they were constantly on the alert to fill their potbellies.

However, the axe had no time to move. There was a flick of the wand from the shadow Irasmus, and the creature convulsed and collapsed. But already a second of its kind was materializing, and then a third, their ungainly bodies tense as though ready to drag down some prey—until the sight of their fellow on the floor sent them statue still.

Faintly, very faintly, and only through the aid of the crystal, could Gifford catch now and then a word; and some of those made him ill. Irasmus had not been the lightweight failure they had so mistakenly turned away from the Place of Learning!

A dozen of the gobbes were present now, all alike in monstrousness of feature—the Dark personified. Irasmus waved his wand, and one of the gobbes scuttled forward, cringing, to bag and shoulder those tomes of stolen knowledge.

The old scholar dropped the crystal from his forehead. He had seen enough—enough to utterly destroy the complacency of his fellow mages. Nor did he, at that moment, believe the ancient spell of forgetfulness in the Pass of the Claw would work against such hell-drawn might as this.

What had they loosed on the world—or, at least, on a part of it? Power—even though Irasmus had been only an illusion, Gifford had felt the crackle of released power, strong enough that its emanations still lingered days later.

The slain gobbe was undoubtedly a warning—one that such creatures could readily understand. But that their summoner would restrain them from their nauseating food quest in the future he did not believe.

The loremaster took cautious steps to avoid the rotting carcass on the floor. Gobbes were of the Dark; some said they were the offspring of Vastor the Ghoul. This time, at least, that paramount demon had done nothing to save one of them; they were, instead, now plainly bound to Irasmus. And there were very few in this world who could withstand their attacks.

Gifford looked at the plundered shelf. There would be, of course, some reference in the general files—probably very slight—to what had stood there. He could only search that out and report to the assembly. However, this was no news any of the human kind could receive without a foreshadowing of fear.

4

THE FOREST WAS AWAKENING TO SPRING. SOME OF THE FLOWERS that gave the first announcement of the season were, indeed, already faded, busy with building a new seed, while the green lace of first leaf buds was afroth on trees so huge they had nearly outlasted Time itself.

Over all sang the Wind. Deep within, at one end of its scale of song, rang the speech of stones and earth; at the other lilted the twitter of birds and the faint, ephemeral patter of flower thought. For the Wind was the keeper and the sharer; and every life that dwelt within reach of its inner voice knew—even as the Wind itself learned—what passed in the world.

Perhaps the Forest was not the "world" as most men would reckon it. However, it kept secret its own mysteries and those of its children; and there had been no intruder within for many seasons. Men forgot, but the Wind and the trees and the earth did not.

That vast tract of woods had its heart. This was no temple raised by those unaware of the singing of the Wind; though there were places where giant blocks of moss-garnished stone lay to mark the dire days when the Dark had massed its battalions, the Light had gathered its forces, and warfare had been waged of a sort no creature now living would give credence to.

That heart was a single Stone, rooted as deeply as any of the trees which ringed the glade that held it and nearly as tall. The Stone bore none of the lichenous blotching that defiled the dead and forgotten shrines; instead, it appeared, at first regard, to be an unbroken dull gray. However, sparks of light flowed over its surface. These followed no pattern, save at intervals, when they ringed themselves about a perfectly rounded hole in its middle. The core of that hole held the utter gray of thick fog, and through it the Wind sang. Sometimes other beings of the Forest gathered to learn what it was needful that they should know.

Once the Wind had ranged far more widely. At a time of great peril, it had been loosed to its full strength, and parts of the earth had been swept clear of that which should not exist. Then the Covenant had been sworn, and the Wind was bound, in its uttermost might, to keep within the borders of the Forest. Yet such force could not be wholly subdued.

There was also the valley. Styrmir was its ancient name, one without meaning now. It sheltered its own people, many of whom, at the swearing of the Covenant, had stood aside, not because of any allegiance to the Dark but rather because their sufferings during the days of the war had been such that they never again wished to use any power.

Though the folk of Styrmir were of mankind, they could not root out of themselves the talent. Ever and again, the Wind sent its questing breath to them; and then, like their ancestors, they would become for a space at one with all that was good in the life of the world. Yet still they held stubbornly apart, forgoing all chance of honing their gifts into tools or weapons, but living perhaps more content than any of their ancestors had done. Here, now, was neither lord nor serf. All shared in the common good; and none ever visited the roofless tower that had once been their rallying place in times of danger.

The inhabitants of the valley saw very few from the lands beyond the Forest, though remnants survived of a road leading down from a pass in the heights above. Several times in the year, those of Styrmir might be visited by wandering merchants to exchange the clippings from their flocks and other common things the outsiders found interesting enough to acquire. For the most part, however, these people of determined peace took no interest in anything beyond their sheltered vale.

Yet there was one clan that still kept the records. Such accounts had become monotonous over the years and contained little to stir the blood, but the lines of family births must be honorably preserved. This kindred were also rumored to have dealings with the Wind, whenever it came visiting, and to treasure scraps of ancient learning about which none of them ever spoke.

Thus was Styrmir, defenseless, yet even so long past the days of the Covenant giving root to talents that could be used if a man were clever—or vicious—enough to try.

It was the quiet harmony of Styrmir that those of the Valarian looked upon on this spring morning. Of the twelve chairs, only eight were occupied—that was another matter wherein they had been lax, as Yost was now forced to make himself face. Few entered as novices these days, for the focus of interest in the wide world had moved on to other ways. Now only those young people, whose thoughts were made restless by too generous a gift of the talent, sought out what was certainly an ambience lacking in action, as far as those still favored by the strength of youth were concerned.

Many beginning students also split away before they finished learning. The last full brother the mages had welcomed among them was just now hurrying into the council chamber, his cloak, splotched with dabs of color, bundled awkwardly about his shoulders. Pausing just within the doorway, he smoothed one of the wall banners into more even folds. Harwice's talent used tools: his large, long-fingered hands were always itching for a brush. For it was he who could bring into mind a picture and then transfer it to just such a background as he wished to illuminate. Yet it had been twenty-five seasons since the artist had taken the Covenant oath to don his cloak, Gifford recalled.

Since Harwice—oh, there had been a trickle of others, both men and women, as the talent seemed unaware of gender when it made itself manifest. Some had been drawn to healing and, having learned all they could absorb, had gone out to restore such of the shrines as had crumbled nearly away. In only three courts, halfway across the world, were there still chapter houses which were listening, feeling, and dreaming posts, though those who served within them had little enough to communicate.

At the sound of his name, Gifford came to attention with a start he trusted none had noticed. These few moments of withdrawal had, he hoped, given him strength to resist any force of the Dark that still lingered in that accursed, now-resealed cell below.

Yost was watching him keenly, and the librarian-archivist saw that this was the time to make known to his fellows the breach in their defenses. He knew he was overfond of dressing any speech in a festival robe of words, so now he made an effort to tell his story as starkly as a sentry's formal report. From somewhere to his right, he heard a breath deeply drawn, though there had been no ripple of movement in all that seated company.

"So—Irasmus—" Yost was far from the oldest member of that assemblage, but the woman whose white hair was as neatly bound to her head as his waved free seldom raised her voice in council. However, it was to Dreamgate Yvori that the seers turned when they needed fragments of far-off history such as might take Gifford days to uncover, for all his excellent keeping of the files.

"He is"—the aged sorceress's speech still held steady against the flow of time—"of the House of Gorgaris through his mother's inheritance, though it has been four generations since Gorgaris has been even faintly remembered. Irasmus came to us through the urging of Kristanis, presented as close kinsman to the Banner of the Red Boar. The Boar has ever stood on the right flank of any force that moved against the Dark; yet that, too, may also be forgotten today."

Yost leaned forward a little in his chair. "No one can question the path those of the Boar have always trodden. But in one of Gorgaris's get— How came such a mixture of spirit?"

Yvori spoke again. "How often it is seen that, the brighter the light in a man or his line, the deeper of dye is the darkness when they fall into evil! With time, all houses may sink into decay; and Gorgaris and his hero ilk are now long gone from any rulership."

"But if the idea of rulership has not gone from his line?" Gifford queried. "We might hold here a key to the knowledge we seek. Irasmus is gone—where?"

The painter with the color-splashed cloak seemed genuinely interested for the first time. "When one would draw true strength, he had best look first to his masters, and then—to his roots."

Gifford tensed, his head turned a fraction so he could see again that banner which had enchanted him earlier in this day now overshadowed by horror. However, Harwice, who could translate beauty from dream to reality, had already advanced, not to precisely the hanging Gifford had admired but to one at its side.

Harwice stared, and colors rose and flowed and solidified. The brotherhood were all used to the manifesting that followed his concentration—it was as though a slice of earth had been rendered immaterial enough to swim the air above, summoned to give up knowledge. There, unmistakably, appeared the vestiges of the old road the traders still cherished. What those in the chamber now saw distinctly was a party of plodding pack ponies and figures moving to keep them closely herded.

The animals moved awkwardly and needed that guidance, as it was plain they could no longer see where they were going. What were those creatures shambling about nearby to keep them in tight order? The loremaster wet suddenly dry lips with his tongue. Gobbes!—monster things never meant to scuttle under the light of day.

All those horrors had eyeholed hoods pulled tightly over their heads to protect them from the fierce rays of the sun, which offered a serious threat. Among them rode an unhooded man, who guided with skill a bony horse. He never looked behind him at the motley crew, seeming very sure that none of them would stray from the direction he set. His thin, beak-nosed face carried a mocking smile which was close to a jeer.

"The Claw—" Someone among the viewers breathed, as if summoning a defense.

"We have slept!" The archmage's voice rang out until, Gifford thought, it might almost reach the ears of those on the road. "The years have tamed and drained us! That is a trader's train—with certain embellishments, to be sure. But, brothers, do you see Master Pretus or one of his choosing among—*those!*" He nearly spat that last word.

It was the woman Yvori who gave him an answer of a sort. "This noontide, we shall say power words for Master Pretus and those of his party, for I do not think any of them still walks his well-known road. Pretus was bound for the Court of Gris. A strong comrade of ours dwells there— Mage Rosamatter, who is not to be thought of lightly in the matter of talent."

"No—our renegade heads to Styrmir," Yost said in a voice heavy-freighted with the emotions he must always control. "Gorgaris held sway there until the Wind sweep. What better place could Irasmus now look for to plant roots?"

The limner-of-dreams took one step to the right and now faced a second fabric panel—the one Gifford had renewed his spirit by watching earlier.

Once again, they beheld the valley, peaceful with the spring, yet bursting with the force of new life. No clouds hung in the sky whose dullness might set a smudging finger on what lay before them. Only, to the far right of that view of the old road, there stood what looked like the jagged fang of some great beast but which was, in fact, a roofless half-ruined tower.

"The Wind—" Those words came shakily, almost as if the speaker suggested something he knew held no truth.

"Yes, the Wind," Yost repeated, his eyes blazing, the faintest of flushes tinting his pale face. "It plays in Styrmir— but only the smallest part of it, and that now and again. The Covenant did not altogether forbid its dance there; yet those who chose to hold that land were talent born, even though they have steadfastly refused to draw upon power. Doubtless there are dreamers among them, and the Covenant does not forbid warnings to be delivered to the innocent. But, more—?" He shook his head, and his upstanding white crest of hair licked the air. "What more can we do? We are sworn—"

A chair scraped across the floor. One who had sat silently on the very edge of the company now stood straight and tall. Though he wore the livery of the place, there was a fraction of difference, as if he had been wont to go clad in another fashion.

"Those unwitting folk will be gobbled up, even as a ver-hawk snatches a lamb from the side of a shepherd's hound. Send your dreams! These soft ones have been ten generations or more steeped in peace. Can you conjure the spirit that could make them erect a wall of defense about Styrmir? Our brother is right—the message gusts once borne by the Wind are all but gone. We are not the only ones held by oaths; what you see—" he gestured toward that view of the valley "—already bares its throat to the knife.

"It remains that we were the ones who loosed Irasmus. How do you answer that?"

The flush on the archmage's cheeks deepened. "We seek now to find what was taken from the vault of Arbobis. You were once a man of war, Fanquer. What came of that long-ago conflict that none on the Path of Light wish even to name? Half a world and the life it contained scoured away! The Wind is bound, and so are we."

"There is this." Oddly enough, it was Yvori who confronted the erstwhile soldier. "Does not the Covenant have an answer of its own?"

Fanquer scowled. "Dreamer, look upon heaven—you shall see it become hell. Think of those fields you see after the hunger of the gobbes has been sated! As for the Covenant, the ones to loose the string of its binding must needs be those with their roots in a corner of the world the Dark once smirched. What have we here? Farmers and herdsmen! Save for one family line, the valley dwellers have deafened their inner ears to the talent as well as they could and abandoned all that might serve them now. Can any of you promise me that some hero will rise to summon an army of Light?"

Yost raised his hand, and the gesture was emphatic enough to bring the company to attention. "Irasmus rides, and with him goes the filth of the Dark. Just what damage can he do with his stolen learning, Gifford?"

"No one can guess the reach of another's full talent," replied the loremaster bleakly. "That he brought gobbes to heel says he is far in advance of any novice—even of some journeymen and women who have served their time with us. What can we do? Will She Who Strides the Wind come at the call of any?"

"Does that One now even take an interest in the things of this earth?" Fanquer added a more troubling question. "She viewed as an insult the plea we made once before that She lend her powers to the aid of the Light. Who of our blood has ventured to seek out any of Her servants in the Forest for twice a hundred years? And do not those of

Styrmir come into this world having, from the very wombs of their mothers, a barrier set within them against any encroachment upon the place of trees?"

"Dreams have no barriers," the old sorceress responded. "Warnings can be sent—"

There came a lightening on the faces of all those assembled, as if a measure of their burden had been lifted from them. Only the warrior laughed sourly. "Send your night messengers, if you will, but they are a feeble answer to what now descends upon Styrmir."

Fanquer was regarding the wall hanging with narrowed eyes. "Those complacent fools have no time left to beat reaping hooks into spears. This I say, and say it plainly: those of the Right Path will hold it against us that it was one claiming to be of our craft who now goes forth as a bringer of death. There remains only a single clan that can be warned by a dream-sending, and they are not more than a handful with no Wind Caller among them. We must fight a battle lost before the banners meet upon the field where steel strikes steel!"

Gifford's eyebrows rose and his lips pursed before he answered. "You would have us on the move?"

A stir rippled the ranks of the councillors, and a murmur of voices arose. The archmage brought them again to order with a gesture.

"Nothing, Light Seekers, has ever been accomplished by arguments not founded on well-based facts. Shall we now propose to follow the custom once used before? Those who can—" he glanced first at Gifford, then at Yvori "—must look backward in time. You, Fanquer, should study well the Covenant, since words of yours were used to frame it. We all have our talents, and, by the will of Light over Dark, let us hasten to use them, for sometimes even a fraying thread may bring down an empire."

With that final admonition, the mages dispersed, save for Harwice, who still stood before the banner's window into Styrmir. Suddenly, the scene of peace and plenty pictured there changed, darkening and closing in to show a road upon which dusk was descending curtainwise and where an ugly, monstrous crew padded purposefully forward. The artist raised his hand, but the archivist's own fingers flashed out to imprison the other's wrist.

"Would you warn them?" he demanded sharply. "I tell you that he who can command gobbes cannot be turned from his chosen way except by a far greater spell!"

Harwice glanced at the keeper of records, and a half smile gave a hint of satisfaction to his smooth and seemingly youthful face.

"How well do you know what now lies in the outer world, Brother Gifford? How long has it been since you brushed the dust of moldering books and scrolls from your sleeves and ventured forth further than the outermost gardens? Not only the actions bred by mankind may change the paths of life; sometimes, as Mage Yost has said, a single worn thread can turn their course.

"That one"—the dream painter waved at the image of Irasmus—"sniffs for power of a sort; but his nose has not yet sharpened into that of a hound! We shall call upon time, even if we cannot summon the Wind to stand as shield comrade."

Harwice reached into a pocket in his robe and brought out a tiny pot that fit easily on the palm of his hand. One stride brought him within reach of the wall hanging. He dipped his forefinger into the pot, to bring it forth colored dark green. At the same time, he began to hum. Gifford found himself caught up in that sound—a Wind song, though the scholars seldom heard such here.

Quickly the finger moved and, at some distance before Irasmus and his train, there sprouted up a hedge, most branches of which were scarcely shorter than a belt knife and twice as sharp with thorns.

Harwice thrust home his creation with the tip of his finger, and the last of the color bled from his flesh onto the fabric of the banner. He laughed softly. "Wind talent, Brother. Even if your dreamers cannot arouse Her, the use of green magic without Her choice will still give the alarm. And there is nothing in the Covenant to say that a man may not sound a warning horn when the Dark begins to waken."

5

HARASKA STOPPED SUDDENLY IN THE MIDDLE OF THE HOMELY TASK of kneading the bread dough. She stared down at the thick paste as though she had never seen its like before, and her tensely held body was stiff as a harvest corn dolly enlarged to human size.

"Grandmam, those blue-winged thieves have taken more than *half* the fruit from the ground trees." A high-pitched young voice announced the coming of a girl, who shook a basket which lacked several finger's depths of being full. She was trailed by two other children, each of whom wore a betraying mustache of berry juice.

Sulerna of Firthdun had nearly reached the table when she realized that all was certainly not well with Haraska. Her grandmother's hands were still deep in the dough she had been vigorously pummeling, but she was staring straight ahead. Staring? No, not quite that, for her yellow-green eyes were almost half closed, as if she longed for sleep.

"Grandmam!" Sulerna called urgently, but she knew better than to touch the well-loved elder of the clan. The younger woman turned to her nephew and his sister, who had edged backward toward the door, the small girl pulling on the wide sleeve of the boy's work smock. Yes, it was also so—Cathrina, being female, would be first to catch the faint touch of— Only this was not any vagrant breeze skipping out for the forest.

"Get you Mam and Grandsire!" Sulerna ordered Cathrina. The girl dropped her basket on the table and ran to obey.

Sulerna now moved to stand directly in her grandmother's line of sight, but still the elder made no stir. Chilled, the young woman shivered and gave a quick glance into each corner of the kitchen, which was the heart of the clan; but there was nothing. The Wind she would have been able to detect herself—though her talent was not as great as some—but this had nothing to do with the Forest or such encounters as she had known before, of that she was sure.

"Now, now—what's to do, girl?" Fatha, her mother, a freshly pulled carrot in one earthy hand and impatience plain on her face, came in the door. Behind her, supported on the two sticks he had spent most of the winter carving to his liking, stumped Firthdun's present master, her grandfather. Sulerna could only point to Haraska, for she had certainly never witnessed such behavior from her bustling and ever-efficient grandmam before.

"Ach!" The carrot struck the floor as Fatha gripped her father's arm, nearly oversetting him. "Girl"—she swung next upon Sulerna—"open the cupboard bed. Cathrina, run for Mistress Larlarn! Father—?" Some of the authority went out of her voice as she looked now to the dunmaster.

"It is so." The old man might have been answering some unasked question. "Do what is necessary." He made no attempt to approach his statue-frozen wife but dropped onto the settle by the low fire, his eyes fastened on her.

"Sulerna!" The snap in her mother's voice brought the girl into action. "Free her hands from the dough, but gently; she must not yet be roused."

While Sulerna obeyed, her mother went to a nearby cupboard and, from its topmost shelf, brought out a small bottle.

Its top was sealed with thick wax, and this she attacked swiftly.

It was very quiet in the kitchen now—the girl could hear her grandmother's heavy breathing, as if the old woman strove to climb a hill in a battering wind. She helped her mother to support Haraska to the cupboard bed. The bottle had been given to the old man, and he was carefully shaking a drift of what looked to be leaves long dried to powder onto the blade of a small fire shovel.

They made no attempt to undress Haraska but settled her onto the bedding, drawing up over her the patchwork quilt which was usually kept rolled at the bottom of the bed. To Sulerna, that quilt had always seemed strange, for she could make no sense of its patterns.

Then a newcomer entered—Mistress Larlarn who, of all the clan, had the final word on illnesses. She came leaning forward a little, with one gnarled hand on Cathrina's shoulder, as if the child now aided her as Grandsire's sticks served him.

However, in spite of her need of assistance—for she did require such—the old healer crossed the kitchen quickly. She surveyed Haraska for a long moment before she spoke in that soft voice which always sounded to Sulerna like the Wind sighing.

"This one obeys a dream-call—yes. Such a summons comes not by day unless the need is great. Light the strengthfire."

Grandsire had thrust the small shovel closer to the hearth, and now there curled out smoke. It bore both the rich aroma of leaves being burnt in the fall and the faint perfume of wildflowers ablow in the spring, but it also held a third attar which seemed to be the breath of the Wind itself which none could ever set name to.

As Grandsire released it to her, the girl accepted the shovel and returned with it and its burden to the cupboard bed. There Larlarn received the smoking implement and began passing it up and down over the inert woman, head to foot and foot to head, while her lips moved in words never spoken aloud in the company of the uninitiated.

"*Yaaahh!*" Haraska gave a cry of horror, such as might be born when sighting a peril from which there was no escape. The healer thrust the shovel with its now-depleted dusting of burnt herbs toward the stricken woman's daughter to be set aside, and both her hands vanished under the overhang of the cupboard. Slowly she began to stroke the forehead of the clan mistress, whose face was now knotted in terror. From the still-open door behind them came a breeze that blew into the wall bed, and Haraska's contorted features relaxed. Yet the old woman's eyes still remained open, focused on something that drained the vibrant, happy life from her face and left a mask of growing despair.

Larlarn's hands cupped over those open eyes, not touching the skin underneath.

"Let the Wind sweep," she commanded. Others of the homestead were now crowded about the doorway of the kitchen. One or two of the women had edged inside, but none of the men intruded. The Wind had chosen its voice; they had only to listen.

"The Shadow rides, the Dark rises." Haraska's voice was the monotone of one reciting a well-learned message. "Styrmir will be the abiding place of all evil, and we"—now her speech held a broken note—"shall serve one such as none of humankind have bowed to for near a hundred hundred seasons. There comes a lord for the tower; and his power— *aaghha!*" Again her cry rang out. "His power shall be rooted within us of peace, from the babe new-born to the great-grandmam. The Covenant be broke!" Haraska reached up one hand now and clutched at Larlarn's sleeve. "We took not the Oath of Watch, and so we shall be the first of the prey. He comes down the Lost Road, no honest trader, but— a ruler of demons!"

Haraska gave a sigh, and her body relaxed, leaving her limp. When the healer lifted her hands, Haraska's eyes were closed, and her breath came fast and with a force that shook her whole body. Larlarn held out a hand and had pressed into it an oddly shaped cup, whose edge was pulled forward in one place to form a spout; then she gave a quiet nod to Sulerna. The girl held her grandmother's head steady while Larlarn worked the spout into the clan mistress's mouth, at the same time stroking her corded throat so they could see the old woman swallow. When that was done, Larlarn pulled the doors of the cupboard bed nearly shut and turned to face those of the clan who had gathered.

"This was a sending," the healer told them with authority, "by its strength from, I think, one of Those Who Dwell Apart."

None of the dunsfolk answered, but a hum arose.

"What have they to do with us?" asked a man who stood close to the door, a branch-cutting tool in his hand.

"The Light must always warn, Geroge!" Larlarn returned sharply. "It would seem the world has turned too many times, and we are about to witness a return of what we have nigh forgotten. Who has flock duty in the eastern meadows this day?"

"Yurgy," Geroge replied. For a moment, the husbandman twisted the reaping hook in calloused hands; then he burst out, "Mistress, does it matter who stands where this day? Do we not call—"

A large hand on his shoulder shook the youth warningly. "Where learned you what each Styrmir man born must know, boy? The Wind is not ours to summon, though it helped to carry this warning."

"We deal not with the Forest—and we have no truck with the ones who chose to stand apart!" Geroge refused to be silenced. "Where are our weapons?" His glance swept the chamber, resting for an instant on each face turned toward him. "Do we just stand, doing nothing to defend ourselves and what was always accounted ours?"

Mistress Larlarn turned away from the sleeping Haraska. "There were always those, and of our own clan blood, who had a foreboding that this day might sometime come. Go out that door, Geroge. Run to the duns of Ithcan, of Brandt, of Katha, and call up an army. No? Then listen! Within our line, we have taught the children the wisdom that others have not dealt out in generations. Yet, even in the days of the Last Battle, what we had to offer was too thin a talent to count much. Death and worse comes upon us now, and none will be left to hold a taper against the fall of night. Those Who Dwell Apart may well believe that they have done their duty by this sending. They are great cherishers of traditions and oaths, and they will stand by the Covenant. And think not that the Forest will take heed of our plight. We shall, indeed, be sheep—bound and delivered to the slaughter!"

The youth brought his hook down against the back of a chair, hacking a grievous gouge in the flawless, brightly rubbed wood. His face was flushed, and his mouth was flattened into a tight line to lock unseemly words within. The healer regarded him for a moment, then turned to the oldfather of the dun. When she spoke, her voice as freighted with the heaviness of one about to shoulder a great burden and already nearing the end of her strength.

"Though it will do us little good, Grandsire, someone should ride for Yurgy. Should the innocent young of a neighbor be the first to feed the enemy?"

Though the day had started out clear, a spiderweb of fog now appeared to be clinging to the heights of the bare mountainside eastward. That precipice was not of the Forest, nor did any of the valley venture there; but men had and did, for the traders who came twice a year still used the pass above. On their last visit, however, these chapmen had reported a dangerous overhang that might in time close off the narrow passage.

It was warm enough that Yurgy had discarded his outer coat and now, in his jerkin, he sat on a rock, very still. He was engaged in something exciting—a trick of Power he was not sure he could do.

The stout reed he had harvested this morning with dew still beading it lay on the ground, twisting now and again until it seemed about to spin over. Within it, a grub was very busy, eating out the sweet pith and leaving in its wake a smoothed tube. The young herdsman had concentrated on summoning that voracious small worker, and his delight that the worm had appeared and the work was being done was almost more than he could contain.

So the old stories *were* right! One who surrendered his own will to the Wind could hope to become a part of all the world in a new way. The boy watched the grub's blunt, brownish head emerge from the far end of the reed, and he wanted to shout; instead, he held his body moveless and let the Wind carry his thanks to the little borer of cores.

Then came a sharp interruption. The wiry-coated bas-hound gave tongue at the side of the flock nearest the old road—and the dog's ululating howl was picked up and echoed by his two half-grown sons.

The boy was on his feet instantly, leaving his coat and food pouch where they lay, and heading down from the rock. The sheep were milling about, and the shrillness of the new lambs' bleats and the ewes' anxious cries made a clamor that broke the usual quiet with a hint of worse to come.

A scream rent the air—not from any living throat, but as if the Wind itself had uttered a cry that was half pain, half promise of peril. And then, where those webs of mist had been gathering on the heights, a spear of light flashed forth, so bright that even the sun could not hide it. Not honest sun glare or the softer beaming of the moon, not true fire flame—that brilliance was nothing of Yurgy's world to which he could give name.

Nor was the light all. There followed an instant of dead silence. The young herdsman, no longer even aware of his flock, wrapped his arms around his suddenly shivering body. The Wind—that low-voiced being that had encircled him so comfortingly through the morning—was *gone!*

Sound came again: a crackling—the earth itself might be splitting apart. That dangerous rock in the pass—had it yielded to some force, falling and walling off Styrmir from every other land?

Now birds climbed the sky, black of wing, their hairless heads mere puffed sacs of scarlet skin—such pollution as neither the valley nor the Forest had ever vomited into the air. There was a breathless feeling, as if both the land and the trees . . . waited.

The fragments of talent, which were the Wind's remaining gift, whirled abruptly in a wild dance about and above the flock, for there were calls even the earth itself could be summoned to answer. Yurgy swayed. His hounds—! Tusker, the sire, was walking stiff-legged down the road, leaving the flock and his duty behind him; while his sons followed, nearly on their bellies as if crushed down by fear.

A sudden movement showed ahead in the fringe of old gnarled trees bordering the curve of the road where it entered the valley: a pack train. But the boy knew, from his first sight of it, that this was no trader such as had ever before visited Styrmir.

Bile rose in Yurgy's throat, but he could not move so much as a finger. Though the mist web did not enwrap him, he was still trapped—trapped!

The fear rising from the animals, by now running back and forth across his path, fed his own growing horror. In the past, strange creatures had sometimes come to the edge of the Forest to be sighted by those of humankind; but the woods children had been merely different, not—not—*evil*.

The huge bas-hound had come to a halt, his offspring behind him. As, in a happier time, he might have saluted the moon, he now threw back his head and bayed—not in warning but rather as if he faced now what neither fang nor claw could bring down. That howl rang so ear-numbingly through the windless world of the pastureland that it shook Yurgy partway free.

The panicked sheep were beginning to collapse here and there; some ewes had even crushed their lambs. Now the young herdsman could feel the force that had kindled the tinder of their fears into a mad flame. This was no Wind, caressing and healing—it was a power arising from the earth and gathering to itself parts of life which none could see. Unable to stand against that, Yurgy moved forward, stiff-legged and helpless as his own hound. And what he saw, through staring eyes he could not close, was so sickeningly unbelievable that his whole inner being was wrenched with revulsion.

Things—things no mortal, even one twisted of mind, might put name to—led the head-drooping pack animals. Then, as if they, too, were hounds, albeit of hellish breed, the creatures launched themselves forward, bore the herd dog to the ground, and ripped the living flesh from the screaming animal. And the bas-hound was not alone in his torment. Several of the horrors raced down the road and, even as had their sire, the two whelps ceased, in a rain of blood, to be.

The sheep had subsided; perhaps the death of their guardians had touched them in passing. Those monstrous butchers had begun to move purposefully in the direction of the flock itself when, as though heeding a silent command, they suddenly stopped and swiveled their heads in the direction of an approaching figure.

The rider who led this demonic crew urged his trembling, sweating horse forward, skirting fastidiously the fouled places where his minions still fought over the scraps of their feast. So great was his contrast to those beings that it could almost make Yurgy believe the events of the moments just past to be those of a troubled night vision.

This was a man, slender of body and bravely dressed in a jerkin from which dangled chains, each supporting a winking jewel. He wore no head covering, but his waves of thick reddish brown hair were kept in place by a wide metal band which, though bare of any ornament, somehow drew the eye. He was clean-shaven—in fact, his skin gave the appearance of having never supported hair. Thus, he seemed young—until one saw the feral yellow eyes beneath his smooth brows. Had it not been for those eyes, and for the cruel curl to his lips, the stranger might have been judged as handsome as a lord's son from one of the old tales.

Now the coldly compelling gaze was bent upon Yurgy. The horseman raised his arm and beckoned with a graceful sweep of a gauntleted hand. In spite of every instinct against it aroused in him by the night, the boy obeyed.

Goaded by fear, Yurgy did next what he was, by the most binding rule of the valley, never to attempt—he strove to reach the Wind. But there was no Wind—only an eerie emptiness and that pull of power he had felt from the herd and its hounds on the first appearance of this man.

Then he was standing at the side of the windblown horse—and its master.

"Greetings—Yurgy."

The soft voice seemed, in an odd way, to deaden the nightmare about the boy. But how did this stranger know his name?

"Who is your headman?"

Did he mean the oldfather of the dun? Yurgy wondered. Guessing that that might be so, he answered hoarsely, "Racal the Sixth of our dun here."

"Excellent." He of the catlike eyes fairly purred. "And now you shall lead me to him."

It felt to the young herdsman as though a haze had risen all about him. He was not even aware that he trod right through the bloody puddle which was all that was left of his youngest dogs; still less did he know that he led the grasping hand of the Dark itself into his beloved valley.

6

THERE WAS SILENCE IN THE FOREST. PERHAPS SOME OF THE VERY oldest of the huge trees could recall its like, or the toss of ruin stones here and there; but there were no others to remember a time when the Wind was stilled—utterly stilled. It might have balled inward upon itself, solidified, and then departed all the dimensions, worldwide, in which it once had life. As for the Valley which had been encompassed by it for so long, this was like the setting of the sun at midday, the shattering of the full moon's glory.

Small creatures ran madly for their burrows or crouched beneath the nearest shelter they could see. Birds sat claw to claw, wing tip to wing tip on branches, enough of them so gathered as to bend stiff wood earthward.

Those glittering motes, which made outward glory for the great Stone, swarmed until they made a thick mass about the hole that pierced the rock. There they pulsed, dimming and then flaring up, as if to offer protest and, perhaps, futile battle.

From the earth below the north side of the pillar came a stirring, a faint scent of long-settled soil reluctantly yielding place to life. Upward thrust a sheath of rolled green leaves, taller and taller, as if here was bursting into the outer world a plant to rival the rise of the trees themselves. Just short of the top of the monolith, the green blade came to a halt.

Sound arose now—not the soothing of Wind song but rather a drumming, an ear-numbing boom that seemed to issue out of the ground itself. The curl of the leaves began to loosen, but there was movement along the living wall of the glade, as well.

Here came one, then another, three, and four beings, all as alike to the untutored eye as if they had been hewn from logs. Their powerful, uncovered bodies were also the color of polished wood, and heavy fur with a sheen like the finest of satin cloaked each. Though they strode on hind legs in humanoid fashion, these were not men and women but creatures of a race the Forest itself had bred and nurtured.

Some of them had twisted a garland of flowered vines about their shoulders or thighs, and the perfume of those adornments mingled with a musky body smell which was not unpleasant. A number of them carried huge clubs—weapons such as might bring an ox to its knees with one well-aimed blow.

Yet their furred faces were not masks of malice. Rather, as they came on, they looked at the leaf sheath by the Stone and then to their nearest neighbors, and their uneasiness was plain.

Once the Forest's children had circled the waiting Stone, those with clubs held them high, then brought down to earth in unison the thick butts of those weapons; and the dull booming echoed again. Others began to sway their well-muscled bodies from side to side so that their vine-twinings were set in motion. They opened their heavy jaws, and there came forth, as if in a single voice, a call that was also a name.

"Theeossa—Ever-Living One—She Who Can Command the Storm Winds—" They added, to that first hailing, title after formal title.

The leaf continued to unfurl, until it spread wide, as might a wing. Then She who had been reborn again after generations of sleep stepped forth and, leaning back against the great rock, ran Her hands up and down it as one might stroke a beloved beast.

No more than the beings who stood in a silent ring about the place of rebirth might She be named human, but in a far-off mountain refuge She was known—known, yes, and now being watched by those gathered there to put to use a weaving of their own talents.

Though Her figure was feminine, showing the proper curves, Her smooth skin was pale green. Her dress was sleeveless and only half thigh in length, and it was girded by a wide belt that might have been fashioned from vine flowers stripped of their leaves and tucked tightly together. She held her head high, and Her hair was so bright a silver that the band holding it back from Her face looked dull and almost tarnished.

And Her face . . . But to those who had come at Her call, She had no true face. Between chin and brow, there was only a greenish mist no eye could penetrate.

"Sasqua." Because the Wind had deserted them, the earthborn could not speak in Her private voice, but in Her tone was the warmth of friend meeting friend. "Daughters, sons, who serve well this world of ours—greeting! You have been summoned as witnesses so that no one can ever afterward say a warning was not delivered."

Before Her, the air seemed to flicker. A section of it became opaque—and not only opaque, but occupied. Another stood there, matching the woman in height. His cockscomb of hair was nearly as silver as her own locks, but his features were not veiled.

The newcomer raised a long-fingered, pale-skinned hand to the Green One as if in greeting; but She, standing with Her hands planted against the Stone, made no answering move. The voice which issued from behind Her masking oval of mist no longer held a soft and welcoming note.

"Evil has rooted itself well within your company—deny it not!"

The man bowed his head in assent, and it was evident that he accepted Her anger as just.

"And yet you sit at your ease," She continued relentlessly, "making no move to finish that which should never have been allowed to begin!"

Now there was a slight change in the other's face. "Final judgment is not for either of us to utter." He answered as one who has long wielded authority.

"This scum, who gathered what he would of your learning, now takes elsewhere what pleases him—and takes it harshly, in blood and death. Yost, he and his works are a seeping sore open at your very border! You may well guess what he would have for himself—your place. Would you have him open one of the Great Doors—call up what he cannot control? How could even so learned a one as you hope to stand against such a loosing? You and your kind helped forge the seal of the Covenant—surely you know what lies behind it, ever waiting?"

The archmage's eyes flashed gold fire. "If we break the Covenant, are we any less guilty than he?"

"It is no one wrapped in Wind who does this thing. Caution has always ruled your kind. You depend upon the sanctity of locks—thus, what is prisoned by one man may be freed by another. Long ago, the Wind I call was made to swear away its full power, and that bargain has been kept. Now this Son of Dark prepares to ravish a whole land whose people have some kinship with us, for does not the Wander Wind visit them? And this evil came from your domain, Yost."

"He is *not* of us! And there is only one way we can strike back and still remain within the Covenant—"

"The old belief that the defense of a land must be rooted among its own people? *Faugh!* If you have chosen your army so, they shall die in their first engagement. That one seeks to open a door, and there will be none left to stand against him, not in that stricken land. Yost, I call upon you against all your oaths, your laws—I summon you now to stand against the Dark!"

As the earthborn uttered these last words, a shimmering played about the man; and he and that which had contained him wavered and were gone.

She who had thrown that challenge did not step away from the Stone more than half a pace or so; Her hands could still rest easily upon it. Now they moved up and down, stroking the surface, and in this manner She made her way completely around it. Still came no sound of the Wind; rather, there remained a silence so steady that the breathing of those watching could be heard.

When She had again reached the place from which She had started, She stood yet further back. The points of glitter that had gathered about the dark-filled hole now scattered up and down the length of the rough pillar. As they moved, they gathered here, fled apart there, until they had outlined two figures on the Stone as plainly as if nature herself had painted them on its face.

"See, daughters and sons?" The Green One looked over Her shoulder at the nearest grouping of the Forest people. "Once I might have called, and the Death Wind itself would have swept this filth from the surface of the clean earth. Oaths hold—but changes may also be made so that they will serve our purposes.

"Listen now to the word I lay upon you. Death stalks the land before our tree borders, and it will . . ." The woman hesitated for a long moment; then she stepped forward once more and laid a forefinger to the head of each of those out-lined figures of light.

"Keep the bonds until the day that will come for their breaking. Unfortunately, the mage Yost has the right of it— I could not wield what I now hold to break the shackles of the Covenant—even our Mother Wind will not be able to do more than bear a faint dream of green-knowing. But, mark you this, Sasqua of the True Blood—there shall come those who can fashion other and greater clubs than your own! Set your watch upon the Wind Stone; at its call, answer. Go not beyond the shadow of the fringe trees about the bounds of the valley, no matter what ill you may witness inflicted on the innocent there. It is not our choice, yet we must, as the mages, now stand apart."

For a last time, She touched those two figures sketched on the Stone. So indefinite of shape were they that one could only be sure they represented bipeds. This time, it was not their heads she sought but that ambiguous portion of their sticklike bodies which might, in a living creature, enfold the heart.

Once more, the heavy clubs struck the ground about the Green One, and this time the females also crooned what might have been a lullaby. Three times they did so, pausing after each repetition, though the woman did not make them any sign.

"Thrice called—" Now Her words were absorbed into the rising of a breeze and, around the Stone, the land came once more to life. Those of the Forest knew the lift of fear. Some of them, for whom the past was swallowed up by every sunset, could never keep in their small heads the memory of what had happened here; but the Wind would hold what must be learned again and, perhaps, relearned many times.

The body of the earthborn now touched, then closed over, those pictures; and, as if the Stone had returned Her embrace, She seemed to melt into the rock face itself. As Her children drew a long breath of awe, the light patterns dissolved into the motes of which they had been shaped, to resume their dance again over the gray surface like dust in a shaft of sunlight.

One of the most massive of the Sasqua raised his head, his broad nostrils expanding as if, against his will, he was catching some foul scent—a rank reek no waft of the Wind would carry.

"The dark one has come—" His message mingled as always with the voice of the Wind, and his face was now a fearsome mask promising ill to what must be met. "*We* hold the woods—we go not into the accursed land. But"—he had come forward to stand by the Stone, being careful that he did not touch it—"let it be known that, if any true of heart comes seeking shelter under the Wind's wide wings, such a one comes in safety. This She has not forbidden, and it is, this one thinks, such action as might be a part of what She would do."

Swingers of clubs, singers of Wind, trickle of cublings, the children of the Forest split apart, and the glade was left to quiet and—for the time—peace.

There was, however, no peace for Styrmir. Irasmus and his straggling caravan had made straight for the broken fang of the tower that rose stark against a dusky sky. Clouds were gathering there, though those were not driven by any natural force. Flowers, which had showed bright as lanterns in fields and hedges, now paled and drooped, their ash-gray petals falling earthward as if an early frost had cut them down.

Time and again, Yurgy half raised his hands as if to touch the ears that no longer served him. No birdcall, not even the frenzied bleating of his plundered flock, were to be heard any longer; but he could catch—and would, had he been able, have shuddered away from—the growled gabble that served for speech to the gobbes about him. Like one held by chains, he paced beside the mage's shambling horse. No longer could he pick up the pain and terror which beat the beast along the path his rider would follow; nor did he try to look up at the man in the saddle. From that direction flowed a monotonous murmur of words that meant nothing to the young herdsman but that seemed to change in tone from plea through excitement and on to triumph.

For Irasmus, this ride down his newly claimed land was an intoxicating experience. He had never doubted—at least, not for the past half year—that he would do just as he was now doing. Still, he found its accomplishment as heady a

draft to his spirit as might be apple cider to the parched
throat of a worker who had spent the morning swinging
a scythe.

This young lout who had been taken so easily—a good
rich drink the mage had taken from him, who was young
and had the full strength of untroubled innocence in him.
There would be more such—many more—for his quaffing.
But he must not be impatient. The one who practiced the
most efficient craft was not always the first runner in the
field.

Nor, after he had reached the tower, did the others who
were brought to him, so rightly named by the Forest Lady
the Son of Darkness, prove to have any defenses. There had
to be examples, of course, such as would never fade from
memory, and the gobbes were excellent tools with which to
mete out punishment, always hungry as they were in this
world not their own.

Thus Styrmir became a place of the living dead—not all
at once, however, for it amused Irasmus to spin out his
pleasure. He could afford to move slowly, as there had been
no whisper of opposition. In fact, upon occasion he wished
that he might suck out all the gifts at once from these land
grubbers, make them watch the devastation of everything
that made up their lives. There were times when his talent
leaching became as dull as having to sit in the Place of
Learning and listen to one of those prosy lore lovers dissect
this and that facet of the power, when all knew that full
control of it lay within their touch. Old men, they had lived
too long and clung too much to the ancient legends; and no
spirit or ambition was left in them. Nonetheless, Irasmus
had been careful so far not to attempt any of the various
methods he knew that would allow him to spy on Yost and
his ancient flock. Slow and sure, slow and sure—he had to
keep reminding himself.

At first, the Forest held no interest for the new ruler of
Styrmir, who was too intent upon gathering from his unwill-

ing captives—and from what they planted, tilled, and cherished—the major portion of the power he continued to store so carefully. But, as his demon servants drove the valley people to repair the tower to be a fit place for their master, he sometimes rode out a little way from that central point of the land he claimed.

The wizard had made some useful discoveries on a number of those occasions when he had thought to enlarge his knowledge of the land. There was one dun—kin, clan, whatever these clods called them—that appeared to possess a greater measure of talent than the others. He had so far left that particular holding alone, not even allowing the gobbes their clamored demand for a share of its flocks. If there were any truth in the rumors that some of these earthworms had any unusual talents, he wanted to make very sure of their nature before he took them.

Irasmus had come to drain, not to be drained. It was a laughable thought that any in Styrmir could stand against the knowledge he had so carefully garnered, so warily tested. Still, Firthdun and its folk stayed unharmed within his net. And perhaps they did possess some instinct keener than their fellows' for, from the day of his coming, they had shut themselves away from even their neighbors in the valley.

At its homestead, that clan went about its usual round of tasks as though nothing else mattered and Styrmir remained as it had always been. He who observed them with such interest had some of them listed. Seven males—one very elderly; another well past the prime of life; several youths of little power, and children.

Then there were the females. No one who had studied at the Place of Learning was stupid enough not to know that there was woman talent that both stood apart from that of males and sometimes was superior to it. Of womenfolk, Firthdun held an ancient of whom his spy birds saw little, as she remained in the house; one of middle years; two of budding youth; and a child. There was, moreover, another female who had taken up residence with them, and she was a point to be carefully considered. What had brought her there on what must have been the very day Irasmus had come into the valley—and what held her there? Of course, as of this day she had no home to return to, because the gobbes had made one of their belly-filling raids and had left the woman's homestead a smoldering ruin behind them.

Yes, in spite of the new ruler's confidence and success, Firthdun remained in his mind like an itch between the shoulders. The sooner he had to do away with it—holding and holders—the better.

Why did his thoughts keep returning to the younger of the two girls? It was as if something he had forgotten pricked at his memory now and again. Very well—tonight he would be back at those books which had been arranged with such scrupulous care in his chosen tower room. From that sealed chamber in the Place of Learning, the supposed scholar had taken, on general principles, the full contents of a shelf but had so far been able to adequately decipher only four volumes. Well, they were enough for his present situation.

His curiosity oddly aroused now, Irasmus turned his mount back toward his stronghold. Turning, he caught an unusually sharply focused view of the Forest edge. His distance from it was such that he could not be truly sure he saw—what? A tree walking, retreating further into the gloom?

Utter nonsense, of course.

7

As THE FLOWERS WITHERED, SO DID ANY COLOR OF CHEER FADE from the land itself. Men and women now plodded leaden footed to the fields, dull-faced children with them; but that which possessed them now brought all to work only to feed its own ravening hunger. Even the crops had a grayish look, and many of the heads of the upward-pushing grain showed the spotting of decay before they even had a chance to ripen.

Yurgy no longer had a flock to urge to the uplands—what remained of that pitiful herd was the sport of the gobbes. He did not have a home, and deep in him that loss was an abiding pain which ate at him night and day. He had not been born of Firthdun; however, the law of fosterage had brought him there when he was barely able to set one foot firmly before the other. The tie was a very distant one but strong enough so that that clan had taken in the orphan.

Other duns in the valley were reduced to ruins. For some reason no ordinary human could possibly guess, the master had not yet sent his force upon Firthdun, almost as though he savored the fear his continued failure to attack must be breeding there. The numb emptiness in Yurgy's mind—for it would seem that he was now brain deafened, even as he had been ear deafened—only let him wonder vaguely at times what kept Irasmus's hand from squeezing the life from the boy's foster dun as he had wrung dry all others.

Yurgy slopped water from the ill-smelling well they had reopened in the courtyard of the stronghold. Perhaps because he was the first one Irasmus had taken into bond, he had remained a member of that crew the mage led.

Now he was aware that the demons' master—and his— had come riding back into the area that ringed the base of the tower, but Yurgy did not raise his eyes from his task. It was only when the crooked, taloned fingers of Karsh, the leader of the gobbes, closed in deliberate torment on his shoulder that he looked up. Distantly, he noticed that even his lord's brilliant richness of clothing was dimmed by these walls that the men and women labored each day to raise higher, set firmer in their ancient pattern.

"Slug." The master's finger crooked. Yurgy could not have disobeyed that summons had he wished to do so—not with the gobbe chief's hold upon him. Somehow, he found himself able to look into the face of the man who was regarding him as a reader might turn upon an open page.

"How many seasons have you?" came the next demand.

It had become harder and harder to summon words— for little had those of Styrmir now to speak of, as the Dark had well nigh swallowed them up. Only now, for a moment or so, it seemed that Yurgy was thinking more clearly than he had for days, and with that sensation came a new surge of fear. The boy coughed, nearly choking, as if a puff of dust had caught him full in his face, but he answered as quickly as he could.

"I was counted scythe-worthy last harvest." He found those words almost meaningless.

The master was smiling. "Not too old, and not too young to delay us much," he commented, though the sense of this remark escaped his listeners. "It does not become any man to waste a tool. Get you to the kitchen, slug, doff those rags of yours, and scrub your noisome body." He raised his hand and pinched his nostrils together to make very clear his opinion of this son of the soil. "Then come with Karsh. You may"—he nodded his head at his own thoughts—"be what I need."

Still bearing the now-full buckets, the chief gobbe keeping shadow close at his shoulder, Yurgy entered the lowest room of the tower. The greasy smell of an ill-kept kitchen was strong, and that reek was laced with the stench that was ever a near fog about the demons. Two women of the valley were busied there already, the first at the fireplace, the other chopping gory meat on the table. The one performing the latter task bore a bruise on her cheek and over her chin, and blood had trickled in a thin stream from the corner of her mouth, leaving a stain she had made no attempt to wipe away.

The workers spared only a quick glance for those who had entered, but the bruised woman gestured to put the pails under the table. Karsh favored her with a horrific grin.

"This one"—early on, the master had somehow made it possible for the two different species to understand a common speech—"he washes and goes aloft." The gobbe jerked his thumb at the nearby staircase. "Let him go bare—the lord has no liking for rags too close to him."

The woman carving the meat jerked the last bucket back out from under the table, not looking at the boy. The other scrabbled with already-grimy fingers in a scorched bowl, then slapped a lump of lardy soap into his hand. This done, they turned resolutely back to their labors and ignored him. Karsh, however, lounged at the foot of the steps, staring at Yurgy's bared flesh as if it suggested some table dainty.

When the youth was as clean as his crude efforts would allow, he tipped the bucket into the sour-smelling drain. A chill struck at him as, though the fire burned well and there was heat in the room, he felt a kind of shame he had never known in his lifetime before.

"Up!" his gobbe guard commanded impatiently, as Yurgy's feet found the steps even colder. There was a small landing at the end of that short flight and a closed door to the right; but the stairway continued, and Karsh signified that he should do the same.

There was an odd change here. The stink of the kitchen was gone, and for one moment of excited hope, Yurgy thought that the Wind had sent a messenger down from the next level in welcome and protection. However, just as quickly, he realized that, while the scents intermingled now to form a cloud which apparently shut away the rot-tainted realities of darksome living, this was not woven of the freshness of flowers or growing things, and it carried no lightness to the heart, no joy for the mind.

The next floor of the tower also had a shut door awaiting; and the steps did not end but were much rougher, newer work that narrowed until the gobbe would have had a hard time forcing his way above. However, the creature made no attempt to do so but only brought his fist down with a drum note against the door, holding the boy at the same time in the grasp of his other hand.

No sound came from beyond the portal; instead, it swung open, and Yurgy faced an inner curtain of black, so dark as to suggest that there was nothing behind it. Karsh allowed the youth no hesitation but shoved him through an almost-invisible opening in that barrier—and into such light and color as he had almost forgotten could exist.

Irasmus sat at ease in a high-backed chair that was curiously assembled from what seemed the crooked bones of some great animal. But it was also cushioned in scarlet, and certainly the sitter could rest in comfort.

A table stood within reach. Placed for easy touching was a round globe of polished crystal upon a smoke-colored stone that looked almost as if it might be a bowl of sorts, for within it whirled and twisted a whisper of color only a little darker than what held it. There were also two tall candlebranches and, catching sight of those, Yurgy stiffened.

Those lifters-of-light had been made for Year's End candles and were to be used only for that short hour and after proper ritual; at all other times, they were kept in the great chest of the tenthman of Well-Watered Lea. But, of course, that dun was long since gone; and the boy himself had seen the tenthman torn apart by whooping gobbes. In the holders now were no candles of the finest and clearest beeswax, as was fitting, but rather crooked, greenish stalks of a stuff that burned clearer than any of the candles or lamps Yurgy knew in the clan homesteads.

Flanking the candles at one end of the table was a pile of books—old ones with wooden covers and tarnished metal hinges. There were, in addition, several parchment scrolls. On the other side were more records, and these were also known to Yurgy—they were the tallies submitted each season to the Harvest Assembly. Two copies were always made, one kept with the candles and the other stored in Firthdun.

The candles, that loaded table, and the presence of the master at ease held the valley youth's attention for longer than anything had done since the mind-drain had caught him. Could Irasmus be in some way releasing that hold? But why?

"Hither—into the light." Irasmus beckoned. Again the boy felt that warm wash of shame. He could not read anything in the mage's expression; still, he had a feeling that he was being thrust facedown into the dirt by something that lay at the far back of the other's yellow eyes.

"Turn—slowly," came the next command. Yurgy tried to fasten his thoughts on what lay in the room as he obeyed. There was a richness here, though all the colors were muted. He saw a shelf on which rested bowls and stoppered bottles; another bore books and rolls of such accounts as were done quickly for shorter record-keeping. Two braziers rested on high stands; from them coiled those threads of smoke which he thought changed the scent of this level of the stronghold. Against the far wall stood a luxurious bed (one taken from Gotthley of Sanzondun), piled high with coverlets and a couple of furred rugs. Then the boy had finished his circle and once more faced Irasmus, to discover that the master had opened one of the Styrmir record rolls.

"You are of Firthdun?"

Yurgy shook his head. "I was but fostered there."

The mage studied him. "Fosterage is given only when there is kinship," he commented. "Where, then, were you birthed, and why did you come to fosterage?"

"I was son to Yetta of the mill; my sire was Ovan. In my first year, there was a storm, and the river took the mill and most of those within it. My mother was second granddaughter to the Firthdun line, and my father's kin already had sons in many. It was arranged for me then."

Again there was a short silence, as if Irasmus were considering something which might or might not be of importance.

"But the truth is," he said slowly, "that you have in you some kin blood. How well do you know her whom they call Sulerna?"

The youth was astounded at the sudden change in subject. "As well as sister kin. I was fostered, but they believed that the blood held true in me—"

"Blood?" The mage leaned forward, his interest fully caught now. "Blood, or—talent?"

Yurgy shook his head, confused, but the master was smiling again. "You may find your way to being a hand of mine."

"Like Karsh?" The boy somehow found the freedom— and the boldness—to demand.

"Not so—look around you, slug. Once I was as soft brained and slave intended as you. There are many ways in which the talent can serve, and others by which it may be summoned. Get you down now to the chamber below this; bid the door open, and it will obey. What you find there is yours for a space—perhaps forever, if you are clever enough."

The head demon was not waiting outside, a fact for which Yurgy was thoroughly grateful. He did as he had been ordered—retraced his steps downward, to pause before the other door, clear his throat, and manage to get out a single word: "Open."

Surprise stirred in him a little when the portal swung smoothly inward. Here was no heavy curtain of dark but, rather, light which was stronger than any finding its way through the narrow window slits of the tower.

The boy took several steps forward and then glanced down at the soft floor covering which soothed his bare feet. This was no lately mown grass, for all that it was dull yellow and seemed as thickly bladed as turf.

Behind him, the door glided closed again. Yurgy spun around, ready to burst out once more if he could; but, to his startlement, he saw that, though the door itself was a barrier against intrusion, there were also two bars on this side—one near the top and one close to the floor. He guessed shrewdly that any attempt at defiance might well be turned against him to seal the room in some fashion, but still he attempted to push those bars into a defense; however, they were immovable, and, though uneasy, he at last gave up the struggle.

The carpeting, which was so like the browned ground growth of autumn, covered the entire floor except for three places where there stood lamp standards as tall as himself. There was a low trundle bed, which might have been taken from under the rich four-poster in the upper chamber, and a table on which perched a small lamp which appeared so far turned down that its flame did not do much against the gloom. A chair was drawn up to the table. At the far side, opposite the bed, was a curtained niche. The boy advanced warily to this area, only to find that it hid a garderobe, as well as a very small ledge on which stood a jug and an empty basin.

The last of the furnishings that he had been carefully avoiding was a chest so heavily carved that, in the uncertain light, grotesque faces and monstrous forms appeared to shift of their own accord, while bulbous, slit-pupiled eyes leered at him.

The hasp bore no lock. Yurgy hated to touch that wood, which he believed very old and which, though well-polished, was overscored with a multitude of leprous-looking patches, more virulent than any mold designed by nature. However, the chest opened easily enough, and the boy looked down at such clothing as one of the far-traveling traders might have owned, different by far in cut from either the smocks and breeches he had been used to all his life or from the color-flashing garments the master affected.

This chamber possessed no mirror to reveal his nudity, nor did he any longer feel chilled. Yet, Yurgy was very reluctant as he drew forth those garments one by one.

He who once must have owned them had been about Yurgy's height, but his girth had been greater, so that the boy had to fold in the clothing and make very sure the belt, which was a part of this hoard, was tightly drawn. The chest yielded boots also but, regretfully, Yurgy had to set those aside, since they were at least a size too small for his bare field-worker's bony feet.

As he fastened the last clasp of the jerkin (which did not hold well because of the width of the garment), he once again gave searching survey to the room and all it held. The wits, which had been so dulled, were surfacing in him again with a keenness he had not known for days.

One thing, Yurgy knew, was clear: this room might have the luxuriousness of a dun leader's, but he did not think he was going to be able to leave it at his own desire. There were the door bolts, to be sure; however, there was also the matter of food and drink—supplies he had certainly not come across in his exploration. He was as much a captive here as he had been since his first meeting with Irasmus.

Once more, the boy made a circuit of the room, ending to stare down at the chest. That coffer was now empty, save for the useless boots he had dropped back into it before he'd closed the lid. Save for the lamp standards, which would unfortunately afford only the clumsiest of weapons, no arms were to be found.

It was the book on the table that caught Yurgy's attention at last. He was aware, from his visit to the master's quarters, that books were treasures. As were all the dun young, Yurgy had been early taught his letters and simple sums but, beyond that, no book knowledge but only the long-gathered wisdom of his elders.

For lack of any other occupation, he started for the table and the book that lay so close to the source of light, beckoning to him. But he had taken only a few steps when emptiness of mind descended on him once more.

It was not the table and the book that drew the boy so strongly now but rather the trundle bed with its smoothly pulled covers. Not waiting to strip off his new clothing, he stretched out upon it and straightway had the feeling that he was in the soft embrace of something—the Wind? Deep-buried memory stirred even as his eyes closed. The Wind—Where had the Wind gone?

Gifford, Yost, and Harwice sat close together at the table, none of them moving, and stared at the oblong of light hanging at eye level before them.

Pictured there was a crude bed and on it a flush-faced boy lying as stiffly as a statue.

"Seek." The archmage did not speak aloud, but his lips formed the word. And seek they did. What they wrought then was not a thing forbidden to their kind, but it could only be called upon for service in the direst of perils.

The mages no longer saw the sleeping boy; rather, they viewed the rich and weird new furnishings of the chamber above his. And there, indeed, was Irasmus, busily referring from book to script-roll, then to a second book. The smoke of burning herbs was so thick that they who watched felt they should have been able to pick up the scent themselves.

"He prepares a tool," Harwice stated. "Should we move?"

"He has already begun his ensorcellment, and to interfere now would be beyond the talents of even all of us assembled in high council," Yost returned.

"But there must be something we can do!" The artist continued to protest, for he had never ere brushed more than the edge of so potent a dealing with the Dark.

"Death would answer," his superior said slowly. "We could reach out and stop the heart of that sleeper. Or—what is planned might be turned against the planner. We cannot, perhaps, influence those Irasmus intends to set about his filthy business now; but we may be able to twist his desires to bring him down in the end."

"But those whom he would make use of—what can we do for them?" Harwice had gripped the edge of the table and was holding it so tightly his nails bit into its substance.

"There is this," Gifford said. "Death is not an end—do we ourselves not know that also? And the evil born within one which is forced upon another is not wrongdoing that the tool must, in the end, pay for."

"The—the realization of this thing"—the painter's voice sank—"that is to be laid upon me."

"Yes; that will be a heavy burden. However, there is deep strength in this boy, and he shall leave that as heritage to those coming after. He shall die—but to live in the arms of the Wind!"

Yurgy turned his head, and now the mages could see him better. Coursing down his cheeks were silver streaks of tears, tears from closed and dreaming eyes.

8

THOSE WITHIN FIRTHDUN NOW ALWAYS GATHERED AT SUNDOWN in the great kitchen, where the rich smells of the even meal still lingered to lighten hearts a little—at least, those of the younglings. But now there was neither telling of tales nor roasting of apples on the hearth; the dunspeople did not know how much longer it might be before the new master struck and all would be gone forever.

The younger men made regular rounds at night. They could not walk the outermost boundaries of the dun, but they made as sure as possible that their animals rested in safety. And since neither man nor beast stepped beyond those boundaries, both seemed to be free from attack, though no one was sure of the reason for that.

Theirs was not the richest dun in the valley—those had gone easily and early. It was certain—the Firth folk were all sure in their hearts—that their escape so far was because Haraska was dunmistress here, along with dunsire. He had never spoken much of his past, but it was well known that, in years gone by, both had ventured into the Forest at the Wind's call, returning to become pillars of strength against evil.

Long days of nursing and nights of careful watching had

been needed to return Haraska to the woman she had been on that morning when the sending had brought its warning. She, who had always been joyful of heart, full of stories to keep the children amused, and clever and diligent with her old hands, no longer spoke much, and then only of very common things. The dunmistress laughed no more with the little ones but rather studied them from time to time and sighed until they, sensing that something was wrong, kept their distance from her. Above all, she clung to Sulerna, fretting if the girl were not in her sight and making her promise over and over again that she would venture no farther than the orchard. Yet, Haraska admitted freely when the others questioned her, she had not truly foreseen any especial evil for her granddaughter but only feared for the young woman in her heart.

Most of all, the dunsfolk missed the Wind. Hans brought out his pipe now and then and awoke trills of sound, the tunes they had danced to at the harvest feasting; and there was a vague comfort in those songs, as if a ghost of a breath of the Wind did still reach them.

Time passed as the people lived in this fashion on the edge of darkness. That Yurgy was lost to them they knew, for he had been seen at hard labor with the men and women dispossessed of their duns, but the Firth folk dared make no attempt to bring him to what now seemed their place of safety.

With the help of Mistress Larlarn and those of the strongest talent, Haraska had twice tried to reach forth for communication with something which was of the Light. However, she struggled to no purpose, and, at last, Mistress Larlarn declared that the oldmother must not use up her precious energy so.

Of an evening, the household had gotten used to sitting in a dimness broken only by the small fire on the hearth. Children rested in their parents' arms watching the flames, while the elders reported each day the amount of work that had been achieved. None spoke of what all knew—that just beyond their holding lay fields of stunted and fungus-fouled grains, choked by fearsome growths of new weeds that gave off vile odors and left stinging blisters on the flesh of any who touched them.

Their flocks were gone and had been since the day Yurgy had walked down the valley at the side of the master's horse. However, they still had two milk cows, a sty of pigs, and a goodly flock of fowls, all of which were kept well within the dun boundaries. Moreover, the kitchen garden, with its wealth of vegetables, throve, and the fruit trees promised a high basket-heaping to come.

But this island of peace and plenty lay only within the borders of Firthdun—and how long would it last?

This night, Haraska sat in her usual chair. A knitting bag lay beside her seat, but she made no effort to reach for needles and wool. Instead, while Sulerna sat on the floor before her, the dunmistress had captured both the girl's hands and was stroking the smooth flesh. The fire flared suddenly as a new piece of wood caught flame, and Sulerna could see the tears drop from her grandmother's eyes as the old woman made no attempt to sweep them away.

"Grandmam," she said hesitatingly, wanting to bring comfort, but how—and for what?

Haraska's clutch on her tightened, as if she believed she must keep that hold on the girl for the sake of Sulerna's life. Those who sat about them had begun to watch the two, and it was Mistress Larlarn who rose up behind Haraska's chair to rest her hands on the oldmother's bent shoulders.

"Sister," she said. She spoke softly, yet so quiet was the room that all within it heard her. "Is it a sending again?"

The dunmistress gave a great wrenching sob. "Wind—!" The sob scaled up to a high cry, near a scream, for aid. Leaning further forward, she caught Sulerna into a tight grip, no longer looking down at the girl but rather into an emptiness beyond, which was being filled by something she fought to escape.

"No!" Again came that shout of denial. "No! Even the Dark cannot move so—"

Slowly her grip on Sulerna loosened, and it was the young woman who had to brace herself to keep the weight of that old body from sliding onto the floor. But Mistress Larlarn and several others moved swiftly to gather their old-mother up. She lay limp, with eyes closed; however, her face on the left was savagely twisted to one side, and her left arm swung as if all control of muscle had gone.

"What—what is it!" Sulerna cried.

Mistress Larlarn shook her head. Fatha put down her young daughter and hastened to open the cupboard bed; her face was also drawn, and her breath came in gusts. Marah tried to hold to her mother's skirts, only to be shaken loose.

There was a sudden voice from one of the men: "Like the second of Wiftdun! We were just sitting, eating our meat at the Midwinter Feast, and he was taken so—but he was none that dealt in dreams. Four months he was as a babe and could not talk, sit, or stand; only his poor, tired eyes followed any who came near him, asking for aid. And we never knew what or who had struck him down."

But Haraska looked for no help from those now tending her. Instead, her eyes remained tightly closed, as if all her will centered now in refusing to look.

Fatha drew the quilt up about her mother's body. All the light and the usual kindliness had fled from her face as she spoke directly to the healing woman.

"Is this some stroke from that death maker who would be our master? Wind Caller she was in her youth, and dreamer for all of us who still held to the old ways. When one would kill a plant past reviving, one destroys a root—"

"Of a certainty, there was a sending," Mistress Larlarn replied slowly, "but I do not think it was aimed at her in direct attack. Rather, what she saw aroused great fear in her for another—" She nodded toward Sulerna.

"But—but I am not a dreamer," faltered the girl. "Why

should the one in the tower think me prey worthy his notice?"

"If he does, he need count his thoughts again!" The well-muscled arm of her eldest brother Elias gathered her close against the strength of his supporting body.

Grandsire, who had been sitting and stroking the nerveless hand of his wife, now turned to stare at the healer. "Mistress"—his strong voice seemed to have lost half its wonted resonance—"there are ills of the body to which all of us can be subject. Think you that an interrupted sending might well bring on what we have seen this night?"

"Fear," the woman answered him straightly, "can harm past healing—twice in my lifetime I have seen it so. What Haraska saw twisted her spirit and drove her near to an end. Look upon her now, Oldfather—see how her eyes strain? She does not lie in any dream. No, she denies with all that is in her what she saw or still sees. This was not a sending such as we welcome; it was—perhaps yet is—a foreseeing."

A murmur arose in the room. One of the smaller children, frightened by the emotions of its elders, began to cry, and its mother made haste to hush it.

"There has not been a true foreseeing," Grandsire said heavily, almost to himself, "within three generations of the dun, nor has my wife ever shown such a talent. Mistress"— he spoke again directly to Larlarn—"can you mind-touch— if such a talent exists—and tell us what ill befalling holds her thus?"

Slowly the healing-woman shook her head. "With the Wind gone from us, that is impossible. I cannot learn what it might know, for it has left our land. Do you not understand?" There was a kind of fierceness about her now. "This monstrous lordling drains us—and sucks life from the waters, the clouds, the very earth! So he fills a well of power that puffs him ever greater.

"Once"—Larlarn's hands arose into the full light of the fire so that all might see them as they moved, though the

gestures were without meaning to those now gathered—
"some elders of my kin—my dun—dealt more openly with
the Wind Stone: that which anchors the Wind to our world.
But the Stone is no longer yours to seek—"

From the cupboard bed came a gasp which drew their
attention. Haraska's body writhed. Plainly she no longer had
the use of either her left arm or leg, and spittle ran from
the corner of her distorted mouth. But her eyes were open,
and her spirit raged in them, trying to force some communication. Her struggles from the frustration of her inability to
do as she wished brought Fatha, Sulerna, and Larlarn to
hold her in the bed, for it seemed she might throw herself
upon the floor.

Twice the old mother gabbled sounds that were far from
words; then she shuddered and grew still. It was apparent
that the folk of Firthdun could not hope for any swift recovery, if recovery at all, from this blow of fate.

The twisted, ever-burning candles in Irasmus's chamber
flickered once, and the dark lord's hands closed tightly on
the record-roll he had been studying—a listing of duns on
which there were also some newer runic settings of names.
Then he threw back his head with a hearty laugh and
reached for the goblet waiting to hand. Holding it first aloft
as if he gave a toast to—something, he then drained it, even
though it was the last of his bruwine, brought with him to
celebrate some momentous event. What greater knowledge
could he have at present than the discovery that his growing
suspicions were true?

Setting aside the goblet, the wizard took up a pen and,
dipping it carefully into the last of the wine, drew on that
genealogical roll a line that connected two names set some
distance apart. Chuckling, he found the midpoint of that line
and proceeded to set below it a short pattern of vertical
dots, scoring the pen into the parchment at the base of the
bar with vigor enough to break the point.

Then that roll was pushed aside, and Irasmus took up

one of the books he had brought with him. This was a slender volume, bound in a strange hide with short, bristly hair.
The pages within were few, and only a sprinkling of them
bore lines of cramped writing. The mage had no difficulty
in discovering what he sought: three such scribblings, hard
to read, but not when he held the book so that the page in
question faced the smoky globe that seemed the center of
all he thought important.

Once more, the flames of the crooked candles flickered,
though there was no breath of air entering the room. Irasmus ran his fingernail under one of those strange inscrip-
tions, as if such a gesture would enable him to get its
meaning exactly correct.

Twice, three times, the lights of the tapers wavered.
However, Irasmus kept to his task; and the flames flared
high and burned clear again. Only then did his head come
up and, with care, as if he might be drawing some information from every wall about him, he made a slow and pain-
staking inspection of his quarters.

This web of his was protected by every defensive spell
he had hoarded over the years. Nothing could—or had—
dared even to try the strength of its armor. Yet somewhere
there had been a stir of talent—and one which was not an-
swerable to him.

Firthdun! But who there? It was the females of the line
who carried the talent most strongly. Once more, the dark
lord opened the scroll on which he had made the entry and
rubbed a forefinger across one of the names he had selected,
his body tensed with strain to pick up even the faintest
suggestion of power.

The old hag! Irasmus switched his gaze suddenly to the
globe on the table, and what he appeared to see instead of
its ever-swirling mist made his mouth curve in a cruel smirk.
So—she knew . . . or thought she did. However, in the end,
her old body was betraying her, making it impossible for
her to give any warning. He would keep watch on her, of
course, as well as on that other one of a descent inimical to

his plans: she whom they called Mistress Larlarn. His prize in that place must have not the slightest inkling of what was intended for her.

Now it was but a matter of time, because part of this wreaking must be done with the aid of nature, or it would fail. A man could—with a great deal of trouble and danger— call up a demon, but he could not physically control time in such a case. And all the necessary preparations were yet to be made, the events arranged in their proper order.

The mage could crush Firthdun and all those it held with no more difficulty than rising from his chair and walking across the room. But that homestead must lie for a while yet in its imagined safety, until— He licked his lips, as if he could envision a banquet table spread before him. Talent . . . With the taking of that dun— No, he had enough slaves, and none others would be so rich to the taste or so bountiful in supply. When he was through with that holding, it would be utterly erased, down to the last shriveled blade of grass— in his own time, not theirs. Those sniveling earth grubbers had chosen this fate, or one like it, long ago.

Irasmus was aware now—and the knowledge added savor to his enjoyment of this moment—that his defenses were at last under test. Let Yost or Gifford or both of them with all the rest try to learn what he would do!

The master of Styrmir rerolled the record sheet and again took up the strange book, muttering certain words as he closed it. At present, his most needful tool lay but one floor beneath him in deep, drugged sleep; and there was, more-over, the matter of Firthdun to muse on now and then.

Wind does not die—it withdraws, comes with teasing puff or hammering blow, then retreats once more. Who can harness the Wind of Deep Hearing to one's will? No power known in this world.

Yet oaths can also bind . . .

None knew whether the Wind was a living entity with purposes wholly of its own devising. But, at this hour, all that listened and added to its strength were suddenly uncertain. They well understood, within the extent of their reasoning power, that the Wind was not only thoroughly awake but perhaps also ready to go seeking peril in spite of the bonds once laid upon it.

A young Sasqua, who had been intent upon reaching a certain place, hungry for what awaited her there, turned, she did not know why, aside from her straight path. Then before her opened the glade of the rock, its Stone aglitter with flecks of light as the brilliant bits held within its surface appeared to swirl restlessly.

Hansa made the hands-up awe sign of her species, even though she knew that she had, indeed, been summoned. Striding forward, she brushed through the ferns, while jeweled insects arose to dance in the air around her. She laid both her broad hands flat to the Stone and, in herself, listened. Twice she nodded: yes, yes—but not yet—the time was not yet. Then that which had drawn her was gone. In her mind a memory door closed, and she went on about the business which was so important to her this night.

9

THERE WAS ANOTHER DREAMER THAT NIGHT; PERHAPS IRASMUS'S wards were not as secure as he believed. What ventured into a sleeping mind in the dark lord's tower was a complete dream, set in each small detail in the receiver's unconscious, so that by his command—or another's—it might be brought into sharp focus again.

Color came first. To the one touched by the vision, the very appearance of those soft, rich hues was soothing—if the Wind ever appeared visibly to human eyes, this was certainly that Breath of Life in its most comforting aspect, seeking out its own.

No, *not* Wind—that was a denial so sharp and sudden as to shake the dreamer from his blissful content. This force might serve in its way, as did the Wind, but it was not that power.

Yurgy could not see clearly, for swathes and ribbons of the color wrapped him, held him for an instant, then swept away to make room for others of their kind. Yet, like a landsman who sowing rare and precious seeds on a waiting bed, each left something behind. Mist-masked faces hung suspended over him as if he lay at the feet of their wearers. They offered no outright threat, but they were of impor-

tance; and the fact that he could not see them clearly began
to erode his sense of well-being. Each who wore such a
featureless face also brought with him—or her or it—a growing need to know!

Now the colors wisped away, and only the hazy, masked
faces remained; then, far in the distance, someone called his
name. Yurgy would have answered with relief, but the summons was gone as quickly as it had come—thin and frail as
a Wind touch, yet heavy with such a weight of pleading
that he wanted nothing more than to go in search—to aid—

"Evil done must bring full payment, even if the doer
does not plan the foulness wrought." Those words were not
faint, like the call of his name, but seemed rather to strike
straight into his ears.

"Remember, at what seems to be the end for you, that
in this matter you were but a tool and not what Irasmus
shall try to make you. Let the knife come cleanly to your
throat, and be free—the Wind awaits. For this is a vile deed,
and from it will issue what will draw the dark one to his
fate, even though you shall then be long gone into . . ."

Once more, the colors ribboned about the boy. This time,
the soothing they brought was very faint, yet to the rags of
that he desperately clung.

Though he had never dreamed true before and had no
way of understanding, Yurgy knew that, though his eyes
were still closed, he was now fully awake. He—he was
Yurgy, fosterling of Firthdun. And where he lay . . . The
boy opened his eyes. This was certainly not the half-ruined
hut that had been his main shelter since that day of all disas-
ters when he had answered Irasmus's beckoning and had
been conscripted into the service of the Dark.

Anger, such as the valley youth had forgotten could exist
stirred in him, and the growing fire of his ever-strengthening
emotion seemed to clear his mind. To his sorrow, he knew
he had not been Wind-touched, no; but that those who had
looked upon him were skilled in dreaming he was sure.

Certainly, they were not of this place, nor of its deeds or thoughts.

Slowly Yurgy sat up and looked about him. No window broke these walls; it could be day or night. But there was light—the dull glow of candle lamps. He stared at those almost stupidly before memory returned.

He was in the tower! And he did not doubt for an instant that he was there by the will of Irasmus and would remain as long as the master had use for him. Why would a slave be sheltered in what was now luxury for any born of Styrmir? The boy held up his wrists—no metal bands, no chains.

Warily, he got up, expecting at any moment to have the gobbes break into the room and beat him for some task he had forgotten or otherwise amuse themselves with visiting small torments on him. He looked more closely at the nearest lamp; it was equipped with a standard about the length of his arm and formed of a dull metal.

Feeling as if any sudden movement might send him back once more into helplessness, Yurgy carefully approached the table on which stood the pair of candleholders. Then, for the first time, he noted the other objects there: a bowl of tarnished metal, a round of bread that looked more like human food than the half-chaff-and-straw cakes of the usual slave fare, and a tall cup.

Food! The sight of it gave him the power of rising hunger, and he was around the table in an instant and reaching for a share. This was one meal that would not be snatched from him by a gobbe and deliberately trampled, leaving him to pick broken bits of crust out of the mire.

At first, Yurgy tore at that round of bread as might one starving, cramming his mouth so full, lest the feast vanish, that he could not even chew. He coughed and sputtered, spraying crumbs about, then grabbed for the cup and drank so that the lumps in his throat were carried down. What the bowl held was cold, dotted with lumps of grease. But it was truly meat, and he disciplined himself to small bites and long periods of chewing to savor a near-forgotten taste.

The first flurry of eating behind, the boy realized there was also a book on the table. His forehead wrinkled; swimming bits of memory made his head ache. Another room, another table, books—more of them—and recorders' rolls.

When the boy had eaten all he could find—to the last crumb of bread, glob of turgid gravy, and sip of watery juice—his curiosity was awakened, and his eyes kept returning to the book. It must have been left for him, but to what end? True, he could read the Valley script although slowly and with effort. Once again his forehead creased, and he caught at a fragment of praise that floated in his seeking thoughts—he had been skilled at his studies.

Yurgy flinched. Master of such learning as Irasmus kept on his shelves? No! No clean-souled human would take pride in such vile achievement.

Nevertheless, he knew that, sooner or later, he must reach for the book, must open it, must discover what lay between its covers. It had been placed there for that purpose, and a compulsion not to be denied or defied urged him to action, even as tall grass bent before the flow of the Wind.

In appearance, it was not like the books he had seen in the mage's chamber. Those had been dull and dark, many of them covered by heavy slabs of wood possessing metal locks; there had also been one with the noxious-looking hide cover, as well as some with lighter backs and lines of lettering to identify them. This volume was larger than any of those. Plainly, it was a book that could not be comfortably held in the hand for reading but must rather be laid on a flat surface. Moreover, the cover was of brocaded stuff, dark red in color but fully as luxurious looking as the scarves the traders sometimes brought. Haraska had one such, of dawn rose with flowers picked out in silver thread, which she loaned to dunmaidens who asked to wear it at their weddings.

Haraska! The hand Yurgy had reached out to pull the

book closer to him slapped the tabletop instead. To think here of the Oldmother was like spitting on the floor!

Still, the rich crimson of the volume's cover drew his attention more strongly with every passing moment. Its color was not the maidenly blush of the early morning sky, matching Haraska's scarf—it was brighter; even to stare down at it began to excite him in a way he had never experienced before.

At length, curiosity won over wariness. Brushing the tabletop carefully, lest an overlooked crumb of bread or dollop of gravy spot that deep-red fineness, Yurgy reached forth both hands and drew the volume directly before him.

The lamp must have flared up a fraction, for the boy had a feeling that, at his movement, the light in the room had increased. Slowly he lifted the cover, to display a page that felt, to his rough fingers, most like stiffened linen of the finest weaving. There was writing there, surely enough, but using no symbols that had any meaning for him. And so it continued as four pages were turned to join the first. Now his interest was made more intense by frustration. He had been meant to find—and read—this book; therefore, he must puzzle out its secrets.

As the fourth page turned, Yurgy simply stared. Each of the sheets now was half occupied by a picture, depicted clearly and with a lecherous skill. The youth's face flushed, and his hands quivered as if to clap shut the cover, sealing each clever and vicious painting away. Only he could not. Nor would whomever had drawn him into this action in the first place allow him to raise his eyes until every detail seemed to have entered his head like a nail pounded in.

Nor was that the only picture; there were more. With the revealing of each, the lamps flared higher and the details demanded to be studied with ever greater care. Never had he seen nakedness so vilely aggressive. And, what was worse, a part of him was beginning to answer—to—to *relish* what he looked upon! His body felt as hot as if he worked, sans smock, under the heaviest smite of the summer sun.

No! one part of him continued to protest, but that was being overborne by this new and shameless eagerness to see what more could be disclosed when the next page was turned.

Yurgy had no memories of his life before he had been taken into fosterage, and any boy working on a farm comes early to certain knowledge. Only, that awareness was a knowing of life as it was—while *this* was the normal order of things twisted by evil into a hideous mockery to be rightly rejected.

The youth did not know when he began to notice the one girl who, by the artist's skill, was shown surrendering to the lusts of a creature he knew to be of an even more hellish nature than the gobbes. He found himself looking for her now in every illustration he uncovered. Then—and, with the one part of his mind that yet seemed his, he knew he had not willed it—his fingertip touched the small, childish breast so blatantly displayed . . .

And felt warm, living flesh beneath his own.

"Yaggha!" The sound came from the wrong side of him, but it signified his disgust. He caught the guilty hand with his other and held it in a tight grip, lest it master him again and—do what? This was only a picture in a book, and a book can be closed.

Using both hands, Yurgy slammed the cover and sank back into the chair. Sweat stood in beads on his forehead; his whole body seemed afire in a way he could not understand. And there was no Wind to calm and cool. Bits of those paintings danced alluringly even yet through his mind, in spite of all he could do.

Mage Gifford sat in his desk chair, also with a book on his knees; however, he was staring down as if the page lay by the toes of his boots. His round face seemed to have lost flesh in the past few days; new lines were etched there, and his lips had a downward droop.

"Do we then have to make this innocent pay for the ills we ourselves fostered by neglect?" That question was fired with a sharper crack than anyone in the Place of Learning had heard from the archivist in years.

Harwice, on his left, uttered a small sound that was only the ghost of a sigh. A sketch block on his knee, he set crayon to paper with a hand that appeared to move of its own accord, limning in swift, clear lines an object or scene; he immediately crumpled the page, and uttered an oath.

No change was evident in Archmage Yost's expression or bearing; yet it might well have been that the fires in his eyes were near to being quenched.

"The valley folk are—were—kin of ours once, not subjects of the Forest, though the Wind they could truly hear." Harwice hurled another ball of paper from him. "Thus it is one of our own whom we leave in the grasp of evil—an evil bred within *our* walls."

"Yes." A single word of agreement from Yost, spoken flatly, and with no emotion. "It is the price to be paid for freedom, for, as is known, a people are only free who fight for themselves and a just cause.

"You have read the runes as well as I. This monstrous act will, in time, bring forth that to which Irasmus shall cling and which will, at last, deliver him into the embrace of the shadow lord for whom he longs. Not that that will bring him any of the power he seeks! We have nigh spent ourselves this night to catch a dreamer who is not trained to the talent. The wise one who might have stood guard with him is dumb and as a child who must be cared for. Also—"

Gifford nodded, his distress even more visible. "She also—"

"The Caller?" Harwice's crayon was suddenly still, and his hands rose, molding the air as the stuff of his art. This time he outlined a woman, about whose slender body flowed nearly invisible drapery—the evidence of those powers She could command.

"No!" Yost was as emphatic with his denial as he had been earlier with his assent. "We but prepare now for what She has already urged upon us. Although"—he paused for a long moment—"She heeds, and I do not think that, in the end, She will refrain from taking a hand—a year or so from now."

"When it is too late!" Harwice snarled. "She was never one to partner another."

The loremaster placed the book on the carpet by his feet. "So be it. But what we have taken upon ourselves must be paid for, and it would be wise to look forward to that day and be prepared."

Yurgy stood up and backed away from the table and book. He had a feeling that he must not take his eyes from it, lest it open again and spill out the foulness it held.

The boy bumped against the trundle bed from which he had arisen such a short time before and fell back upon it. His hands rubbed back and forth across his eyes, though what he saw now was not through them; just as the jingle, clamor, and seductive crooning which circled him struck deeper than by the ears clean nature had given him.

Sulerna . . . The youth hunched his shoulders as if he took a storm of blows he could not escape. She—she had been foster sister . . . as much his kin, in his belief, as a womb sister could be! He wanted to tear from his mind the thought he was fighting now.

"Wind?" In the heart of Irasmus's own domain, Yurgy dared to try and reach for that which was gone forever. But there could be no aid from that source—not here!

In spite of the boy's great turmoil of spirit, his eyes, his hands still pressed tightly over them, closed, and out of nowhere there came at last blessed peace.

"Think you this act well done?" Yost asked. He did not turn his head toward Gifford, and there was a chill in his question.

"Brother, though we cannot break his chains, we can give him at least some relief from the pinch of them. And we know that Irasmus will not guess what we do."

"Not yet!" The crayon Harwice held snapped. "This I say: let the full strength come soon, brothers. These torments are of the Dark, and no true one among us wants such trials of the spirit to last."

The moon was full tonight. The sparks on the Stone shone with a silver fire as their interweaving grew faster and more agitated. About those swirls of colored motes was something that hinted for the first time of menace. Above them was the hole, tight-curtained by darkness; while down from the sky whistled the Wind, to search out that entrance, twist through it, and be swallowed up by the unlight as if it so attacked a bitter enemy.

Hansa emerged from among the trees, her large feet moving with a grace unusual for one so large and bulky. Her furred shoulders were wreathed in heavy circlets of flowers, whose scent filled the air as she moved. She was smiling dreamily, as her kind knew smiles, and she hummed; so it seemed as if even the fury of the Wind about the Stone was stilled a little.

Straight up to the Stone she came; and her hum of contented joy grew louder. The mad dash of the light specks slowed, changing pace; and they began to cluster into thicker lines and bands and rose to frame the dark hole.

So tall was the Sasqua female that she had to stoop a fraction until her thick lips could come into line with that shadow-centered disc.

"Awee, awee-ee." Hansa's hum had become a song. Her arms lifted as if she now held a precious bundle against her breast. "Awee-ee, awee." It was a lullaby she voiced, the oldest song known to her species; and it held more than a little of the talent that was theirs alone.

The hole changed. Its dark veil disappeared, and the Forest's daughter was looking at the face of a human woman whose countenance was twisted with fear and stained with blood, yet whose eyes held a determination that held off even death.

The Sasqua showed no surprise. Instead she sang again, "Awee-ee!" in triumph and joy. The woman's bruised and swollen lips moved, but no sound issued from them. Only her eyes met Hansa's; and present and future touched for a breath's space out of real time. Then the curtain fell once more.

But Hansa still stood before the Stone, drawing her fingertips lovingly down its surface and singing, softly now "Awee—" for a cubling not yet born.

10

Yurgy crouched in the chair by the small table, even as an animal might strive to squeeze its bulk into a hole too narrow to hold it. His hands still blindfolded his eyes, until the pressure against his closed lids was enough to cause real pain. But the book remained closed—truly closed. If only what lay within it did not continue to leak into his thoughts, spreading a poison he could not escape!

There was no night or day in this windowless tower chamber for, by some use of power he did not understand, the lamps flamed always, seeming never to exhaust their oil. He could but stumble across to his bed and throw himself down with eyes sealed tight, sometimes biting at the fingers that wished to busy themselves turning those foully ornamented pages. Lately—he could no longer keep any tale of time—he found that the scrambled script at the fore of the volume made sense in places. Nor could he banish from his mind the vile suggestions made by the pictures.

He tried—oh, Wind, how he tried! Yet never but once had he tried the way which, he inwardly believed, might help him the most: to picture the kitchen at Firthdun, Haraska at her baking, others of the kin busy here and there. That longed-for safety had been so divided from him now that it had nearly become a fragment of a dream.

After only a moment of his continued struggle, the boy had become aware he was not alone. Someone had been waiting for just such a chance to read his home memories—and for a purpose wholly evil. He fought fiercely to forget what he had once been and how he had so peacefully lived amid kin goodwill. Sometimes, instead, he tried to recall the fields in which he had helped with both sowing and reaping, to catch and hold with all his mind strength the brilliant passage of bird or butterfly, avowing aloud as he did so, "This is *real!*"

However, even if they were real, such memories brought him no strength. He returned to the Styrmir that had been, only to have it almost immediately vanish. In place of the heart-lifting vision of home, he beheld forms and witnessed actions that made his body heat, twist, and turn on his bed until he had to stuff a thick corner of the coverlet into his mouth to keep from crying out.

Yurgy might well have lost all control over both mind and body, except that surcease did come at intervals, in a sleep born of the drain of all energy.

Sulerna sat beside Haraska, tenderly wiping, from time to time, the drool that threaded from the crooked corner of the old woman's mouth. Always the young woman was aware that, if her grandmother's eyes were open at all, they fastened only on her. Sometimes her jaw worked, splutters of saliva flying, and it was plain that Grandmam would speak but that some barrier kept her dumb.

More and more, Sulerna came to believe that Haraska was trying to deliver some sort of warning. She said as much to Mistress Larlarn, only to be secretly daunted when the healer agreed with her.

"Yes, that could well be it. If she is permitted to do so by the Great Power, she may yet be enabled to give you her message." Thus the girl became as careful a nurse as possible and seldom left her patient's side.

Though the kitchen was now part sickroom, the dun kin still gathered there of an evening to share the small scraps of rumor or knowledge they had managed to gather. They were careful not to openly stray beyond the boundary marks of Firthdun or try to contact such pitiful near ghosts of those they had known as might plod along the roads, hauling a wobble-wheeled wagon that held all that was left of lost prosperity. Still, no matter how dull brained and listless those of Styrmir had become, it did seem that, when not being herded by gobbes, they sometimes commented on events concerning the master and his tower. Not that any obviously believed matters as they now stood would ever change again; yet at whiles they would pass on cautions as to this or that action or attitude which was better avoided.

It was young Jacklyn who, having kept hidden from sight in one of the berry bushes which hedged the lane, brought home a piece of news that did have meaning for those of Firthdun.

" 'Twas Oblee as said it," the boy announced with importance. "He and Jannot was told to bring in the fowl from far side, nigh the forest edge. The dark lord did send one o' the demon faces with 'em, but them gobbes—it seems they be a right lazy lot and, when the master's eyes be not upon 'em, they takes it as easy as pleases 'em. Well, this day there were another party of gobbes—hunters. And they was carryin' somethin'—

"Grandsire"—he turned to the man who now stood for the dun in assembly, even if none such still existed—"two o' them demonish things had 'em a head, swingin' from a pole they carried between 'em! 'Twarn't any head of folk like us, neither. 'Twas big and hairy all over, with teeth as long as a double barn nail—leastways, that's what Oblee said. The gobbes was a-laughin' in their nasty way—even jumpin' like they was tryin' to dance. When they seen the other gobbes with Oblee and Jannot, they yelled somethin'

in that snarled-up talk o' theirs—they never talk straight—
and they all started for the tower.

"Somehow, He knew they was a-comin'—like he always
seems to. They puts the head down before him and waits,
teeth a-grinnin' like they thought he'd be a-passin' out
sweeties. But he didn't be takin' their gift kindly at all—He
points that there wand at 'em, and they scream and twist
and roll on the ground yammerin'. All the rest of their kind
backs off, lookin' like they expects to get some o' the same.

"Then"—Jacklyn reached what seemed to him to be the
main point of his report—"that One, he twirls his wand,
and out of the tower comes—*Yurgy!*" The boy paused for
effect, enjoying the complete attention he was receiving.

"*Yurgy!*" echoed several voices.

"Aye!" Jacklyn confirmed with relish. "And he weren't
dressed in no rags, neither. He had on good cloth breeches
and a jerkin.

"Not a look he spares Oblee or Jannot or the wizard's
pets, mind you. He just stoops and picks up that head by
its hair—has to use both hands, he does, like it be main
heavy. Then he just turns 'round and goes back into the
tower. The master follows—and now he does be lookin'
pleased."

"Yurgy serves—*him!*" Sulerna could not suppress her
doubt of that portion of the boy's tale. Haraska's good hand
suddenly caught at the girl's apron, keeping her from getting to her feet. The Oldmother's watching eyes seemed to
have a leap of life flame in them.

" 'Twas him as brought that black one down on the valley," commented Elias, the brother closest to Sulerna in age.
His body might be almost whip slender, but it was well
known to all that he possessed not only a quick and easily
roused temper but was a master of wrestling tricks and one
not to be rashly challenged except by the ignorant. Elias
himself had never favored Yurgy; the foster brothers were
close together in age but in all else as separate as day
from night.

His sister turned on him quickly. "Yurgy is no gobbe!"

"It may be"—Elias watched her with a slightly malicious expression—"that the master likes someone bowing and scraping around him as is not a twisted monster—"

"Say penance for your words, youngling!" Grandsire seldom raised his voice; however, when he did, all within hearing listened. "Has there been any hint that anyone of the valley serves this raiser of demons willingly? Belike Yurgy met him first and was seized upon because the dark lord could wring out of him what he would know."

"He should long ago be questioned out by now," muttered Sulerna's brother, not to be silenced till he had spoken his mind. "They said he came from the tower and took the head within, nor did he look on any others there—they might have been naught. Is that not as you told it, Jacklyn?"

The younger boy nodded vigorously. "Oblee, he said as how it was told that Yurgy be never seen save together with the master, and for days he be not seen at all. Always, when he comes among others, he stares ahead as if he sees what other men do not. Dorata had it from her sister that he has a room of his own within the tower and is served with decent food, such as be set before the lord himself. She had so much to say about it all, when she got started, her man had to give her a swat to shut her up when a gobbe came near."

Mistress Larlarn pulled her shawl tightly about her shoulders, as if she had been touched by a chill. "This night, dun kin, do we speak power words for Yurgy. Do not think he is gone from us by his own will, for he is Light born, and thus perhaps his fate is far worse than that of the ones who have been set to building or field grubbing. He comes of the true Old Blood and, in his childhood, the Wind once touched him fully; though none knew it then, not even himself, save—"

She paused, and Grandsire nodded gravely. "We stand as strong as we can for the Wind, Mistress. Always have we had truedreamers in each line of birthing; but, at one time, your kin were greater still—Forest born!" He saluted her reverently, and she acknowledged his gesture with one of her own.

"The head—" The healer who now changed the subject. "It would seem that the gobbes may have broken the Forest barriers." She smiled a little; then her face assumed an almost sly look, as if she were about to enjoy some action those about her could not guess.

At that moment, an incoherent cry drew their attention elsewhere. Haraska, free of close watch, had sought to sit up and had nearly fallen to the floor. Mistress Larlarn and Sulerna waved the others back and, together, they once more settled their charge in as much comfort as possible. The kin drew away toward the fire, but not until Sulerna caught the name "Sasqua." She then remembered Haraska's tales of the older days when men and women, and children as well, sometimes ventured safely within the Forest and there met the Wind in all its splendor with nothing to fear from its strange servitors.

Meanwhile, a good distance from the threatened dun the Wind lifted years-laid leaf carpets, ripping roughly through the branches of great trees and nearly snapping tender saplings. It sang no longer of content and well-being; instead, its voice resembled a beast's snarl of ever-growing fury. Still, there was that which kept the mighty power from its desire—old bonds, wards centered in the Stone of the glade. In that place, the sparks of light would this night remind none of the moon's touch. Rather, they darkened and, if they did not truly drip, they yet showed the glisten of splotches of newly shed blood.

The Stone remained the anchor, and the bonds held. Even in anger, its full force could not turn against its own kind—that side of life of which it was keeper, not killer. Thus, its first burst of rage quieted, and all aspects of the land that had felt it knew relief—for now.

Yet blood called payment for blood. Threading through

the lessened voice of the Wind came the heavy beat of clubs drumming against earth, rock, or any surface near those who held the weapons. The drummers, also, the Stone held—but not the being who came in a kind of dancelike motion over the uneven Forest floor.

If a living leaf, or even a tree-high pile of such fall castings, could produce the faintest of greenish ghosts, so might this night walker be described. It had no true form, unless one could picture a well-leaved branch that could bend hither and thither. All growths rooted in reality appeared to draw back and away from the entity, much as they might seek distance from a flame that threatened them.

Once in the glade, the ghost fire did not approach the Stone straightaway; rather, its swinging dance led it in an ever-narrowing spiral toward the gray pillar, on whose surface the sparks now glowed fiercely bright. Three times the wood-bred creature circled that which it did not try to touch. In the hole, there was a riffling of the sight-barring stuff that kept out the world beyond. Shadows touched shadows, and nothing would have been clear to a watching eye, had there been any to witness that ritual. As the ghost whirled, another sound arose in the Wind, seemingly born of the dancer's erratic movements and matching its actions.

Often the Wind carried tatters of voices. Sometimes, such were messages meant only for certain ears; others were either spoken out of memory or had not yet been uttered anywhere, save in the future the Life Breath foresaw.

"Blood will be paid—" The glistening droplets on the Stone's side spattered, and their angry hue began to fade. But the fire dancer became taller and taller, thinner, until it was the girth of a war-spear's shaft. The lower end snapped off the ground, moving upward until it formed a horizontal bar; still its substance grew no thicker than the mist of its first forming.

The shaft appeared to balance, as if it were now indeed gripped in the hold of a battle-seasoned warrior, a weapon that he knew well would not fail him. Then it hurtled through the air, and one point of it pierced the hole. The rest of the shaft followed; and the Wind gave a single great howl, such as might have been a screamed demand.

If demand it was, however, no answer came.

"What does this fool? Evil I will grant him, and perhaps more of the Dark Knowledge than any of our caste, even back in the old days before the Covenant, ever drew upon. But—now he rouses the Wind, and blood has been shed within its own sacred place!" Gifford's troubled face was that of a man who had lost all the good cheer meant to be his birthright.

"Foolish or evil ruled, he follows a plan." Yost did not turn from the window panel of the hall to face his companion. "You saw how deep is his entanglement in that. Yet one can become so set in a single chosen path as to be unaware of any others. This act was not of his ordering, nor"—the archmage hesitated—"would it be the command of any in the dimensions of this world. But Irasmus seeks to open other doors. Has he not already drawn upon another level in bringing the gobbes to his service?"

"That hell crew!" Gifford sat straighter in his chair. "Brother, we have thought much upon what we may or may not do in this; but have we forgotten that the Dark also schemes and plans in its shadowy halls? The gobbes were raised by demonic ritual of Irasmus's performing, true; yet one was dead when they entered our sphere. Can it be hoped that, in drawing them hither, our would-be dark lord greatly overestimated his powers? Or has he brought in other players about whom we know nothing . . . and he less than he believes?

"Those ghoul's get were able to enter the Forest past its wards—at least to the outer fringes of it—deeply enough to strike a grievous blow there. Did we not believe that those guard spells were beyond any breakage?"

"We assumed that would be so—given *her* temper," Yost answered dryly. "Still, those creatures of the utter foulness did enter there, and killed—and certainly not by the command of their present lord." Now the archmage did swing away from the window. "Brother, all things age and lessen with time. Could it not be that, even though Irasmus might become what he has long desired—a mage of mages—there are forces, whereof we may know nothing at all, that are using him to further their own plans?"

Yost grasped the back of the chair that faced the archivist's, his knuckies standing out like hard knobs of skinless bone with the force of his grip.

"We deal with vicious phantoms now, Gifford, and hope alone can help us. Already lives are being interwoven that will bring changes past reckoning—my own, at least."

Gifford's face displayed his inner misery: that which had been eating at him since the first of their discoveries.

"Why have we kept aloof here, and what have we allowed to be planned?"

"What fate has forced upon us," Yost returned. "Thus, when payment is demanded of our brotherhood, none can deny the justice."

"Grandmam—" The old woman's hold on Sulerna with her good hand was painful, more so than any the girl had known before. Sulerna tried to catch and hold those staring eyes. More and more, she had a feeling that Haraska was indeed a prisoner in her wrecked body—though one aware of her plight—and that, through her ever-pleading gazes, she fought valiantly to give some vital message. For that her grandmother *had* a message—a warning—Sulerna was convinced; however, apart from her private speech with Mistress Larlarn, she had not mentioned what she believed to the others. What was more, her remnants of talent assured her that the message was meant for her.

Haraska's struggles were dying away; and she was relaxing, despite the torment the girl could read in that fixed gaze. Once—once a touch of Wind breath might have made all clear; but now the Wind was gone from Styrmir forever.

Her eyes closed at last, and the old woman's breathing became more even. She had worn herself out by that last effort and was no longer conscious now. Sulerna dared to loosen the hand which had so branded her upper arm, freeing herself from its fingers, one by one, as gently as she could.

Someone came up behind her; and she felt the pressure of another grip, this one laid insistently on her shoulder. When she looked around, it was to see her older brother Elias, his expression troubled.

"We must be doubly careful now," he stated. "If it is true that Yurgy is bound closer to *that one* than the rest of his slaves—well, this dun is his home, and he knows every possible door, so there are no secrets left to aid us."

Sulerna shook her head firmly. "Yurgy will never turn on us," she declared. "Never he! Think of how the story was told—that he moved all but witlessly at the master's command, looking neither right nor left. The dark lord has slaves aplenty; perhaps now he needs such who are more than the dull-minded things our people have become. Do you not wonder if, mayhap, there is some reason why we yet remain free—"

"Yurgy?" Her brother's laugh was ugly. "He has not even a breath of the talent, nor ever did! Listen to me, Sulerna: keep close to the dun; be ever near one of the elders. I am not one to welcome a sending, but this lies heavy in my mind."

"I shall do so, of course," the girl replied, somewhat coldly, "but, as you know, as I seldom leave the side of our grandmam, there is little need for me ever to go outdoors."

11

YURGY LAY SPRAWLED ACROSS HIS PALLET, STARING WITHOUT PUR-
pose into the nothingness that appeared ever, these days, to
roof his chamber. He could hear no movement from above
or without, and he might almost believe that the tower,
holding himself alone within, was otherwise deserted once
more and left to the ravages of time and weather. He never
saw who—or what—delivered his food; however, when he
would rouse at intervals and look at the table (in spite of
all his efforts not to do so), he would see a filled bowl and
cup, with perhaps a half-loaf twist of bread. And hunger
would not allow him the strength or courage to refuse what
was meant to keep him alive.

Nonetheless, he did shrink from laying hand to that
food, for eating seemed to lead always to his taking up the
book once again and leafing slowly through it. What was
worse, he could now, by some chance or design, read all of
what was written in those outer pages.

Only once had the boy been freed from this prison that
gnawed away at his spirit. That was when—he only dimly
remembered now—he had gone down the tower stairs, to
become aware of a mass of people, of screeching gobbes,
but, most strongly, of the master.

There had been a thing, not unlike a great ball dribbling blood, that had lain nearly at the dark one's feet. Without an order being spoken, Yurgy knew what was to be done. He picked up that gory trophy and found he was holding a head—not of either man or gobbe, but still a head, hacked off at the neck and freshly killed.

Later, the youth came to believe his wits had been overlaid with some illusion, for he had not been at all curious as to what he carried back into the tower and up to Irasmus's chamber. The master had followed closely and pointed with his wand at the table, which then was clear of all the tools of his unnatural work except candles.

By that light, his mind having cleared to some extent, Yurgy might at first have thought he had brought in the head of an animal. But he could see now that, in spite of furred skin, its countenance was more akin to that of humankind's than to that of the gobbes or any beast.

The sorcerer's eyes were alight with interest. Out of a small chest, he brought the globe he so cherished and set it to face the slack features of the dead.

The valley youth was loosed into further freedom from the daze that had held him as solemn words rang through the room. As Irasmus spoke, he emphasized each word with a tap of his wand's tip on the table.

"Sasqua!" There was a note of contempt in that address. "Woods animal! What were you called?"

Faintly and from far away came a whisper of a name. "Lacar."

"There is no Wind here to whirl you away, Lacar. Where is She who is supposed to call you Her child in your time of need?" He laughed. "Well, you will serve someone's purpose this day—mine."

The mage did not even turn to look in Yurgy's direction, but the boy moved under a control he could not break. From one of the shelves on the nearest wall, he selected a plate as large as a platter. Having set this on the table, he grasped the clotted hair of the head and placed the grisly object upon it. Its eyes were wide open, and Yurgy could believe that death had not fully claimed this creature—that it still possessed a fraction of both sight and mind.

Irasmus drew both candelabra closer to the plate. Once more, Yurgy obeyed unspoken orders and fetched a number of small boxes he had difficulty in carrying all at once, though that seemed to be the master's need.

Carefully, the youth set these containers in a row, while Irasmus, keeping his hands well away from the table and what it bore, pointed with his wand to the first, then to its neighbor, and so on down the line. The lid of each box snapped up in turn. A fine dustlike film rose in the air, though there was a difference in the shading of colors as the motes gathered into a multicolored cloud that formed above the severed head and began to spin.

Whatever the Dark Lord had thought to achieve, however, he was not to finish it. Though the candle flames had brightened when he had begun to chant, there now came from nowhere, to strike through that glow and dim it again to near nothingness, a thrust of raw radiance so terrible that Yurgy cried out, his hands going up to shield his eyes. He heard another scream, perhaps uttered by Irasmus.

Then around the boy roared an arm of Wind, to strike at him, almost bearing him from his feet. With it came a piercing howl that filled his head with a pain he thought would burst his skull.

Mercifully, that assault on the ears ceased nearly as quickly as it had struck. The brilliance that had heralded that sound also subsided; and only the subdued glow of the candles remained.

Yurgy found himself lying on the floor. Irasmus still stood by the table, and his malignant smile widened even as the boy caught sight of him.

On the table, there was nothing left. Not only had the head vanished, but the row of boxes had disappeared as well, leaving behind only blackened smears. And the wand the dark lord so cherished that it was never far from his reach had diminished by half its length.

At that point, the sorcerer did something odd: he turned away a little from the table and bowed—some person of note might have been standing there against the far wall.

"Most impressive!" The mage used the silky voice Yurgy had long ago come to fear. "That which is Yours lies once more in Your hold; but I do not think such would have had much worth my hearing. The Sasqua are Your faithful beasts, Lady, and they serve in death as well as life. Accept my apologies for requiring action that must have sore taxed Your strength." Irasmus inhaled deeply. "Ah, one can smell such power—"

Yurgy could scent it also—a metallic odor in the air.

"To waste force," the Dark Lord continued in a conversational tone, "is it ever wise? However, be assured Your fosterling did not die by any order of mine. I merely thought that even the smallest scrap of knowledge can often be garnered to future profit. You have bound the Forest against us, Lady—which suggests another problem. Had You a wish for gobbes so that, this day, there was no barrier against them?"

Much of the mage's malicious humor vanished. His lifted lip might still have been meant to suggest a smile, but now the sharp-pointed teeth of a predator showed.

"If You did not summon my servants, then I suggest, Lady, that You study well what has happened. I do not believe that Yost plays tricks with You or those You claim as Your children; therefore—who does?"

Yurgy had learned that anger from Irasmus could produce an almost-palpable feeling in the air. What he caught a suggestion of now, however, came from a vastly different source and one even farther removed from his kind. Then it was gone, and he realized that they two mortals were now alone.

The sorcerer reached out as if to take up his wand, but

he did not quite touch flesh to the wood. He crooked a finger at the boy.

"Take that to the fire; it is worth nothing now."

Irasmus watched carefully as Yurgy did as he was told; then he centered his attention fully on his captive.

"Time, perhaps, will no longer serve us. So be it! You shall do what you shall do."

There was still a Wind of rage—albeit rage kept in tight bonds—alive in the Forest. The drumming of clubs continued as if to feed that ire, and the Sasqua gathered.

The Forest's children were no longer the amiable creatures they had been for the numberless generations their kind had walked the woods. For the first time, they felt a new emotion: an anger as deep and devouring as that which the Wind itself could summon from its inmost being.

Through its fosterlings, the Forest listened, seeking as one with the Wind. Almost nothing remained, save a body just within the tree wall and the stench of evil from the Valley. Ill will was a feeling unfamiliar to the gentle giants and, after it had come to nest with them, it brought them disturbing dreams at night and made them restless and aggressive by day. Often, some would seek out the Stone in the glade and sit before it, watching; yet they knew no way of calling or asking—they could only wait.

Once more dismissed from the Dark Lord's chamber, Yurgy rested on his pallet that night, fighting sleep as if to yield to it meant death itself. He sensed that the master was alert and that perhaps the fate of the head had caused him to speed up some plan.

The boy at last closed his eyes, though he struggled against it, sure now that some talent not unlike dreaming pulled him deeper under Irasmus's control when he dared even to drowse.

It was always then that he saw the faces.

The horror of those was the worst, for they were connected with the bodies in the book's vile pictures. By an obscene coupling, the countenances of those he loved with all his heart were paired with the forms of the humans shown surrendering themselves joyfully to utter depravity.

But sleep could not be forever denied, any more than the boy could refuse the food that appeared out of nowhere. At first, he would sit apart and gaze at that unwonted bounty, and the emptiness in him was a pain. But what if it were by the means of those meals that Irasmus controlled him? He could not be sure.

At last, the youth was driven to take a drink. And once the watered juice was in his mouth, easing his thirst, he could not hold back his hand from the bowl, then from the bread. . . . So he cleared away all to the last crumb, cramming the food into his mouth and swallowing it as speedily as he could, ashamed of his lack of self-control.

However, he would not open the book—he would not! Perhaps, at that moment, Irasmus's will was busy in another direction, for Yurgy was able to rise, stumble across the small room once again to the pallet, and throw himself onto it, breathing as heavily as if he had run the length of Long Field. Still, he had not touched the lust-inflaming volume. Nor did he dream again.

The boy could not be aware that, far from putting him out of mind, Irasmus was now concentrating on him. Preparations had to be made in the room above, and the faint uneasiness the master had known since his experiment with the Sasqua head had failed so dramatically kept him busy throughout that afternoon, night, and the following day. Now the second dawn was drawing near.

The mage had checked everything twice over. This was his own private matter, having nothing to do with the Forest or what might have been awakened there. He uttered a last incantation, caressing the ball with both hands as he did so. His will might have been feeding what lay within, and that power, in turn, strengthening him. Now he spoke with the authority of one who could not be disobeyed.

"Journey forth, youngling. You are not altogether what I would have to serve me in this, but you have been tutored, and you are now geas bound to what must be done. *Go!*"

The pallet in the room below held a mass of twisted covers, but nobody rested there any longer.

For a wonder, during these past ten days and more, Haraska had not roused during the night. Yet Sulerna's sleep had hardly been deeper than a doze—she might have been waiting for a call from the old woman.

Yawning, the girl slipped away to the far side of the room where she could wash face and hands in the waiting basin, then unbraided her hair that she might brush those wavy lengths. No real light burned here to show the glints of russet shot through the darker-brown locks; and the girl did not look into the square of mirror fastened to the wall above the washstand—she knew well the face that would look back at her.

Sulerna was also aware that her skin had lost its tan because she had been kept so strictly indoors. In her now, there burst a longing for the dawn, for the right to run barefooted through dew-pearled grass and drink in the fresh air outside. Even if the Wind were gone and the land dead or dying beyond the boundaries of the dun, the girl felt drugged by the many potions that shared cooking-space on the hearth and by the herb-scented wood smoke of Mistress Larlarn's twig fire. This chamber served as both kitchen and sickroom these days, and all its odors were strong.

The girl did not reach for the hairbrush; instead, feeling with a new intensity the unfreshness of one who has slept too long in shift and petticoat, she bypassed the heavy clogs set by the door. But—her hand had risen to the door bar, which was not in its proper place. Startled, she eased the door open, and it yielded to her without a creak. No one roused to challenge her going. Before her lay a patch of mud where the water bucket had slopped over. Impressed there was a single footprint with one toe enlarged. She recognized the shape of a bandage—one she had fastened herself to ease a bruise for Jacklyn. Why had he ventured so? Unease gripped her now.

The household had carefully set out the protection patterns they knew, so she need have no fear of anything crouched in wait nearby. All such wards were attuned to the kin of the dun, and no alarm would be raised by her passing unless early warnings had already sounded an alert.

The gravel of the path was sharp to the girl's bare feet; still, the feeling of freedom though now touched with rising concern, which had enveloped her since she had slipped through the half-open door kept her moving, until she chose to tread instead on the plants framing the way. Their mingled fragrances, and the sharper scents of their crushed leaves, banished for her the last of the close house smells.

Sulerna reached the end of the garden and turned there quickly to avoid the gate that led to the now-blighted outer world, for to pass that boundary would trigger the wards.

The men of Firthdun had been plowing yesterday, for every palm-sized piece of land must be used to raise food—as long as their enemy did not stamp them out of life itself. Ground doves, already awake nearly an hour before sunrise, had found a hole in the hedge large enough to let them in and were fluttering fast over the freshly turned earth. It was Jacklyn's duty—his and Marita's—to keep the birds from pecking up the precious seed.

Sulerna grinned and flapped her skirt, whose edge was already damp with dew. Knowing Jacklyn well, she could guess that perhaps he had been out on some business of his own the night before. From his birthing, her older sister's first son had had something in him which the night called. It might be the shadow of a talent, Mistress Larlarn had suggested at last, although not even the healer could guess the reason for the boy's need to ever be seeking moonlight. The kin had never been able to teach him to control his strange urge, but they had made him aware—when the

Wind still came—that he must keep within the boundaries they set.

Until now—Sulerna looked out over the recently plowed field. For the present, the thieving fowl had not worked their way far from the hole they had found. However, leading away beyond them, pressed clearly into the newly broken soil, were footprints. The girl was startled. Her nephew well knew the ways of the dun, and to cut across a just-sown acre was the mischief of a much younger and less-well-taught child.

Frowning, she scrambled over the gate, climbing its bars instead of trying to open it. The cloud that hung ever over Firthdun darkened in her mind, if not before her eyes. She hurried to follow the boldly marked trail. Uneasiness stirred again in her and fed the beginning of fear.

Jacklyn had crossed only a corner of the field, and his tracks vanished into a barrier of thornbushes through whose forbidding tangle she knew better than to try and push herself.

"Jackie," Sulerna called. "Jackie, where are you?"

Seeing that bramble barrier, the girl felt increasing fear. Soon the gangs of slaves would come, herded to the nearly sterile fields that had been the pride of once-prosperous neighbors. She remembered the child's tale of hiding in just this hedge to listen to any who passed. Having obtained one exciting piece of news to offer his elders, and make himself the center of attention thereby, Jacklyn, his aunt could well believe, was trying the same trick again.

Sulerna stood very still, listening with all her might. There were always sounds aplenty when the gobbes drove their captives to some nearly always unprofitable labor. She heard nothing, but didn't dare call out again. Only one chance was left her: to somehow trip the nearest-set ward and so arouse the dun. However, her work had always been in the house garden and the dun itself. She knew, as did all the kin, the whereabouts of the major wards, but she knew, too, that the men who had to risk their lives in the fields had others known only to themselves.

As the girl stared ahead at the thorn-studded brush wall before her, she tried to imagine just where such a ward could have been set. Plainly, from what Jacklyn had said, he had had no fear of those alarms when he had eavesdropped on the work gang. Too, he had had a reasonable excuse for hedge diving: he had been harvesting berries and, though the season was early, the dun could use every possible foodstuff.

Slowly Sulerna began to ease along the hedge, sure she was heading in the right direction. Then she saw the half print of a foot pointing reassuringly ahead. However, such marks were moving further and further from the dun itself, and that she liked less and less.

She was thus almost prepared for the sudden shriek of pain and terror that arose from nearly in front of her. She caught at the brush, paying no heed to the thorns, and staggered back as a section wider than her own body came free from its roots—recently hacked so and then set once more into place.

The girl plunged forward as a second cry became a piteous whimper. Scratched and torn by what remained of the barrier, she stumbled out where the old trader road made a loop. Jacklyn was there, lying very still, and Sulerna was sure she saw a splotch of blood staining his coarse smock. Forgetting all else, she made for the boy.

Then out of nowhere came those arms. The flat of a hand slapped the girl's face on one side so that her head whirled. She tried to struggle, but she might as well have already been bound, helpless and unable to defend herself, as hands tore savagely at her few garments.

Now she could see the face of her attacker. Beastly, misshapen, gobbe-fashioned as she expected, it was not. She tried to scream, *"Yurgy!"* as he gave her a second vicious blow across her mouth and knelt over her downed body.

12

Dull gray sky hung over Yurgy. The boy lay dazed, staring up into the bowl that held a sun always pale these days. But the tower—where—how—?

Then his whole body jerked in sympathy with a sound, a desolate gasping cry such as fitted the bleak world about him. Awkwardly, as if his muscles had forgotten how to obey his will, he levered himself up.

No! This was part of a nightmare born of one of the pictures in that book!

Only, the terrible image did not fade, as was usual with any dark dream upon one's awakening. The youth could see the girl, hear the faint, bubbling moan that rose on the trickle of blood washing from between her swollen lips. Against his will, his eyes moved, but with pitiless slowness, as if what they allowed him to see must be seared into his memory forever. Her white body, bloody, bruised—this was his doing—*his!*

Still, in a sheltered corner of his awareness, Yurgy faintly knew he did not bear the rotten heart and mind that would lead to such a deed as this. He was Yurgy—and, in that moment, all the entanglement of illusion and domination was swept away. There was no Wind, but also no Irasmus or pictures; there were only he and—she—

On hands and knees, for he did not have the strength to stand upright, the boy crawled to the girl's side. Her eyes were open, seemingly fastened on something no one else could see high above them. Her head did not turn at his coming.

"Sulerna?" Her name was a whisper, when he wanted to shout to awaken her—and himself—and to let him know that this could not be the truth for either of them.

His foster sister only moaned and continued to stare at nothing. Her body was so slender, those now clawed and bruised breasts so small—hardly more than a girl child would show before her first moon time. And below those—

Yurgy raised his head as high as one of the forest wolves and, like them, howled, but for shame—a shame that could never now be riven from any mind.

Thus, just as Sulerna had not been aware of his attack, so Yurgy in his turn knew naught of the one moving in behind him, until a painful yank on his sweat-matted hair brought his head further back.

A face hovered above his, one so twisted with rage that the boy's wits seemed too dim to set name to it. Then came the downward flash of a sickle. Yurgy did not try to offer any defense—there was no other answer but this for what he had done—and he was hardly aware of the bite of the blade through his throat or the gush of hot blood that followed. Though he heard, dimly, through the mad cursing of his executioner, something else . . . a ghost of a breath . . . yet, still, somewhere—

The Wind.

Elias kicked the body away from his sister.

"Sulerna—Sulerna!" His first calling of her name sounded too vigorous, too loud, and he feared he might, with the lash of a harsh voice, drive her into further withdrawal.

But the girl's first reaction was fear as she tried to slide away from her brother across the brittle, broken grass, throwing up an arm in a vain attempt at self-defense. Elias did not try to touch her—perhaps she would shrink in pain from any man, now, no matter what kin he was or what aid he wished to offer.

"Sulerna"—he lowered his voice to near a whisper—"it is Elias; let me help you."

Fright still lingered on her battered face, and she edged even farther from him. He had to get her back to the dun— what had happened here might be the beginning of the end for all of them. But he dared not attempt to touch her. Instead, he gathered up the rags of what had been her clothing and gently covered her body. That much, it seemed, she would allow him.

"Is—is she—dead?" asked a child's voice, high and cracking with fear. Elias had forgotten Jacklyn, but now his nephew, a smear of blood along his head, ran across the field to hold to him fiercely, gabbling in terror.

"No," Elias answered shortly.

"But Yurgy"—the boy had come forward and looked beyond his kin—"he is?"

"There is no more Yurgy to be remembered among the kin." Elias's rage made an oath of that. "Jacklyn, get you Mistress Larlarn, and Ethera"—he named his own wife— "and Grandsire."

It was the women who seemed able to tend to Sulerna— and to break through the horror that had frozen the girl— so that she could be laid on pole-stiffened blankets and taken back to the dun.

Elias and the eldest of his line remained, and Rush and Vors joined them. The four men half encircled that other body, and Grandsire dropped a roll of earth-stained blanketing he had been holding.

"Leave him to be found and, if what has happened here is not already known to the Dark Lord, it certainly will be. If *that one* moves now to wipe out the dun, we are already too late. Yet there is always hope.

"We have kept to ourselves," the Oldfather continued, "yet still he has found a way to pluck one of us out of safety. Let the body of this—thing, which he has so corrupted, be taken and, if the work can be done well out of sight, thrown into the root cellar beneath Mistress Larlarn's holding. Then cast down upon it any covering that may long endure!"

In the dunhold, the children had been brushed out of the way and, about that improvised stretcher, the women of the household gathered. Sulerna had returned to them now—she repeated their names in a whisper one by one, then sighed, and her eyes had closed. It would seem that warm and comforting darkness had at last claimed her.

"Sulerna?" As one, the women turned. Haraska was sitting up in the cupboard bed. No longer was her face drawn to one side, and she helped herself rise using the arm that had lately failed her.

"Grandmam!" Ethera was the closest and hurried to support her. "You—you are healed!"

The strangeness of it all held them: fear, pain, and deep wounding had stricken Sulerna down, while Grandmam had risen from the near dead.

"No!" Haraska made a negating motion with that long-paralyzed hand as the injured girl's mother opened the door of the cupboard where, on the top shelf at the far back, were kept certain mixtures known to the women alone.

"No!" The Oldmother ordered again. She had reached the edge of the bed now and held its quilt about her as a cape. "Not the black drink!"

The bottle was already in Fatha's hands. "Sulerna has been"—she paused as if the next word was beyond her ability to utter until she nerved herself to the task—"*taken*. It is not right that she be forced to bear the fruit of ravishment if means are at hand to rid her body of such a monstrous thing."

Mistress Larlarn moved beside Haraska, and they clasped hands as might war women shouldering together to face a skirmish.

"There is a reason." The old woman's voice had weakened a little from her unwonted exertion. "That sending

which left me unable to warn— Did you never wonder
whence it came?"

"You foresaw—*this?*" Sulerna's mother still held tightly
to the bottle as she nodded her head toward her unconscious daughter.

"Why think you I rebelled against such knowledge until
my body broke?" questioned Haraska. "Now listen and
heed well. We are women here together, and the worst of
all men's vileness has been wreaked upon one who is dear
kin. However, I swear, by the Moon of my First Offering"—
she spoke very slowly, and her words entered deeply into the
minds of all who heard her—"that what Sulerna bears now
within her body will not, in the end, be for evil but for good.
That much was promised me this very night by a truedream.
Thus, tonight, when the moon shines full, we shall take our
loved one to the Women's Place where we spend the night
of our first moon gift each month. There we shall place her
in the light—"

"But she is no longer virgin," objected Ethera.

"She will be what the Wind Caller determines she will
be. We are near the end, kin-daughter, of our safety here—
this thing was done as part of malicious planning. But this
I have also come to believe: we shall raise up champions
such as rode with the Wind in the ancient days, and for
such aid, payment there must always be. Blood has already
been shed; it may be that all Firthdun shall cease to be.

"Ethera!" Such was the force of her name being called
by the old woman that Elias's wife was startled. "Ethera,
you are also with child."

"Am—am I so?" The young woman flushed. "I was not
yet sure—"

"You may be sure. You shall call the daughter who
comes at the proper time Cerlyn. She will live surrounded
by fear in her first days, thus training her talent the stronger,
but the Wind shall favor her. I was not shown the end, kin-
daughter, but we are all part of something being built stone
by stone, even as was that accursed tower down Valley—

save that the Light, not the Dark, shall be with us in the end."

Suddenly she collapsed, as if a strength, which had been loaned for a mere moment, had been withdrawn. Mistress Larlarn eased the frail old body down upon the bed once again. Sulerna's mother continued to hold the bottle, looking from it to her daughter; then, as her gaze moved on to Haraska, some of the stubbornness leached out of her grim face. She must accept that what they had heard was dreamer's truth and that they would have to face a daunting future.

It was decided among them hastily that, if the men of the dun were to learn of Haraska's words, it would be by her telling and not theirs. Mistress Larlarn suggested that they say the Black Drink was too strong for Sulerna in her present state and that they must follow the Oldmother's instructions and seek strength from the moon—matters that had been, from the beginning, purely women's affairs.

No mention had been made of Yurgy when Grandsire returned with only two of the men. The rest had been sent to make a show of their usual daily tasks, for all of them suspected they were being spied upon. Jacklyn crept away to the darkest stall in the stable and there cried until he could hardly see. The heaviness of his guilt in that hour put an end to all his joyous innocence—and to his boyhood itself.

"So be it." Yost looked into the hanging panel of fabric, that was again a window showing the events of this day just passed.

"So be it!" Harwice struck his fist against the wall until blood marked the stone he pummeled.

"The dream"—Gifford might not have heard either of them—"that was no sending of mine."

"I think there will be very little dreaming for a space." The archmage spoke heavily. "Irasmus believes his plan safely under way; at present, he is perhaps more interested in the connection of the gobbes with the Forest.

"You say you sent no dream, brother." The misery on the old archivist's face was as real as any flow of tears. "Think: to whom do these Firthdun women now appear to turn? Each to her own, Gifford."

"But *She*," protested the loremaster, "She has always kept Herself aloof and has ruled the Forest, never the Valley—though, by Her power, the Wind blew there once."

As he replied, Yost fixed his gaze on the bloody splotch left by Harwice's impassioned blow to the stone as the painter spoke his oath. "Irasmus has dared use his strength to force his will upon a woman—obliquely, to be sure, but the ravishment came by his desire.

"Yes, *She* has ever claimed the Forest and not the Valley; still, She also commands the Wind, and that force blew there at its strongest when She did call. Firthdun was once Her shrine—or have you forgotten what lies so many years behind us? Now, with or without our renegade's orders, his creatures have taken the life of one of Her chosen—and he himself has moved against a human whom She might well hold in favor. We can only wait and see—Time can be both an enemy and a friend.

"Meanwhile"—the archmage now touched the wall stain, as a warrior might make blood oath to seal his purpose—"we must continue to search our most ancient records to discover who—or what—moves Irasmus now, perhaps completely without his knowing. One cannot fight an enemy until one knows his name, face, or kind."

Gifford drew his cloak closer about his shoulders. He had lost more flesh of body, as well as pleasure in living, and he always felt cold now.

"I search; so do we all. We dare to break seals on the forbidden chambers, endangering our beings by such probing. If we could achieve only a single crumb of enlightenment, it would be worth the effort and peril.

"The Dark—" the loremaster shivered visibly, in spite of

his close-drawn cape"—sometimes I think I hear it chuckling in the corners of the rooms I comb. Others have reported hearing voices speaking in unknown tongues. We have tried very hard not to release anything, though we do not even use the permitted search spells anymore. Yet I can offer nothing that is meaningful."

Harwice looked down at his battered knuckles. "You search the records. I and my two novices have opened lofts in which paintings lie in dust so thick we must fight through what is very like a sandstorm to see clearly. I—"

"Brothers!" The three men turned. Behind them, the panel was once more innocent embroidery. Danful, now the youngest of the novices, stood there in his shirtsleeves, which were nearly as black with grime as his face.

"In the room of Archmage Khanga"—the youth was all but spluttering—"Brother Rees has found a Dam Seal!"

In a moment, the mages were all on the move, following their young guide to see for themselves the most potent seal of spells ever known to their kind.

The search for the power interfering with Irasmus's plans had not been confined to the Place of Learning. Though Irasmus had read only the smallest fraction of the books and scrolls he had stolen, he had been studying those assiduously through many nights. His ploy with Yurgy had helped to bolster his belief in himself, and he had watched in his seeing globe with avid attention not only Sulerna's taking but what happened afterward.

That those dolts had thought to throw the boy's body into the root cellar the Dark Lord found amusing. It was already carrion and, as such, would draw not only his watch birds but also any gobbes within sniffing distance. A slave burial for a slave!

All these things had unfolded in the globe which, as had been promised, had served him well. Indeed, the only desired image the sphere seemed unable to reveal to him was the answer to what was still only half a question: why had the gobbes invaded the Forest and thereby, at least in part, endangered his schemes? Irasmus still blinked when he remembered that light, which had either destroyed the severed head entirely or taken it where even his own enlarged and ever-expanding talent could not find it.

Now he stacked and restacked his oldest books (though setting apart the one which was nastily hair covered), calling precisely to mind a scrap of spell here, a bit of ritual there, and refusing to be frustrated.

An hour—even two in certain corridors in the Place of Learning! The rogue mage would give much for that; but merely to seriously consider ways of performing such exploration could threaten his most carefully stored power. In those halls, now forgotten even by those who had concealed it, lay such a wealth of lore that the thought of it made him feel a nearly physical ache of hunger.

So much could be lost, falling between cracks of years. . . . From the tentative fingers of seeking he had dared to put forth, Irasmus was sure that this very tower had once housed more power than he had managed to discover in the rebuilding. Only, he could not now risk any interference with the dun and its people. Nature had a power of her own, and he must wait out the months until his plan in that direction would be complete.

Last of all, there remained the gobbes who had invaded the Forest. The Dark Lord had purposely remitted none of the torment he had visited upon them on their return here; thus, relief at hand from pain now might be of more importance to them than some later nebulous punishment—or even reward—offered by an unknown.

Though he had not yet had time to fashion a new wand and imbue it with power, he had the globe. Making up his mind, Irasmus picked it up and set about carrying out what might, or might not, be a very necessary action.

13

PERHAPS, GIFFORD THOUGHT AS HE ENTERED THE LOWER LEVELS of the ancient edifice, which descended by one curl of stairs to another, a building could become *too* old—cunning and reclusive in its own way, as if it took on, year by passing dusty year, an awareness of sorts. Working in squads, the scholars had begun their search, starting from the sections they all knew well and working their way into those which had been most deserted, save by any of their number striving to follow a trail of learning across far centuries. After the past days, when the brothers had delved and probed here, the loremaster, who had once complacently believed that the archives were his own particular territory, had made such discoveries as set his tired mind abuzz when he tried to record them in order.

How old was the Place of Learning? Gifford had never been able to find any record concerning its foundation. Perhaps that account had been concealed during the Days of Chaos before the Covenant. However, on the seals of doors the mages had read names that had long ago passed beyond history into the realm of legend.

Even now, one group of the seekers approached such a lore hoard: the sealed archive of Archmage Khanga. Reputable scholars had more or less agreed that that name was not a true one but rather a lost password of sorts.

A number of lightballs gave full luminence where the rest of the brothers gathered with those who had made the discovery. What those spheres shone upon was no door— not even the outline of a portal was traced on the web-hung wall. In the center of that space was something wrought by human hands as a warning.

The Dam Seal itself was known—at least the representation of it was, as Gifford knew, listed in the more ancient accounts. But its actual appearance differed greatly in detail from any drawing on the page of a book.

A skull was a common enough symbol for death. But this grim object bore fangs and horns, showed an unnatural arrangement of bones, and even suggested—if one continued to look at it—that it had never worn flesh at all. Moreover, its dome was perhaps a third larger than any human braincase would normally be.

Forming a frame around the skull image was a maze of intertwined runic characters of ancient mode. Directly above it were engraved the warning characters by which the reporter of this find had identified it: the personal insignia of the myth-shrouded archmage.

The present explorers formed a half circle, none of them approaching the device. Though draped with a curtain of webs spun by the eyeless spiders of the lower ways, the seal itself was as clean as if just polished by some dutiful hand.

Even a mage could be touched by the chill of fear—if he or she were a true holder of talent. The archivist wanted none of this thing. Nonetheless, it was part of his domain, and to leave investigating to another was a weakness of character which did not lie in him.

The rest withdrew a little as Gifford approached it. A Dam Seal was set only to restrain some entity that was too potent to be allowed loose. In this place, that being must have been a major power of the Dark.

"Back with you all!" Gifford commanded. The loremaster heard the shuffling of feet and guessed that he was being speedily obeyed.

Three of the traveling globes of light swooped down to ring him in an aura of blue radiance. There was no door— there was only the seal. . . . The archivist wiped his sweating hands down his cloak, then unhooked the clasp and let the cloak fall, wanting all the freedom of body he could obtain.

Three was one of the numbers of power, as even a novice knew. Jutting from the skull were three massive horns, the middle one directly above a hollow that might have grounded a nose, the other two each overhanging a bottom-less pit of darkness that could have housed an eye.

Three—no, so easy an answer could not possibly exist. Then followed nine: three upon three upon three. Yet how could a man with only two hands deal with such a series?

Horns, eye sockets, nose pit. But what if—? Gifford's head rose higher. This monster had been set here by a man—that he must believe. And what remained of the man? Only a diamond shape above, divided down the middle and bearing what he recognized with a small shock as the repre-sentation of a Sasqua's head. The lorekeeper felt oddly reas-sured at the sight, for the portrait of the gentle Forest giant tempered the sinister otherness of that eerie skull.

In the old days, of course, there had been no barriers such as now divided the realms of the modern world; and the Forest might well have shared its wisdom with the Place of Learning.

"By the Great Powers," Gifford intoned slowly. "By the will of—" Three names he repeated; then he was on the edge of boundaries he himself could not pass.

The echo of the last name was still sounding. The lore-master raised hands in patterned gestures, using all the force of his will to keep from trembling. Only then did he dare to press a forefinger on each of those horns and, after a moment's hesitation, to touch the representation of the furred head above.

He was concentrating hard, yet he could still hear the

sound of soft chanting behind him. Once—once someone might have called so upon—the *Wind?*

Even as the archivist's thought turned in that direction, Gifford heard —*it!* Not the powerful thrust of its preparation for battle, no; rather a thin, strained effort, as if it had to fight hard to reach into these depths at all. But it was the Wind, and it carried with it scraps of knowledge.

The Dam Seal shivered, bits of it flaking away as if Gifford had clawed at it with his fingers; then it shattered and was gone. However, there was no opening behind but merely a second seal—one which brought a moan from those gathered about.

The Wind was gone, as swiftly as it had come. The mages had learned the answer for which they had been searching. Now the second seal was, in its turn, fading very fast. The loremaster knew terror then. Was the power it represented at this very moment seeking anchors among those assembled here, just over the threshold that the Light had set uncounted years ago?

That was one name Gifford would never say. Anyone who dared call upon that force aloud placed himself and all the world about him in deadly peril of a fate worse than the finality of death.

So the scholars stood waiting, and each strove to call upon their talent, summon each defense ever learned. Fortunately, it seemed they were, for the present, witnesses only; they would not be swept up to serve all that was most abhorrent to them.

"There came Wind." Gifford broke the silence first. "It was with me—"

But Yost, seemingly unheeding, cut across his brother's speech. "So now we know," he announced. "Perhaps it is better to know, though I think that, for us, knowing will not bring instant surrender! Also, if Irasmus thinks to call upon *That*, he is a fool beyond all fools. As yet, it cannot break through. It can only feel for crevices in the barrier, venturing forth to catch what it may against the day of its own triumph.

"Yes, Loremaster"—now the archmage acknowledged Gifford's words—"you felt the Wind. Even *She*, in Her own place, keeps watch upon Her own; and the safety of Her woodland has already been broken. Give me room."

The archivist stepped aside, and Yost drew his wand from its pocket in his cloak. The crystal that formed its point flashed fire drawn from the globes—liquid light that could be ink of a sort. Then, as the mages began chanting again, their leader drew another sign on the wall—one which was right and proper for this place.

The women of the dun had faced down the men, and since this was a matter in which from of old they had had the sentencing, the choosing, none of the men had approached Sulerna. Instead, they had busied their hands fashioning crude weapons from their farm implements. Almost all under the clan roof seemed certain that they would not have long to wait before Irasmus struck with all his followers to beat the folk of Firthdun into the dust, as he had all their neighbors.

Now the women—even the girl children who had only recently paid their first Moon Due—took turns carrying the stretcher on which Sulerna lay, still drowned in terror and despair.

The moon was very bright, and the sanctuary was wreathed in the moonflowers whose fragrance soothed, seeming to heal a little their sorrow of mind. In the middle of the hollow that lay open to the sky and the Threefold Lady's symbol, the dunswomen set down their burden. Haraska took her place at the head of the stretcher. The oldmother had insisted she must come with them, though Mistress Larlarn and Sulerna's mother had had to support her between them for most of the short way.

The ravished girl's mother gently withdrew the coverlet so that her daughter's body, now washed and treated as best could be, lay nude, nearly as white as the blossoms nodding over her.

The women sang no song of welcome, nor did they give the death wail. No maiden came tonight to be accepted, nor did a woman full of years depart. Never had they so served any of their kind, but they could believe there was good reason to do so now.

Sulerna opened her eyes. Her hands moved slowly into the moonlight, as if, by some favor of Her Above, the girl could draw about her a covering fashioned both of the moon's rays and the blooms around her.

For the first time, the girl spoke clearly. "Yours, Treader of the Far Skies—what I bear within me, let it be wholly Yours." Her hands smoothed over her still-flat belly. "I yield this new life freely to bring about that which must be done so that the Light will not flicker and die forever from these, my kin."

Wind swung those vines on which the flowers grew. It brought only comfort; it did not speak with the inner voice, and it promised nothing; yet they all raised their heads and felt its gentle touch on their cheeks.

But Sulerna seemed to be listening to something the rest could not hear. Her expression was that of one who was giving heed to a lesson, and the hands lying over her womb tightened protectingly; then the faint murmurs that spoke in her ear alone were gone. Turning her head, she closed her eyes, and over her Haraska drew the coverlet once more.

Silently as they had come, the women of the dun departed the moon shrine. Yet this time, as they took the road, they seemed to feel on their heads like a caress the tingling touch of the Wind.

None of their fellow fiends had laid hands on the two gobbes Irasmus had disciplined since his wand had struck them down; but several of the demons had taken stakes and pushed the writhing bodies to one side of the courtyard, where they had lain night and day. If such creatures could know hope, these must have lost it long since, just as they had forfeited the power of speech through endless wailing.

Some of the human slaves paused from time to time in their duties to glance surreptitiously in the direction of the luckless pair, but those of their own kind dared give them no notice.

As the Dark Lord emerged from the tower, every creature in sight scattered. With an uplifted hand, he beckoned to Karsh, the leader of this squad of hell spawn; and the gobbe chief came toward him with what was plainly the utmost reluctance.

In spite of the nearly exhausted twistings of their bodies, the two monsters on the ground somehow held their heads now so that they could watch their master.

Or was he? Swiftly Irasmus put high guard on that thought.

No human could produce the guttural sounds of the gobbes' own language. Irasmus balanced the globe carefully between his palms so it was visible to his slaves.

"You are mine," the dark mage said with very little emotion. "You were bought with blood, as was demanded by the archdemon who sends those of your kind to serve elsewhere."

He paused, as if expecting some answer from the pair under his spell. Both of them showed opened mouths, one of which was now leaking greenish spittle, but neither uttered a sound.

"You are mine, sealed so. Yet you have done that which I did not order. Had you served Him from whom I bought you in such fashion, what would have been your fate?"

Only the creatures' bulbous eyes moved, rolling in their misshapen skulls. Irasmus did not stoop, but he lowered the globe, at the same time taking a stride or so closer.

"You went to the Forest." The Dark Lord spoke simply now, as one might to slow-witted children. "You dared force the barrier of the Wind, or—" he paused, to continue with a question "—was that shield in some manner opened for you?

Then you slew one who serves a greater power than perhaps even your master would dare face." Now his lips twisted, as if he could not repeat a name he knew well. Karsh, still behind him, coughed, and the two gobbes on the ground rolled their heads wildly from side to side.

Irasmus's gaze was on the murky depths of the crystal; however, nothing therein changed. Well, he could hardly expect a quick or easy answer.

"Perhaps the Wind drove you into its outer hold. But you had time to take a trophy. Was that intended as a gift for me?" No answer came from the captives. "No—better as a warning or, most likely, as bait such as a fisherman impales on his hook. It remains that you did this because of orders, and"—he swung the globe closer, from one contorted body to the other—"not any orders of mine."

He began to chant in sharply clipped words like oaths strung together.

Now an answer came for him—not from the two creatures weeping bloody tears but from the sphere he held. At first, it seemed that he saw a tangle of threads there; then that mass displayed purposeful movement.

The would-be master looked down upon a symbol, and only all the power he could call upon kept him from dropping the sphere. Nearly the full sum of the power he had husbanded so jealously was required for him to stand against the will of the Dark entity whose sign he saw for a brief instant or two before it tore itself free and was gone.

The dark mage had dealt with minor Dark Powers for years, secretly at first and then openly. From this land and its people, he had drawn the talent and inner strength, as one might suck milk from a woman's breast.

Why! Why! The word hammered in his head. This Presence had no dealings with the Wind or Her who called it; perhaps it harbored contempt for both those powers. And certainly no one in the Place of Learning could have sealed a pact without all those mages of the highest talent being made instantly aware of the ripples ringing out from such a confrontation.

The bodies of the two offenders he had come to question jerked in one last convulsion, and then they began to shrink. Pools of stinking ichor ran from beneath their crumbling carcasses. Irasmus stepped hastily back, but Karsh cried out wildly. His cry became a weird lament that resounded from every direction as the other gobbes picked up the sound and added their own wails.

Why? The reverberation of the question in his mind deafened Irasmus to what was taking place. Unless . . .

His usually half-lidded eyes snapped fully open, and his mouth became a circle of wonder at the thought. The Dark Ones had been defeated long ago, the greater Powers having been driven into another world and time when the Covenant was sworn. But he also knew there had always been others like him who were able to claim kinship with the unhuman. Perhaps his own actions since he had come to Styrmir had attracted the attention of such an Overlord.

Very well—with most of the Dark Ones, bargains could be made—and such a pact could raise a human to the rulership of a world.

This breakage of the Forest wards could have been willed, not as an act threatening him but rather as an experiment. For the moment, he could only watch and wait.

14

THE GROUP OF FIVE STANDING MOSS-STAINED, TALL ROCKS LOOKED
like a giant hand lifted skyward, fingers apart, leaving a
nearly level hollow between that might be the palm of an
appendage so huge it could well represent a petition addressed to the sky above.

Other stones also stood here—rows of hewn blocks that
must have once been fitted smoothly together into walls.
Only the green moss showed life and growth; no forest creatures—no animals or birds intruded. Silence was complete.

Beyond the crumbling walls, a party was assembling. Male
Sasquas were now hesitating restlessly beneath the shelter of
the last fringe of trees. Unease notwithstanding, they remained.
Now females, some bearing cublings, joined them.

Neither lord nor inferiors were known to the Forest's
children, nor even kin such as existed for the humans. The
Sasqua were a fiercely independent, almost-reclusive people,
each of whom kept within his or her own chosen section of
the trees unless some occasion such as this drew them together. Usually they were also mild of temper, for their great
strength was enough to overawe most other creatures who
shared this land. However, their gentleness was sometimes
but a mask—as was true this day.

Two of the most powerful males shared the weight of a stretcher made of vines lashed between good-sized saplings. The form borne on this litter was covered with a woven blanket thickly studded with white and scarlet flowers that were opened wide to the sun.

While most of the Sasqua now squatted down, the two bearers continued along a wall until they passed between two of the fingerlike rocks. There, with a tenderness they might have used to a wounded comrade, they drew away the bloom-studded coverlet and shifted the corpse of one of their own to the palm of the stone hand.

Not the complete body, for above a mangled, blood-clotted neck no head showed. The escorts arranged their charge until the deceased rested, almost lovingly clasped, in the hand; then, as they withdrew, a pair of the females advanced in their place. Both the she-Sasqua bore reed baskets heaped high with blossoms, the fragrance of which arose like the smoke of a smoldering fire into the air. The females, in turn, stood aside while the males used their offerings to once more blanket the body, avoiding with care that ragged stump of neck. Thereafter, more flower bearers approached, and the he-Sasqua retreated.

Their aim directed toward the hand, the flower bringers tossed their harvest into the air. A soft keening arose, scaled upward, and died away. A breath or two later, that sound was succeeded by a vast sigh that might well have been the lament of the Forest itself.

As the woodland's tribute faded, some of the Sasqua left their places. One of the two who had helped carry the stretcher now raised a mighty club.

With all the force of his mighty arm, the Forest's son brought the crude weapon down upon one of the blocks near him. A deep boom sounded, like the single note from a great drum.

They remained in silence, plainly waiting. A second blow was struck, and joining it rose a shrill fifelike note. Far in the past, the peace of the wood kin had once been shattered, and they were returning resolutely now to actions buried deep in racial memory.

And they were answered, for the Wind arose, whirling the strewn flowers into a disguising cloud until the palm and its pitiful burden were hidden. Overhead, the brightness of the day was fast fading.

A brilliant beam of light flashed with lightning force from one of the tall stones near the hand. As if that monolith were a portal into another time and place, a woman stepped forth from its radiance to join them.

She wore no rich robes, and Her face was veiled by a green mist, but they knew Her. The stones echoed back the Sasquas' hail: "Theeossa!"

The Sasqua knelt, reaching hands out to Her. However, while She inclined her head in acknowledgment, Her first business was with that which lay on the palm of the hand. Gravely She saluted its burden. Above the assembly, a gust of the Life Breath paid tribute.

So! The Lady's Wind-borne thought came to them, more sharply than any speech might sound. *So—already the evil strikes—and at us!*

Now She shifted position, no longer viewing either the dead or the living as She raised her arms high. She brought her palms together above Her head in a loud clap.

Other noises answered Her, rising from the glade and those in it. The topmost branches of the walling trees shook under the buffeting of the Wind.

"Seek," the Earthborn commanded. "Seek—and find!"

With a roar, the Wind obeyed. Then She once more turned Her attention to the body.

The Covenant has been broken—blood broken, my children. Raise your wards and hold them well, for who knows what comes with tomorrow or the days beyond?

One of the nearby females who had been among those scattering the flowers had remained on her feet. She faced the Wind Caller, eye to eye and chin up, all awe—for that space of time—lost.

"It has been said"—the Forest's daughter spoke as one whom some truth now used as a mouthpiece—"that refuge in the Forest may be offered—sanctuary—for any fleeing the Dark. This was once so; do we now depart that custom?"

Slowly the Lady shook her head. "You remember well, Hansa. And this do I now say to all of you: give haven to any who need it. Accept what comes in fear and pain, for it has greater worth than even we can foresee; and it may bring down the Dark Lord."

Wild Wind whirled, swooping over the highest branches of the trees. Its thoughts were its own now; perhaps She who had summoned it knew them, but the rest of the Forest waited. The skin of the Sasqua tingled. Once—oh, once—it had often been so. Was it to be thus again? Their great clubs thumped on stone and earth, driven into motion by the excitement racing through their veins.

The Wind returned. Leaves were whipped from the trees; the blossoms about the body were sucked up, swirled in a mad dance about, then released again. And he who lay there in the hand of mercy was now complete, his head resting where it should. The Sasqua's deep-chested cries vied with the withdrawing Breath of Life to do full honor to their own.

There yet remained a task to be done. The woman spread Her arms wide once again. About Her thundered the Wind, its shouting voice enough to deafen all in the Forest. Gusts broke away to form separate currents.

Though they were now silent, the Sasqua waited, for the death they mourned was only the beginning. As a spot of blight could spread to consume a leaf, so had the serenity of the Realm of Trees been shattered. Oaths long sworn had been broken; Lacar had died at the hands of the Misshapen Ones. And who had brought them into their homeland?

Somehow, even eluding the direct gaze of Her children, Theeossa moved Her hand, and She suddenly stood upon a pinnacle of stone. Clubs swung and thudded in salute. The cudgels moved as one and seemed to possess a life of their own, though in the outer world they were considered but lifeless wood and no match for superior weapons.

With a final howl, the Wind contained its power. Theeossa laughed and allowed Her arms to fall limply to Her sides.

"Watch and ward must be kept," She enjoined, Her manner abruptly as stern and cold as the rock on which She stood. "There has been a stirring beyond the Dark Barrier." To the surprise of Her listeners, the Lady laughed again. "When fools play with fire, they often find themselves cinders! He, whom our present dealer-in-evil would call, has other—and what he considers greater—matters to concern him. He also has a long memory, and he well recalls what befell before the Covenant. Let this man-child, who plays so blindly with forces he cannot begin to know, beware: a Great One of the Dark is not disturbed without consequence!

"The monsters came *here*"—the last word was expelled as forcibly as if She had spat it—"seeking not such a Great One but their own petty lord. Some quirk led them to believe they could free themselves from bondage with a blood price, even as they were bought. . . .

"I say it clearly: the Forest bears no taint for this killing. But remember you—watch and ward!"

Once more, an eddy of Wind looped about its Caller. Her body did not yield to its touch, but Her hair waved banner bright. Mist streamed from Her figure, enveloping Her, and She was gone.

In his cluttered studio, Harwice sat on his favorite stool. Within reach lay a length of smoothly planed silvery wood, while a row of paint pots sat uncapped and ready, their colors glowing. Yet the hands of the artist mage rested on his knees, and he stared at the wood and the gem-bright pots as if he had never used such tools or tried to produce a painting before.

Suddenly he uttered a furious oath, and the shaft of the

brush he held snapped. He threw the fragments onto the floor, and his scowl of frustration deepened.

The plank waiting before him bore a half dozen faint lines, a sketch Harwice had drawn at dawn.

It was bright enough now, by the Power. But the painting . . . This was his talent, and it had never failed him before. He shivered at the thought of any seeping-away of what he had commanded for so long.

In Harwice's mind's eye he could discern two youthful faces—indeed he could see them clearly—but he had somehow lost the precious power that, by his colors and brushes, would make them live. A boy and a girl, they did not exactly mirror each other; still, there was such a close likeness that any viewer would say they shared the same bloodline.

Frustratingly, he had not been able to endow the pair with the likeness he wanted. Here he wanted no flattering fairness of countenance; rather, they were marked by the lines of harsh life, a grinding existence. But their eyes held a keen and brooding intelligence. Whether they knew it or not, their birthright was certainly talent.

They were of Styrmir, those two; but they displayed none of the satisfaction with life, the belief in the future, which had once been known there.

"Harwice?"

The voice startled him, breaking his intense concentration. He did not turn to face the speaker, but his expression was close to a grimace of pain.

As his visitor moved closer, the edge of his cloak brushed against the array of paint pots, jarring one from its stand and sending it to the edge of the small table. With an exclamation, the newcomer pointed a finger at the teetering jar, whose contents were threatening to slop over its rim. Straightway it settled into security again.

Gifford gave a sigh of relief. The room was already growing dim—as Harwice had not bestirred himself to light any lamp—but the archivist walked close enough to the board so he could inspect the sketch. He turned at last to his frowning brother.

"So you have dreamed," he commented softly, clearing his throat as if some emotion pinched there.

The painter scowled at him, though that obvious displeasure did not disconcert Gifford.

"Why do you ask? Are dreams not within the bounds of your talent also?"

The loremaster closed his eyes for a moment. His face showed an expression of weary sadness that had quite banished the glow of content it had once worn.

"You have seen them plain." Gifford's voice was low but intense. "Their birth shall be heralded by kin death and evil, and they shall be brought forth in darkness; yet still the promise of Light to come lies about them both."

The archivist's hand, stained with ink where the other's was daubed with paint, did not quite touch the surface whereon was depicted the face of the maiden.

"Falice, who shall walk in beauty, sing with the Wind—and be what none of humankind could aspire to be since the earliest days of all."

Harwice no longer regarded the drawing, for his face was buried in his hands. "I do no more—let it rest as it is." He spoke with harsh finality. "The shaping of those lives shall lie within themselves; I meddle not with such power."

"You have not meddled," Gifford reassured him quietly.

"I have dreamed, and then I wanted to bring my vision to life, though I was not permitted to carry it through."

"The Light decides in the end," said the lorekeeper. "If the curtain is lifted for you to see a glimpse of the future, do not deny it, brother." He sighed. "Did you not also foresee the downfall of the Great Scale? The pans are now down at hand level for any to tamper with."

Again Gifford raised a hand toward the double portrait, but this time his finger indicated the youth. "Fogar—who from his birth will be given over to the fosterage of evil and who shall know temptation thereby. Yet I say to you,

Harwice, he bears that within him which shall hold steady at the end."

The artist might not have heard this heartening prophecy, for he arose, picked up the slab of wood, and strode to the far side of the chamber. There he set the painting to face the wall, and he turned his back upon it with grim determination.

Sulerna's knitting needles flashed skillfully. They had been carved from bone until they were so smooth and slender that the finest yarn could be used—carved by Elias, who since her ravishment had kept apart from her. Her brother seemed these days to be ever hurrying elsewhere when she would speak with him. Indeed, his eyes would not meet hers even now, though he sat only across the hearth from her.

The young woman's needles were being plied with housewifely craft, yet what they had to work with was but the ravelings from worn garments. In a similar effort to repair what could no longer be replaced, her brother was striving to mend a broken harness strap.

The folk of Firthdun had to make do with very little these days; yet Irasmus had made no move toward destroying them. Fear had become a member of the dun kin and sat always, a ghostly guest, with all of them.

Sulerna dropped the knitting on her knee and her hands covered her belly that was swelling—unnaturally large, she had heard whispered. In spite of her condition, she had taken her place in the fields with all the women. Moreover, she had gone with them on nights when the moon was full to the White Lady's grove to offer petitions for the safety of the dun and those within.

The girl's feet swelled, and her back ached, despite the potions Mistress Larlarn forced upon her. Resolutely, she had barred from memory the act which had so altered her life. To her former playfellows, it was as though she had become a stranger from whom they shrank. And lowness of spirit was harder for her than the pains of hunger that pinched them all at times. She, who had been a-dance with life, crouched now beside the hearth, always feeling a chill, as she strove to contrive small garments from the rags Haraska had collected. And Sulerna danced no more.

It was not so for Ethera, her cousin, who was also carrying, but who bore her discomfort with pride. Watching her, Sulerna wondered at times by what whim of an unknown power their lives had been set in these allotted patterns.

The great looms had been dismantled and set aside, and the same had been done with the linen-break and spinning wheel; for, despite all the efforts of the men, lambs were born dead, and the flax stalks were soggy with black rot.

Irasmus was at the bottom of it—of that everyone was sure. Why he waited, unless he derived some twisted pleasure from watching their struggle and decline, none could say. But Firthdun was dying, slowly and painfully, and, with it, all hope of any help to come. Did any of its people, Sulerna wondered, really expect the Wind to return?

15

A PARCHED SPRING PASSED INTO A SEARING SUMMER IN STYRMIR. Though most of the beasts had long since vanished, there was a crop of sorts to be harvested. However, those things that did grow in what had been fields of grain were now strange root things, thick and solid as wood.

Such growths could be eaten, and they were; but their eaters grew more and more stooped, lank, and vacant eyed. Children—and there were very few of them—showed the blown bellies of ones who had never had enough to eat, and they dug ravenously in the dark sod for grubs and worms until those, too, vanished.

Yet Firthdun stood. At first, the dunsfolk had seen the enemy as Him in the Tower. These days, though, they were kept awake many hours at night when one or another of their guards summoned their aid to face, not gobbes under the orders of their bloodthirsty master, but the skeletal beings who had once been friends and kin.

When those of the dun could, they tried to share, only to realize that such giving would make them the target of their own people and that those, in the end, would show no more mercy than the wizard's demons.

"It may be that he sees this as an easy way to bring us

down," said the Oldfather, as they gathered one night. The kitchen, which had once been the warm center of their lives, now felt like a last refuge held against a powerful enemy.

Elias and his field partner nodded their heads; they were wearied to the point that not even anger could rouse them any longer. There seemed nothing to talk about save their situation; mostly, when they gathered at night, there was no talk at all. The women sat with their children in their arms or else with empty hands, for there was very little to be done, save to spend each waking hour from dawn to dusk with the men in the fields, giving all the encouragement they could to crops that were hopelessly stunted.

This day, the laborers had found another break in the hedge along the road, but one which had plainly not been made by human hands. A plant had grown without their noticing—sheltered by the briars and reaching long roots under their defenses—and had discharged a poison so that the wholesome vegetation withered and died.

Such was the plant's tenacity that the field-workers had had to change partners several times as they had struggled with it. The result was that some now bore bandaged hands covering skin blistered by its acid sap. Yes, Sulerna thought dully, it could well be that Irasmus had no reason to destroy them himself. He had only to wait until the country the dunsfolk had served so long did it for him. Even their kin might bring fire at night and, using crude weapons, drag them down.

Tired—the girl was always tired. She knew, and could no longer refuse it, that often what was best for eating that day found its way into her bowl. Her hands supported her fast-growing belly, and the weight of it seemed to drag her ever forward. Ethera displayed a similar shape, but perhaps she was more strong of bone, for she did not appear to be so heavily freighted.

Both of them drank the brews Haraska and Larlarn prepared. Such potions did, indeed, relieve the aches in the back and the bouts of nausea that had earlier wracked them both but that had wrung Sulerna out into a week of near collapse.

What hurt Sulerna most, was that, when she took her place among the workmen in the fields or helped with a task that needed more than one pair of hands, the others held aloof.

Jacklyn avoided her as much as possible. He was no longer a heedless little boy, and, even as time had added inches to his height, so had lines graven themselves around his mouth and eyes such as should never mar the face of any youth. His aunt had spoken of this to Grandmam, and she had been honestly answered.

"He feels that he owes a kin debt, Sulerna, and at his age he knows not how to repay it. He will not talk to the Oldfather, nor to his own father, and to speak to women is less possible, for he believes he has lost the right to approach them."

The girl was truly roused, then, to think of something beyond her own condition. "But no fault in this was his! How could Jacklyn stand against—against a man who had already knocked him senseless at the first blow? He carries no debt—"

"Save," Haraska reminded her, "he was where he should not have been, and you were drawn after him. Do not try to argue with him, girl. Jacklyn may be only a youth in years, but it is a man's pride that keeps him going through adversity. And he may yet have another—and braver—part to play."

So the days passed leadenly. Sulerna tried to continue working with her needle, as did Ethera, on tiny clothing cut out of what material could be spared. Yet between them stood a wall, for her sister-in-law was free and happy— while she was chained by a Dark will. And now she had ill dreams, at times, to torment her at night.

Then one night she crept out by herself, urged by a call she could not understand, to the Moon's shrine. There— under the waxing light—she lay down, and she dreamed.

Fire and darkness were all about her, and pain was within, but through it there came the Wind's own command: *Run! Run!* And Sulerna could see the goal that had been set her: the edge of the Forest beyond. She thought she could not keep to her feet, such agony lanced through her, yet somehow, though the Breath of Life did not support her, she ran. She fell, just where the trees rose about her. Ahead, a tongue of green light stood upward. Then she was on her knees, while branches beat against her bare buttocks and the pangs continued to wrack her.

Where she sank to the ground at last she could not tell, save that about her was something of the White Lady who walked the skies. And she knew that all would be well for more than Sulerna alone, whose great fatigue would be gone forever.

There was another bearer of burdens in Styrmir—one whose patience grew thin as he sought along strange paths for that portal he must have.

The book with its bristle-hide cover was much in his hands, for most of that lore Irasmus had stolen from the Place of Learning was of neither use nor interest in a quest like this.

In those days, he lived for nights when the thunder rolled and the lightning flashed, darting livid fingers out of the air over the Forest and reaching for the valley. Strangely, however, when those flashes beat around the nearly barren land, it seemed that they were lessened, vanquished.

Irasmus was certainly not disturbed by such petty expressions of spite, as he deemed them. But the gobbes could not be urged out of shelter. He had, at present, no reason to see how far he was able to assert his authority over them. His trust in their attachment to him, though, was now always in question at the back of his mind.

During the storms he chose to ride toward the Forest. Like ashes swept aloft by the heat from a roaring fire, small flakes of power were borne by those tempests. Irasmus had early created a system within himself to draw in any power, making it his own—or so he believed.

To the Dark Lord, the howling of the Wind carried no message save, perhaps, for a frustration that he himself was not its prey. However, the Forest held a strange wildness.

Irasmus bit his lip as he rode. During the past summer, he had, with infinite care, fashioned another wand, and wore it belted on as a soldier would bear a sword.

But he did not draw the wand forth on these night rides. Instead, at intervals, he reined in his frightened horse and tried to draw a greater measure of power to himself by force of will, attempting to see into that dark mass which might hold—anything.

It was on the third such excursion that he brought himself to dare what he had long thought of but had not been able to force himself to try. He drew the wand, and the rain slid along it in a strangely thickened flow as if it had attracted the notice of the storm.

He waited until the dying away of the last bout of lightning. Then, as one might employ an outsized brush, he used the wand to draw in the air. Thus—and thus—and thus—

His mount had stopped its fidgeting and stood as still as a statue. Irasmus's own body, however, was so tense with a mixture of boldness and fear that he felt nothing at that moment but the wand, keeping all his concentration on what that opened in his mind.

The answer he expected came only in part and raggedly, as if it lacked the force to manifest as he would have it: an anchorage to a source of power greater than he had ever hoped to contact. The wand wavered in his grip, and at last he either had to sheath it or drop it. But the last glimmer of power radiance was gone.

The mage sat hunched in his saddle. No, he dared not give way to disappointment—he still had his resources. The lightning cracked one last great bolt as if to strike him down; then it was gone, but it seemed for an instant to leave the faintest trace in the night, pointing in his direction.

It could well be a warning but, even more, it might just be the goad to his memory, the guide to his way of thought. Where could such a signal lead him?

The wizard's horse came to shivering life under him, and he swung back toward the tower, unaware of a snap-light glow near the ground as he cantered past a thick clump of rusberries.

"He is gone." The fury of the storm easily covered that whisper.

Five of them, stinking wet, were huddling together for meager protection from the rain. This was not too daring a meeting. It had been learned some time ago that, since the invasion of the Forest, the gobbes were no longer so brisk about their master's business. Certainly the apparently mindless service rendered by the land grubbers might have led their overseers to believe there was no reason that their charges need be watched too strictly. Not, however, that any of the Valley folk gathered there this night did not hold his or her life in both hands for such recklessness, as they well knew.

The meeting was not one of tightly bound kin from a single dun. As the farmsteads had been driven into the earth, so had their members' identities themselves cracked and broken. Those who had once been looked upon with respect might no longer hold any positions but, rather, listen to the suggestions of herders or harvest hands. The scales which held the old life had become completely unbalanced.

"Why did *he* come?" The voice was that of a young woman. "Has he been hunting?"

"He would have those demons of his on our trail," growled her neighbor in the darkened hollow which hid but did not shelter them.

"What he seeks lies in the Forest. He did not send those misbegotten monsters there—that we all know—but they have followed his will since then. The Forest—"

"The Forest"—this was a much older voice, that of a

man who paused to vent a hacking cough before he could continue—"there dwells the Wind. Would you say that such a man-beast as he of the tower has dealings with the Great Breath?"

The Wind! Instinctively, from what had been learned in early childhood, their heads came up, hoping for that light touch on cheek or brow or the warm rapture of being, out of their many separate entities, gathered into a complete living whole.

But there came no Wind—only the slanting squalls of rain and the fury which raged over the Forest and was all too readily heard.

"Who called the Wind?" Once again the man with the cough posed a question. "Well you know who keeps green growth in their fields, food on their table. There has been no treading to the nothingness we know done to *them!*"

"If"—now the young woman spoke once more—"they have some pact with him, then why would he strike the maid Sulerna?"

There was a bark of harsh sound, very far from laughter. "Are you, indeed, a believer of *that* tale, sister? We all knew who led evil in upon us. And did not that same power take him up and make of him cupbearer and close servant? Yurgy is of their blood, and undoubtedly now also of the wizard's. How do we know that that boy has not been many times a messenger, offering this term and that to tempt the folk of his foster dun? And who dares to swear that Sulerna did not look upon him warmly so that he acted as the Dark Ones always do?"

"None has seen him since," suggested another male voice.

The cougher hacked again, then spat. "Perhaps he had served his turn and has been sent hence, even as were those gobbes. Motram, here, saw what became of them—"

"I saw." The answer was stark, and the memory it evoked was enough to silence them for a moment.

Then another spoke. "This asking and not-answering

does not get us to what has brought us here. Jadgon, why the summons?"

"Are we humans, or are we the spineless worms who bear allegiance to him? Winter lies before us! The last of the herds have been slaughtered, and three quarters of the smoked meat taken by the gobbes. The devils rake from our baskets the long roots and the ball ones, too, which are the best we can harvest now. The bushes have been stripped—once again, under the gobbes' watch—and then the berry baskets have been taken. Even our dogs have been eaten by those horrors, and when has anyone seen a bird—save those raw-headed death eaters that serve him? We cannot live on this sick soil and nothing else—unless we are worms, in very truth!"

A murmur of agreement rose from all around him.

"Do we then," Jadgon pressed on, fired by the passion of youth and a just cause, "go up against him with such weapons as we can shape from flail or scythe?"

"You forget—the Forest." The woman who spoke did so quietly, almost in reproof.

"What of the barrier there?" snapped one of her hearers.

"Garstra brought back a full branch of gold plums she found lying within her own land, as if borne there by no chance but on purpose. Little Zein came upon a pile of more cones than he could carry, though the other boys brought them all in. The gobbes entered the Forest to kill, but we have kept the old peace as best we can. Who knows what may have noticed that?"

"Do not pin your hopes on Wind swings now! We are lost to the Wind. Or"—and now this voice came close to the snarl of one of the long-lost dogs—"perhaps it is one more pleasure of the Dark One to tempt us. No, we keep to our plans."

"But who will be holding MidWinter this year?" questioned the woman who had spoken of the Forest.

The one afflicted with the cough gave his harsh bark.

"Who? Why, them as had a harvest—that's your answer, Rasmine. And all know who that may be!"

"They had to kill most of their herds—"

"Smoked the meat, they did, though—and I didn't see none of it going to the Tower as tribute, neither! They picked their fruit clean, and be sure that's well put away, too. The wheat fared not so well—but they've had a harvest, yes, they have. And 'tis only right that they share it with their neighbors, all square and proper. Or maybe we can *move* them, like, to just give us the whole. Now, spread the word—we've plans to be made!" And the disposed scattered to carry the word.

16

Though the Place of Learning was wrought of very ancient stone, and, outside on the mountain peaks, winter
raged, there was always warmth in the rooms most used,
just as provisions seemed to ever be stretched so that no
one went underfed from the table. Yet this stronghold was
not the serene place for study and service of the Light that
it had been built to be those nigh-uncountable centuries ago.

Certainly there was no peace for those who went about
their tasks with determined energy. From novice to archmage, the brothers were still searching, but their seeking
now lay in a different direction.

Gifford had lost more weight, and his once well-fitted
clothing was belted in in rolls and creases about him. He
had also developed a nervous habit with his right hand
when he sat, as if he were quickly turning the pages of an
unseen book.

"They move." The terse statement was made by Fanquer, who had seemed, during these past months, to become
once more the fighting man he had been in his far-off
youth—even though he wore no mail nor belted on any
sword.

"Yes." That single monosyllable came from Archmage

Yost, who had appeared to take on something of the stiff negativity of a phantom.

Gifford lifted his head. The seeds of tears were planted in his eyes, and he did not try to look straight upon any now gathered there.

"No choice." The old archivist's voice was as broken as if he stood by the death stone of all he had cherished most. "He has tried—through the Night Steps—to invade us three times. Now he returns to his earliest plan, which was hardly more than an idle fancy when first he thought of it. It must have come home to him that Styrmir, in the end, may answer only to those of its oldest breed. Thus, he has determined to have one such to stand at his right hand."

"Only there shall be two," corrected the woman Yvori. "I say to you now, sisters and brothers in the Light, that if one of the twain be taken by Irasmus, the second must go free—and that means only to the Forest."

Harwice was pacing back and forth along the wide stone hearth. "The Forest may not welcome—"

"Painter," Yvori interrupted him with a smile, "do not let your fears color you a picture of the future in the somber tones of the storm cloud, without a thread of gold from the returning sun! We of this place have pursued the nurturing of our talents through instruction. However, there are those, and always have been, who are born with the gifts we must strive hard to develop. I say this: the time of death and blight has run too long. We were told by Her Who Calls the Wind that only a people can produce those of their own kind to save them. Now the day arrives when Irasmus will act—but we, also, shall be ready. We cannot save the boy child—the dark mage has woven his web too well. But for a girl child, there is the Moon Gift."

Gifford's sorrow still filled his eyes. "Sister, it is well understood that, at times, your own powers wax in a different fashion from that which is taught here. What do you plan?"

She who was known as the Dreamgate, did not answer

him—rather, she asked him a question. "Can dreaming still reach into that place?"

The loremaster lifted his hands in a gesture of despair. "I have tried—"

"*You* have tried, but what we would do is of women's secrets, and for that I call upon my sisters here." Four of the cloaked figures moved silently forward. "When the time comes, Gifford, you shall dream, for that is your talent, but power shall be added. It would seem, from what we have heard, that these poor wretches of the valley plan a MidWinter feast. Irasmus allows this because he is aware that, at such a time, the remnants of the valley folk's powers are stronger, and he can milk them for himself. Now he wants all the power he can summon; also, his slaves have played into his hands—"

"You mean this plan of theirs to sack Firthdun during the feasting?" Fanquer asked. "Irasmus would allow that— yes, I can see why. For, with them under his hand at last, he can get this unfortunate whom he will fashion into being his shadow and his lesser self."

"They move in two days' time." Yost broke his silence.

"And together we shall be ready to do what must be done," returned Yvori calmly. "Remember you: two deaths will pay, but that which is so dearly bought shall be hallowed by the Light."

Thus the scholars agreed, prepared—and waited.

The Wind had not yet driven snow to blanket the countryside, yet the frozen earth mounted a chill assault against all who moved. And tonight there were many who tramped stolidly across the ravaged and befrosted land. Man, woman, and child, each carried armloads of wood and baskets of now-edible dried grass. This year, they bore no sheaves of wheat, nor any other stuff which had once represented Styrmir's wealth. But what they could bring, they did.

However, there was another group, made up of men and a woman or two who had been so hardened by the death of loved ones that pity had leached out of them. These, too, headed for Firthdun, committed to what they would do there.

The grim party had the weapons its members had labored on in secret. These were borne openly, since the gobbes, who hated the cold, would be huddling around the fire in the tower courtyard. The creatures would be holding a feast of their own. Those who moved against the hated dun had already put on the spit there a surly old boar, last of its species, that they had tracked, caught, and found rations for a week.

In Firthdun, Grandsire and Haraska stood together. They looked carefully into every face, not only to make sure that all the kin would understand what was said but also in order that each countenance would linger in memory if, after tonight, it was seen among the clan no more.

Sulerna, her burden now almost more than she could bear, did not watch the two elders. Her sister-in-law Ethera's time was not yet by a week or so more, the women guessed; but Sulerna's pains had started in the late afternoon. Though, when each struck, the girl chewed a rag that had been steeped in an herbal potion, she felt with each passing hour as if a giant hand had picked her up and was striving to tear her apart.

"They come to kill." It was Elias who broke the silence. "Have they not said it, even to our faces, that we shall not prosper while they die from want? Our women—"

"Elias," Haraska remonstrated, "remember, your hate, much less the shedding of blood, feeds that fiend who has lived off us for so long. Even now he squats in his web, thinking how he will use this time—and us—to foster greater and longer-lasting violence. We have had the dream-send, distorted and broken though that was." The old woman paused and pressed her hands to her breast.

"If blood there be"—now those hands clenched themselves into fists—"then He shall win, and the Light here may go out forever."

Such a warning was not well received; the young men stirred but did not hasten to perform their usual patrol. White-faced, Jacklyn moved for the first time in months toward Sulerna. For a time, he neither touched her nor looked at her, but, when she haltingly arose, he was there, his shoulder under her hand to steady her. So thin had the boy become that she could feel his bones. Jacklyn was a stranger, she thought sadly, yet she would accept all he had to give.

The ragged crew of attackers broke through the slight defenses of the dun. Grandsire gave the signal, and even the smallest of the children made no sound as they passed through the wide door into the open. Several invaders— those with the best weapons—hurried to ring the little ones and to threaten them with gestures and shouts. Meanwhile, the rest of the contingent found and brought forth the one farm cart for which the clan still had a horse and quickly harnessed the frightened beast. Then, keeping the captives under guard, their fellow sufferers raided Firthdun, as quickly and expertly as the gobbes had stripped their own homes of every stalk of wheat and curl of wool.

Those of the homestead saw the cart roll off, while behind it trudged the women and the older men, laden down with all they could heap into the sacks they had brought. It was only then that the leader of the raiding party gave his orders.

"MidWinter, neighbor Firth Mother," he sneered. "Surely you do not hold apart from us on this night. We are all your kin, near or far born—and this is the time when kin gather!"

"That is so." The very quietness of Haraska's reply daunted the mocker into momentary silence. "But, Goodman Viras, we have among us one who cannot march to any man's orders." She pointed to Sulerna. The gesture was easily seen, for already torches had been lit to make sure that all in Styrmir did at last suffer alike.

"She carries Yurgy's get!" The man was bold again. "The Dark Lord had some use for him in his time; perhaps such will also be true for her. Jansaw"—he addressed a young lout who looked burly enough to have pulled the cart and all its stolen goods by himself—"get you that barrower, dump the slut in, and we'll be off."

Jacklyn cried out and tried to stand between Sulerna and the men but was battered aside. She, doubled in pain and refusing to utter any sound before these worse than gobbes, did not see him again.

This year, the MidWinter celebration was not, it appeared, to be held near the ominous tower. For some reason not known to the celebrants, the flames of the great fire were rising not far from the edge of the Forest as the party with their captives reached the milling crowd.

Sulerna roused enough to realize where she lay. Haraska had told of broken dreams, and the girl herself had had one which she knew she must not share but obey as if it were an order. Perhaps it was one—a command from Her who Rode the Clouds.

The revelers had smashed open the casks from the dun and were busy dipping out, even with bare hands, the last of the strong cider. Meanwhile, another group had gathered about the cart, and now there came a scream from the horse as the beast went down under a lightning storm of badly sharpened knives.

Those raiders who had constituted themselves guards began to slip away to join the mass about the wagon and to help in butchering the luckless occupant of its shafts.

Sulerna could no longer stifle a small cry. Then she realized that she lay on two of the blankets from Haraska's bed and that her mother and Widow Larlarn were kneeling beside her.

So caught up was the girl in the blasting onset of the worst pangs she had yet felt that she was unaware the tumult of the nightmarish merrymaking was dying down. Harsh growls from gobbes were answered by cries of pain, and straight to the knot of women gathered about the girl in labor came Irasmus.

Sulerna's mother cried out and strove to place her body between him and her helpless daughter, to no avail. The dark mage gave the merest flick of his wand in the woman's direction, and, as if struck by an immense fist, she was smashed to the ground.

Sulerna cried out again, partly from pain, but more from knowing what now lay before her. Widow Larlarn was busy over her, but the agony was such that Sulerna was aware of nothing but its red horror. Then, seemingly from far off, she heard a squalling cry, and a terrible silence enfolded her.

She opened her eyes. The fire was blazing high, and the gobbes were leaping around it; but Irasmus had moved closer. In his hands he held what he had seized from Widow Larlarn, and now he shouted. "See what I hold, all of you? This one shall be as my shadow, holding fast to my every wish. You shall look upon him as if he were my son, indeed—"

Now—oh, now! Thank the Moon, whose beauteous face, though tarnished by the smoke from the fire, was yet bright beyond, they had set her down in this, the very edge of the White Lady's light. Haraska leaned close over her, and the old woman's breath was warm on her face.

"Get you gone, heart-daughter. We shall do what we can to cover you."

Sulerna was still encased in pain, and she well knew that she had lost a great amount of blood. But there was still hope left—and life. Then hands raised her and, though she had to bend half over, she could stumble. Jacklyn—only his small, hunger-bitten body was enough to keep her moving.

Irasmus—in the distance, she could hear his voice, and he was chanting now, intoning over the newborn child.

On, with the blood drabbling her legs, and pain, always pain. Then—the loom of the tree fringe. In that moment, a hunting howl broke from the demons behind. Blood! The girl knew only too well that the liquid life drew them more quickly—and implacably—than any other spoor.

She staggered at a push from Jacklyn. "On!" the boy urged. "*On!*"

But his support was no longer her aid, for he was gone from her side. Sulerna fell to her knees. On—yes, even if she must crawl! And crawl she did. She was in the edge of the Forest itself when she heard her nephew cry out, "By the Wind—!"

Then came a scream so wrenching that it somehow gave the girl the impetus to worm her way between the vast trees, striving to protect what still rested in her belly from any harm.

Time was one for her; the past was gone. Only purpose was left, and that drove her fiercely among bushes, around the trunks of trees. The girl held to some of this forest growth when the birth pangs began to strike hard again.

Light showed ahead—not the hot wicked caper of flame but cool as the gliding footsteps of the moon. Moaning, Sulerna drew herself into an opening which circled about a great Stone—a Stone which beckoned, beckoned. Somehow the girl pushed and pulled her unwieldy body almost to its base.

Then came the Wind, and the pain lessened as if it were now walled away from her. But she was feeling once again the tearing coming of another new life, and this time she could not even raise her hands in futile aid for herself.

Another cry sounded, small, alone. Sulerna's hand was able at last to find the birth-slick body and try to hold it to her breast, but the effort was too great. In that moment, the baby's hand moved, and tiny fingers grazed the rock.

The Wind—the blessed Wind—greater, more wonderful than the girl had ever dreamed it could be—curved around her exhausted, dying body. . . .

A tall shadow moved into the glade, and the Wind welcomed—welcomed and gifted—its owner. And Hansa, holding her own small son on her hip, reached down a great fur-covered hand and lifted the crying human infant to rest against one of her ample breasts.

For a moment, the Sasqua female stood staring at the Stone. The body at her feet . . . well, when this child of strange birth grew, she would pay the rites for her mother who was. But now the Forest's daughter was the baby's mother who is—and would continue to be.

Part II

17

"SASSIE—SASSIE! ONE OF THE NIGHT WOLVES HAS BEEN TEACHING you tricks again!" Hands on hips, the girl stood looking around, though there was little to be seen but the boles of trees, which towered to the skies, and, here and there, a moss-grown rock protruding from the earth.

"*Sassieeee*—" Purposefully, the seeker caught Wind tone in that call. She knew that the small Sasqua female could not defy one who was ready to use Wind search for her, even though to do so was cheating in the game they played so often.

Reluctantly, the she-cub crawled out of a really perfect hiding place, where the brown of her fur had blended so completely with the tree bark as to seem a part of it. She dragged her feet as she came, and her brows were drawn together in a Sasqua scowl of pettishness.

The young woman held out her arms. Sassie lost her touch of temper, coming eagerly to be hugged and petted and told that she was a fine big girl but that it was not right to run and hide from Falice, who had been hunting her nearly half the morning.

"Sassie hide—you hunt." The cubling grinned. "You no hide good"—here she laid her hand on the girl's bare arm and smoothed it—"skin too white, too easy see. Need fur, you!"

Falice laughed. "Fur would feel good when the winter comes," she admitted. During the years she had spent with Hansa, she had, after much experimentation, learned to cover at least part of her slender form after a fashion. She now wore a kilt of twisted and tied grasses, trimmed here and there with a purple flower; but the rest of her body only the Wind warmed or cooled.

Her hair was dark here in the shadow of the trees but apt, in the few patches of glade-sun, to show a gleam of lighter, near-golden strands. Its waist-falling length had also been interwoven and tied, that she might not be scalped by the reach of any low-hanging tree limb or high-growing bush.

A garland of the pale-lavender flowers, which were to be found at this season alone, swung about her neck, just low enough to cover her high, small breasts. As she stood, clad so and holding the true child of the Forest in her arms, she looked half woods-possessed herself.

The Sasqua kept no records of the passing years. When Falice could hardly keep to her feet and would cry for Hansa if a bush or tree trunk came between them, there had been Peeper to share her life. But he grew much faster than she, and the day had come when he had gone off to join the other young males. However, when his foster sister saw him at intervals, their bond of shared childhood still held.

Then Ophan had arrived, but, by that time, Hansa's human foundling was a *big* girl—one at least large and mature enough to help care for the Sasqua female's second son. Again, the seasons had flowed swiftly until he, also, went to seek his own kind after the way of the Forest's sons. And now Sassie was here—when not in hiding!

Falice herself had no desire to go too far from the temporary camps the she-Sasqua constructed, perhaps for the use of a night or sometimes for more days than the girl had fingers. She could not imagine a world in which her foster mother did not exist. Hansa had cuddled her smooth-skinned cubling when small, praised her when larger for learning the lore of the Forest (Falice drank in such so quickly, the Woodswoman was certain the girl was favored by the very Wind), and taught her the ways of the Folk, both the right and not right.

Each Sasqua (Falice had never tried to count how many of them she had known in her season-circles in the Forest) had a certain portion of the woodland for his or her own. None intruded upon another's holding without a sending through the Wind—and then only for a special purpose. That the human continued to share Hansa's territory was strange, but she herself was stranger, though all the woods kin had accepted her peaceably from the first.

Some boundaries she never crossed. In one direction, the trees appeared to thin, and the Wind warning against going that way had been very sharp and clear the one time she had thought to explore westward. The Forest held other strange places, too. The girl had been shown one long ago by Peeper where the rocks did not lie scattered but were rather set to rub sides with one another, leaving only a hole for an opening. A sense of unease had kept her from going further, though Peeper had stepped boldly into that gap and snarled a mock challenge into the darkness beyond. This stone stack was not a thing of his people, and whoever had fitted it together was long gone.

However, when Falice had grown taller and her breasts curved enough to be seen, there had come a night when Hansa had stroked and petted her as if the human girl were still a cub. Then the Forest woman had used Wind speech, carefully, so she would be understood.

"You are no longer a little one, my fosterling. I have seen you this day wash yourself at the spring, and there was fear in you. But that is not needful. There has been a change in your body that all of us who can bear cublings know. It would seem that this time is now also upon you. Therefore, you must go apart, for you are not of the Sasqua, and our ways are not the ways of all the world. This night, you must go to the Wind Stone and there be accepted by the Great One as full woman—for such is the custom of your people, Falice."

The girl had twisted her hands together. Yes, she *had* known fear that morning when she had gone to bathe at the spring and had found that which was evidence—or so she thought—of a hurt she had not been aware she suffered.

Even as Hansa had finished speaking, the Wind had closed about the girl as support and guide, and she had had no chance to ask once more the two questions she had posed so many times, to have only evasive answers from her foster mother: Who were her people, and from whence had she come?

But, just as the Wind caught her in a closer embrace, the knowledge she had long sought began to unfold in her mind. This did not take the form of a memory. Instead, she was being shown a picture, and, watching that image instead of her path, Falice went steadily forward.

A land without trees, except for a few here and there; open spaces; strange pilings of stones, not unlike the one to which Peeper had led her, set amid those cleared patches. The girl could not see clearly—it was as if she looked through a space of time (that was an odd thought)—but she did view people who were like her, save that they covered their bodies with clothing that looked much better made than anything she had been able to construct. There were also brightness, flowers, and the song of the Wind, so clear and joyous that she longed to run forward into that different, though beautiful, world. Instead, the Breath of Life brought her to a glade.

Many clusters of rocks were to be found in the Forest: some standing, others lying, a rare few containing many stones. But none of the groupings Falice had seen was kin to the one that faced her here.

The Stone was taller than she—perhaps only the tallest of the Sasqua could have ever stood equal to it. Partway up the side was a round hole nearly as big as Hansa's two sturdy fists clasped together. The rock was light gray and strangely bare of any crust of moss or trail of vine. The most curious thing about it was the sparks of light—of every color she had ever seen in bush, flower, tree, or beast—that bespangled its surface. And these were in motion, as if they were fireflies that used the Stone as a hive.

The Wind, which had brought her here, withdrew. She felt its presence; but it had ceased all sending to her, for what she would learn here would not be of its teaching.

Slowly Falice went forward. Twilight was gathering fast, and the sparks on the rock face appeared to adjust themselves, becoming brighter. The hole in the center remained dead black, as though a tight cover had been fitted over it.

At last, feeling a little dazzled by the constant play of the lights, the girl dared to raise her hand warily and touch the Stone. It was warm under her fingers, almost as if it were the living flesh of a hand that had been reached forward to draw her closer.

The hole held her now. She wanted to see what lay hidden within its miniature night. Placing both palms flat against the Stone, the girl pressed herself yet higher. There came more warmth.

She rose on tiptoe, her right hand moving toward that shutter of darkness. Now the Wind rose again, enfolding her yet not forbidding her to do what she wished.

Falice rested her forehead against the top edge of the hole and stared into its depths.

In his cell-like room, the youth stretched his arms, then winced. Irasmus never used the power of the wand on him; however, the wizard had a cane capable of raising wheals that sometimes took days to fade. Two candles stood sentinel at either side of the narrow table at which the boy sat, and they burnt with the unusual brilliance of all those the Master dealt out to him. Between the candlesticks lay a book, opened to a page whereon diagrams were drawn in red and black. These figures were also emphasized at their points of meetings by lettering the youth could read but which made no sense.

In fact, very little of the life within the Dark Lord's stronghold made much sense to Fogar. The youth was not slow of wit; at times, he believed he understood more than the mage guessed. Though of land-grubber origin, he was not sent out to labor in the nearly barren fields. Instead, Irasmus had early taught the boy his letters and continued his education—sometimes driving home key concepts with the cane—to this day. However, as Fogar had become inescapably aware (though he kept his insight a secret), the Master was deliberately blocking him from understanding the various spells contained in the sorcerous books and rites. The unwilling apprentice saw patterns drawn on the floor and heard arcane mutterings, but, for all he could comprehend, Irasmus might have been one of his own raw-headed birds cawing in place of speech.

The gobbes were no more stupid than the boy, though Irasmus seemed to look upon them as tools and weapons. Certainly they never took part in the curiously aborted ceremonies Fogar was called upon to attend. But there was no way to learn from them, either, except by the same means he had learned with the Master: watching, slyly and carefully, while guarding against any self-betrayal.

Fogar despised the demon slaves, whose appearance, smell, and behavior were revolting, though his earliest memory was of being fostered by them. But their constant threats of ill usage had long ago taught him to play the broken-spirited yokel with them.

The Valley folk, who seemed even more like mindless beasts than the gobbes, appeared to be afraid of him. No reason existed for such fear that he had ever been able to discover, but then this tower was entirely too full of secrets. Thus, though he was always surrounded, Fogar was alone—except for the dreams.

Hastily the boy damped down memory. When the Master sat before his dusky globe, he might well believe he had the whole of the land and the lives of all who lived therein spread out like a map for his inspection. But Fogar alone had the dreams!

Again his mind nearly betrayed him. Bringing to its fore the action of which he had dreamed last night, he concentrated deeply—to no avail. Fiercely he refused to be distracted, and again he looked down at the page of the book.

Only—the youth licked his lips nervously—was Irasmus again playing some trick to test his so-called apprentice? Perhaps he knew the boy had tested *him* from time to time in small ways! Slowly Fogar tapped the nail of his forefinger on the tabletop in a certain pattern, which to the uninformed might express nothing more than impatience.

No—he could not sense the darkness that always clung about Irasmus and, to a lesser extent, to the gobbes. Taking the chance that he was not under observation, Fogar bent his head a little to translate the crabbed printing on a portion of the drawing. Yes! It was so, and it was like opening a door—if only to a crack's width for an instant. Irasmus had, indeed, deliberately garbled the writing on this diagram when he had directed his pupil's attention to it two days ago—a typical ploy in the mage's learn-this-but-no-more method of teaching.

The boy's discovery was like thirsting and being offered a full cup of clean water. Still, he kept up his pretense, frowning and muttering as if totally perplexed. However, having seen to the true heart of this spell, Fogar felt like a mason who had been given a pile of perfectly squared stones and an order to build.

That rush of enthusiasm lasted but a moment. He did not jerk up his head, as his body desired, for he had no reason to stare at the wall above his pallet. But he felt a—*presence*—its attention centered upon him.

Games—always playing games! The youth had seated himself here deliberately some hours ago; no one would wonder that he was now ready for bed. Blowing out every light on the first set of candlebranches and all but one of the flames on the second, Fogar undressed. He then washed at the large bowl of water, though his attention was always seeking the intruder. Finally, knowing no way to make that shadow reveal itself, he lay down and pulled the coarse sheet up over him. His last act, which he dreaded but which he knew had to be done, was to blow out the final candle. Then he waited. He had no idea what sort of attacker lurked, but he had certain skills he could call upon in self-defense—or so he hoped.

The sparkles in the Stone were flashing as they raced to outline the hole, and Falice saw that she was the object of their actions. However, they did not aid in lifting the barrier against her sight. Instead, they formed a thick border around the opening, and the girl did not really need the Wind to tell her that this circle was being drawn for her protection.

Inside the hole there was a vague stirring, though more than movement could not be seen. The girl had the sensation that her vision was being drawn out and out, as though whatever lay within that opening—or on its other side—was a great distance away.

Then the curtain dropped, and Falice saw a building of stone blocks nearly as tall as one of the Forest trees. This was remarkable enough, but it was encompassed by a land such as she would not have believed existed. The ground was sour and held little life; here and there a misshapen plant showed but no trees. It looked full of unclean death.

Mercifully, her glimpse of that accursed place did not last long. She had a moment of light-headedness, such as might have come from being whirled about by the Wind in one of its less-generous moods. Then she was being drawn toward that high-reaching building and to one window in which showed a faint but beckoning gleam of light. She found herself in a room, small and harsh with its bare stone walls and scanty furniture—but also occupied.

Falice's view closed in on a table whereon lay a square

object. This she did not recognize until her attendant Wind supplied the word "book," with the explanation that in such a form were records kept in this land which knew not the Wind, with its all-holding memory.

A being (*man,* said the Wind in her mind) sat looking at that book. The girl drew a deep breath of wonder. She knew Hansa and the deer folk, night wolves, and tree cats, as well as the trees themselves; but here was one who was like herself! Had she, at long last, found her people? Her lips parted, but she did not utter the sound she wanted to make. For, almost as quickly as she had realized her kinship to this stranger, was she aware of a creeping evil that seemed to ooze from the walls of his room, carpet the bare floor, taint the very air he breathed. This was a place to which the Wind could not reach—a cursed place, like the land outside.

The man was, she believed, a youth—perhaps close to herself in years. When he stripped off his garments, she thought that at least two of his wiry, slender body would be needed to match the bulk of Peeper. Cautiously, she cast forth a tendril of the Wind sense that had been hers almost from birth.

This dwelling was evil, but the man she watched—no, he was not truly a part of that darkness, not yet. She sensed that the time might come when he would make a choice and perhaps turn, of his own will, to the Dark. At the same time she realized this, a fierce denial arose in her that such might be so.

The girl could not send this kin the Wind to strengthen and cleanse him of any shadow of evil. In any event, the final choice must be his alone. Yet there were ways of freshening his world with the Breath of Life, even if its full power could not reach him. She knew his face now, as well as Hansa's, and she could wish him well each day; for so did the Wind carry comfort to those who were troubled. At last the stranger put out the thing that made light (another wonder), and his room was in night. Falice, a faint ache between her eyes, drew back from the hole, which was now black once more.

Taking a step backward, the girl suddenly stumbled and fell. Her approach to the Stone had uncovered part of what lay there. Twice she had served with Hansa when they had come across one of her foster mother's kind, long dead, in the Forest. The bones were laid, to the smallest bits, in their proper places; then the doer of honor called down the Wind's protection.

Why so much had come upon her this night Falice could not have said. However, she gathered the bones and laid them straight and, as she worked, she became aware that the frame she put into order was like her own—it had belonged to no Sasqua.

Carefully she set the bones in their places, then stood while the Wind whirled about her and the sparks of light on the face of the Stone flashed.

"Go with the Wind, stranger." Falice repeated the proper words. "Let your way be ever that of the summer breeze, and gather you what you will of the Light."

Each full moon time thereafter, Falice found her way back to the Stone. Some nights it had scenes for her to see, and many were sickening in what they showed. But she understood it was needful for her to view such horrors, in order to know the nature of the enemy.

This day was Sassie's now, and the two of them were playing the cubling's favorite game. However, tonight the moon would rise full, and once again Falice might go adventuring.

18

THE COUNCIL ROOM WAS UNTOUCHED BY THE PASSING YEARS, BUT those gathered in that chamber—all their arts of energy hoarding notwithstanding—showed differences in both condition of body and level of vitality.

The change was most apparent in Gifford. His scholar's stoop was more marked, the wisps of hair escaping from beneath his cap were faded and thinned, and any hint of the wonted good humor and satisfaction with life had been wiped away from his now down-drawn features.

"How long?" The archivist's voice, once so assured, revealed a loss of vibrancy.

The archmage did not look up from the invisible lines he was sketching on the tabletop with his forefinger.

"Who can tell? How long does it take to corrupt a man?" Now—or so it seemed to Harwice the artist—the figure traced by Yost on the dark surface suggested a tower. "That he has held out so long—indeed, from childhood—against absorption argues a strong inner core, or—"

"Aid of a sort, yet not from us!" flashed Fanquer. Of all the mages, the former soldier betrayed the least change. "Brother"—he spoke directly to Gifford—"did any of your surest-sent dreams arrive unmangled by Irasmus's wards?

Have any of us taken a further hand in the game? No, I think that someone else is making his move—or *hers*. It was never well to try the temper of that one who commands the forest Wind."

"She has her own ways," stated Gertta. "Remember, though—it was through Her we were assured that the second of the Old Blood reached safety. The maid is untaught, as we would reckon teaching, but she has lived freely in the arms of the Wind, hearing always its voice.

"You spoke of dreams. The Wind deals with visions also, and Falice dreams without knowing why. Fogar, for his part, is crammed with knowledge—perhaps too full crammed, as the Dark One may discover! The boy's learning is like our own; while his sister's knowing is the memory of the Wind, for she rides the Breath of the World, and it remembers, always and all things."

"Why does Irasmus persist in his dealings with the unholy?" one of the others ventured. "He still tries, now and again, to break through our barriers and rummage among the forbidden levels."

"Because, I think," the archmage answered, "that that yet-Darker One, who might wish to use him, has either been busied elsewhere or is playing with him, testing to see how strong a talent has been shadow snared."

"There is also the matter of the hidden ones." Gertta, spoke again. "The Power that dwells in the Lightless Land is mighty, but have we not all known from of old that a single small error in laying a spell will not only break it but perhaps also rebound to the discomfort of the caster?

"Our rogue mage is aware that he has still within his slave hold another of the talent-blessed Old Blood. That he has not sought her out is possibly because he thinks to keep her in reserve for some final purpose. He is puffed up with all he withdrew from the land; but he was too impetuous at first, greedily seizing all he could summon near him.

"Do not forget"—Gertta paused for emphasis, her dark eyes sweeping the assembled scholars—"that, half a season ago, the gobbe Karsh was struck down and his broken body left just outside the Forest. A force that can destroy a demon is not to be overlooked! Irasmus felt so, too; and he made a great issue of that slaying, beating the countryside to bring out any unknown foes who might still lie hidden, though he found nothing but the ever-thinning ranks of his slaves. He did not attempt the Forest—and we all know why."

Fanquer sat back a little in his chair, and his lips twitched. "The Shadow Lord flinched from a shadow," the old soldier remarked with some complacency.

"He will find Her no shadow, but a too solid wall of defense about Her Forest and its people, if he hurls himself once more against Her power!" snapped Harwice.

While this debate was in progress, Gifford had seemed not to be listening. Instead, he had drawn from one of his cloak pockets a roll of parchment he now opened with care, for it was crumbling at the edges.

"Two have talked of dreams." The loremaster spoke as if he voiced his thoughts aloud, but his words revealed he had heard his fellows' discussion. "There will be a new dreaming. We have striven, over the years, to reach Fogar, and we have managed this much—he inwardly shrinks from what he might become. Moreover, Irasmus, ever jealous of his own, does not share knowledge easily. Now we shall awaken in his captive a new talent. And wherefore?"

Gifford pulled from another pocket a stylus that he now brandished as if it were a wand to rival Irasmus's own. "Because our one-time brother, while he has seemed a patient man, will not settle for less than all: a full confrontation with That which he serves. He believes the Great Dark One to be generous to its servants—though he does not see himself as a minion but, rather, as companion or even master of the Nether Lord he thinks to call up. It has been a long time since he made any move toward that goal, but we shall touch him with a spark that will set his ardor once more alight."

Yost had leaned forward a little, his attention centered

upon the outspread roll. "The script of Jastor!" the archmage exclaimed, his voice deep with reverence. All around the council chamber, indrawn breaths of wonder greeted his revelation.

"Our tireless searching"—the archivist gently used the stylus to smooth the scroll flatter—"has at last brought us a key which, if we can employ it properly, will open a new door for Fogar—and stir Irasmus into action. This knowledge shall be used tonight by all of us in concert, for our dreaming must be powered by the strength of our united brotherhood to breach the deadening barrier about Styrmir."

Fogar set aside the goblet that had been brought to him by a slave. He also cleaned the plate that had been left with it, but his eyes were still occupied with the cup and the liquor that swirled darkly within it. He smiled inwardly, so that his understanding could not be detected by any who spied on him. Ten days ago Irasmus had ordered this particular beverage be served to him. . . . The boy frowned. Why had he been then—and why was he still—so sure that this new addition to his board meant no good?

He caught at an elusive wisp of memory—of a moonsilver shape standing beside his pallet, a form he could only "see" when his eyes were closed. Hard upon its appearance, a strange scent had swept into his nostrils, growing fouler, as if putrid ichor were being forced under his very nose.

The night following these phenomena, the goblet had been newly included with his evening meal. It had at first, as he had raised it to his lips, smelled of a mild herb. Then, all at once, the boy had nearly strangled at the corpse-rot stench rising from the cup.

He had accepted the warning—why, he was still not completely sure. Yet the silver one who had come to him had radiated an aura of peace and goodwill, even personal concern, for him, Fogar, Demon-Son.

What Irasmus had intended the murky drink to do to him his apprentice could not guess. However, the next day he had carefully assumed the fear and befuddlement of one hardly above a valley clod in learning when he was ordered to assist in a minor spell, and he understood very well that the wizard was frustrated by his awkwardness. Irasmus had stopped the boy's recital of the incantation less than halfway through and had, instead, set him to work with the gobbes. The creatures were overseeing the digging, by the former farmers, of a large hole in the side of a hill—a business that had begun two days previously. The Master had given no reason for this occupation; but the demons, plying their ever-ready lashes, had kept the wraithlike Valley folk—men, women (and Fogar)—steadily at work. Nor had Irasmus summoned him that night for any obscure instruction.

Twice more the goblet had appeared with its ill-smelling drink, and each time the youth had managed to feed its contents to the one gullet in the room guaranteed to relish a foul feast—the garderobe.

Now, as Fogar retired to his pallet, his head was full of questions; yet he knew no one he could trust to answer them with the truth. A long time had passed—a number of seasons, really—since the Dark Lord had shown interest or enthusiasm for any project as he had for this delving into the ground. He was like a man seeking a fabled treasure, sure he was on the verge of its discovery.

When the first layer of soil had been listlessly shoveled away by the feeble laborers, a section of earth had been revealed in which were imbedded a number of stones, some cemented by clay to each other. These the gobbes ordered to be sorted out from the loads of earth and placed to one side. The only feature that distinguished them from ordinary stones, as far as Fogar could see, was that these rocks were flat as plates and generally all of a size.

Irsamus had actually ridden out to view this labor late on the third day, spending some time at the pile of stones but neither dismounting to examine them closely nor having any held up for his inspection. The boy noticed that the gobbes did not touch the rock discs either, and that they inspected their carefully raised pile only from a distance.

Fogar smiled. Very well—Irasmus had his secrets, a number of which his apprentice had quietly uncovered over the years. The boy knew that, for all his discoveries—and these were not a few—he could never confront the dark mage openly. Still, he took a certain pride each time he managed to acquire another piece of the puzzle. This game of stones certainly had a very important meaning for Irasmus; thus, it must be Fogar's part to listen, look—and learn.

He stretched out, weary from the steady labor the gobbes had commanded that he alone do—picking of the rock discs out of the earth-winnowing basket and delivering them to the mound of their fellows.

His arms cramping at the memory, Fogar gave a final stretch to ease his still-taut muscles. For a moment, as he raised his hands—why did he still have the feeling of hefting weight even when he no longer sorted the strange stones? But he was too tired to wonder long as sleep came quickly.

It was moon night. Silently as one of the White Lady's own beams, Falice slipped into the glade and, parting the ferns at its base, faced the Stone. She wondered if this would be a "seeing night"; however, of that the Wind never advised her. Still, she went determinedly to the monolith, laid her hands against its warmth and comfort, and looked once more at the curtained hole. Excitement caught her—yes, the sparks of light were gathering to form the frame. She might see again, only—ah, Wind, let the vision not be some horror such as she had been forced to witness before! The girl knew the evil master of the tower very well—not only by sight but also by spirit—for his thoughts as well as his actions were borne to her in snatches by the Wind.

The young man interested her the most. She knew that she had once been sent to warn him by revealing the nature of the vile and dangerous mixture she had seen the mage concoct; she was aware, too, that the youth had seen her—

at least in part—on that occasion. Then, twice more, at the Wind's bidding, she had pointed her will toward certain books and planted in his mind the need for seeking those volumes out.

Tonight? This was different! Falice tried to pull herself back from the Stone and discovered that it would not let her go. Instantly she knew, as the captive's tower chamber was revealed to her, that she was not the only visitor this night. A person? Some shadow of the Dark sent to keep watch on him? No, this guest was an extension of power, such as the Forest's fosterling knew the Wind could produce. Slowly it came, not in full gust as the True Breath, and it seemed to find some obstruction to its entry. But— Falice drew a deep breath of wonder—about that force clung such an aura of rightness, of Light, and of the answering of a need, that feeling it was like meeting the Wind in another guise.

Straightway, without thinking, the girl gathered of the Wind about her what it would allow and mind-hurled herself through the Stone's window.

Falice experienced a strange shock of contact, as if two things, different in themselves but sprung from the same rooting, had met. Then a glow of light appeared above the sleeping youth. His arms had lain limply across his body, but now as she watched, though she was sure he still slept, they arose.

The hands of the dreamer came together to form a cup and, out of the air from no source the girl could see, there poured, as if it were falling water, a blue-green light. Though this liquid luminescence cascaded into the boy's palms, his wrists were also braceleted by glowing rings of the same force; then the radiance appeared to sink into his flesh and vanish. At that instant, her slight link with the other power was broken. The Wind whistled about her, and she knew that what had been worked for here had been wrought: into the hands of that one who was like her, yet unlike, had been placed either a gift or a weapon.

*   *   *

Irasmus had been staring at the murky globe before him, but his real attention was elsewhere. From his coming to Styrmir, he had laid down defenses. Some of those tactics he had acquired in the Place of Learning; though these were not to be trusted, since they had been shaped with the mental tools honed in the storehouse of the scholars. However, the talents of the valley folk upon which he had been battening so long now made Irasmus feel that his own powers were far greater than those of most of the mages under Yost.

He had also continued his probings to penetrate the forbidden levels in the archives; though these attempts had been baffled, so that all he had managed to garner were bits and pieces of knowledge he had spent long hours attempting to fit together. Despite the vigilance of his former brothers, he *had* learned; but he had been able to trust none of his discoveries until now.

This night, however—the Dark Lord's hands, resting on either side of the sphere, curled into fists—his fortress had been invaded, by *what?* He had been aware of slight intrusions in the past, and there had certainly been traces of a determined picking at his locks by the archmage and his fellows. Now, it appeared, a new player had entered the game. Once more the sorcerer scowled at the seeing-stone, which had shown him nothing but confusion—a whirling storm of flakes of Light like the palm-sized blizzard captive in a child's snow sphere. And that cloud of whiteness—conjured by what talent?—had enclosed Fogar.

As Irasmus thought that name, the face of his apprentice appeared in the globe in full detail. There was no sign that his heavily drugged sleep had been disturbed. The master had not been able to use that rein on his chosen servant too often; for the draught left the boy dull witted in the morning and apt to make errors, some of which might be dangerous, in his studies. Perhaps—but no! Irasmus was very sure that the child he had chosen at its birth—one uniting in himself two lines of ancient talents that only one family still held—could not have been a mistaken selection.

Firthdun . . . The men of that line had been disposed of on that wild MidWinter night by the gobbes. Two of the women now labored in his tower and, though he had tested them over and over, neither appeared to be mentally above the level of idiots. There had been a second pregnant female in the dun; however, she, too, had seemed a lackwit since witnessing how Karsh had amused himself in his own unique way with the male who had sired her get. The Forest had been close by at the time, but Irasmus was certain that the girl had had neither the strength nor the opportunity to slip away there.

The wizard arose and went to the dun rolls, which he had inexplicably kept even after all the holdings had at last been wiped from the land. Unrolling the history of Firthdun, he found the scroll had been nearly destroyed by time and knew that its writing could not be read much longer.

Except by such steps as he could take.

Placing the globe atop the roll, Irasmus spoke aloud the Order for Reporting. It was not names that appeared one by one in the ball, but rather faces, to be dismissed with the flick of a finger. Dead, dead, dead; in the slave pens; dead, dead . . .

Still he continued to watch. There came Fogar, right enough, but after him more dead. The other once-pregnant female swam into view, her face, wiped clean of wit, turned up as she slept with mouth open. She was old before her time, sapped and sere, and she differed very little from those truly dead save that she yet walked.

Her child? Irasmus concentrated more deeply now. A scrawny girl. Talent? He sent forth a questing thought—and was startled for the first time in years. Had he, indeed, chosen the wrong child? But how? All his careful plans for breeding the tool he wanted had been carried through, even as he had laid them!

Where is this one? His question was quick.

The picture that came in answer showed one of the hovels where the miners sheltered. *There!*

Well, he had not been able to experiment with Fogar as he might have done, for—at least until his long-term plans were brought to fruition—the boy was needed living, intelligent, and able. But here was a game piece whose existence on his board he had not guessed: another child born at the propitious hour. Not of the proper parents, to be sure, but one who still had a spark within her. He would, of course, take no chances that he would not be in complete control of this one, and as soon as possible.

Once again, the sorcerer asked for the globe to show him the child's face, and he studied it, a slight frown between his eyes. The longer he looked, the more some deep-buried memory fought to reach the surface of his mind. All the folk of Firthdun bore a certain resemblance to one another; his records had told him that there had been inbreeding by choice, unless one of their males had been especially set upon bringing fresh blood into the line.

Yes, he had certainly seen that face before, and not when dulled and glazed of eye. *Eyes*—

Irasmus all but started up from his chair. Four seasons back, the gobbes had been ordered to beat the bounds. He was sure he had all the human slaves under his control, but it was always prudent to check now and then.

Those demons had found two ancient crones hiding near the road leading to the pass that he himself had closed. A pair of old women—but they had stood off the gobbes, who had actually seemed to fear them. The wizard had been summoned (now he shook his head from side to side—how *could* he have forgotten this?); yet the women had been rendered helpless with one sweep of his wand. The gobbes, frustrated by their inability to act, had been particularly vicious.

Only when the half-grown girl had come running from between the rocks had he realized there had been three people here. Pointing his wand had reduced the girl to slave material, and she had been dispatched to the nearest camp of such human drudges.

So—at least he had learned; but he was angry. It was not fitting that an adept at his level of mastery would fail to recall a matter of such importance. Irasmus turned to the globe and began a series of passes and ritual phrases. The revelation of the child's existence and ability had not been a deliberate breach in his defenses, but it was a warning, and one he would not let lapse from memory again.

19

FOGAR AWOKE BUT DID NOT IMMEDIATELY OPEN HIS EYES. HE could hear the gabble of the gobbes rising to his second-story room from the courtyard below. Such a gathering usually preceded a hunt, but where was there prey for the ever-hungry horrors now? All spirit had been crushed from the humans; certainly none of them could even have thought of attempting escape.

Now the boy did open his eyes and sit up, determined to find out what had roused the demons to such a pitch of excitement so early in the morning—the light seeping through a narrow, once-blocked wall slit high above his head was the faint gray of just-disappearing dawn.

His eyes were drawn to his hands. He had washed them the night before, laving away all the dust and earth of his day's labor with the stones. Not many of the rock discs were being found anymore, and consequently the gobbes were urging their excavators to great efforts.

Now Fogar spread his fingers wide and turned the palms first up, then down. Among the stones he had stacked in the days since Irasmus had set him to the labor, there had been a very few, widely scattered, that had felt warm to the touch. That rocks so well hidden from the weak sun should hold any heat surprised him, but he had certainly not reported his discovery to the sorcerer. Master and apprentice had begun their hidden combat slowly, but Fogar was by this time accustomed to playing a role and keeping any secrets he might chance upon locked as tightly and deeply in his mind as he could.

His hands—there was something—

Forehead wrinkled, the youth crooked each finger in turn, bringing them closer to his eyes, yet he could see nothing except several bruises and a half-healed scratch or two. Then why did this sensation persist that, drawn over the flesh were flesh-tight coverings? He scraped with a nail at the invisible coating, with no change in the feeling. Had the Dark Lord managed after all to enthrall him so completely as to have made a change in his physical body? And for what purpose?

The clamor of the gobbes, scaling higher in pitch, set him to dressing and washing briefly. As usual, the dishes and that telltale goblet had been removed sometime during the night, and in their place had been set a twist of dry, gritty bread. Still, no kind of food was ever to be refused in Styrmir these lean days.

This meager meal in hand, Fogar headed down the flight of stairs and came out into the courtyard. The wizard's creatures were gathered there. Their making of faces even more monstrous than they usually wore, as well as the shaking of a weapon by one or two, suggested they were, in truth, preparing for a hunt.

Sometimes one could pick up bits of knowledge from the gobbes. He stood to one side, watching their self-exciting capers, and chewed doggedly on his crust of bread.

As Fogar had expected, Irasmus came down to join them, appearing just as one of the former dunsfolk led forth a head-drooping horse—the only mount left in the Valley. The mage was smiling—a faint, menacing curve of lips—that meant he was, for the moment, in good humor; and he had already beckoned to his apprentice before he was in the saddle.

Master and servants took the familiar road to the hill that had been worn almost level by constant digging. The onetime farmers were lined up, prepared once more to winnow gravel instead of grain, their crude wooden tools and baskets in a row at their feet. None of those human wraiths, Fogar thought, showed any interest in the newcomers.

Then, by chance alone, Fogar caught a sidewise look from one of the work-hunched slaves. Though quickly hidden once more beneath drooping lids, those eyes were not dull and flat, at least not for the instant when he had accidentally met the girl's gaze.

Oddly enough, his hands stirred, though he had made no conscious effort to reach out to her. Why should he? The land grubbers, as he knew only too well from past encounters, hated him nearly as much as they abominated the gobbes. To the folk of Styrmir, the boy was what Irasmus had declared him to be—Demon's Get.

There was nothing unusual about this valley maid, save that she was younger than most of the work detail assembled here this morning; she was just as thin and as dirt begrimed and snarl haired as all her kind. Still— But Fogar had no time to continue his study of the girl, for Irasmus raised his wand and pointed it straight at her.

Her body shook visibly, as if its owner's will tried to fight against some compelling force. At last, with obvious reluctance, the girl shambled forward. Two of the gobbes moved in from left and right and draped chains about her, pinning her arms to her sides with the rusty metal but leaving her hands free. Only when they had immobilized her did the wizard ride up, to gaze steadily down at her.

Though captive now, the dun daughter no longer stood with lowered head; and again the boy caught a hot gleam in her eyes. He was only too aware of how the clan members could hate, but he had certainly never seen such ill will so blatantly displayed to the Dark Lord.

Irasmus spoke first, his voice almost caressing, as if he wished, for some sinister reason of his own, to reassure her.

"You are Cerlyn of the dun of Firth."

Fogar started slightly, but not enough to draw any attention. He, also, as had been whispered spitefully to him, could have claimed Firth as his clan, had not the mage stated him to be of demonic descent. The youth had long thought that all his true kin, save for a handful of slave women, were dead; assuredly the men had been wiped out on the night of his birth, or shortly thereafter.

"I am Cerlyn." The girl spoke clearly, with none of the muffled speech usual with the numb-souled slaves. She stood steady, staring up at Irasmus.

The sorcerer's earlier good humor seemed to have evaporated; now the faintest trace of a frown shadowed his face. This brazen chit, he felt, presented a puzzle—one which, when solved, would prove to be a problem that had crossed his path before.

He spoke an order to the gobbes, who moved away, keeping at a prudent distance from the horseman and jerking the girl with them. Irasmus's smile returned as he watched them go; then he turned to Fogar.

"Hither." He snapped his fingers at the youth, who moved to his side. "Catch this, and do not let it fall or you will greatly rue it!"

From the breast of his doublet, the wizard brought forth what his apprentice had never before seen anyone but its owner lay hand upon—that murk-hearted ball. The thing had always seemed his most prized possession, yet now he tossed it to Fogar.

Evidently, the sphere itself had enough power to make the boy respond as desired, for such a state of surprise was he in that he had only half raised one hand, yet the globe settled into it.

The Dark Lord was watching him closely, but Fogar had been warned enough by the unexpected action on the part of his master to be able to control his own startled reaction.

This was no small task, however, for what he held might have been a glob of frozen slime, whose foul feel seemed to creep outward from his palm to encase his hand.

Irasmus nodded. "Neatly done. Now—" He held out his right hand, his reins gathered into the left, and, without any movement on the part of the boy, the globe arose into the air and swept back to its owner.

"You have never been overbright or clever at your studies"—the sorcerer's smile was still in evidence—"so I have granted you a gift that will help you now. Go and sort out yonder pile of stones, using the hand in which you held my seeing-glass, and place those that answer to your touch in a separate pile. At least you can do this much—and see that you do it at a good pace, for time is now of importance."

With that command, he turned and rode away. Two of the gobbes edged nearer and snarled at Fogar, but he, accustomed from of old to their game of "making like master," refused to pay any notice to their threats and set to work.

Cerlyn trudged forward as if she were being taken to any ordinary task it might suit the demons and their overlord to assign her. The role of lack wit and broke soul that she had been taught to assume—her teachers having impressed upon her from the first the need for keeping any act of hers from arousing interest in those around her—was as convincing as she could make it.

Death, and torment worse than a clean departure from life, had surrounded the girl ever since she could remember. The most appalling event had been the frightful attack on Mam Haraska and Widow Larlarn. In some manner—she had never learned the details of that act of superb bravery—she had been saved from the fate of most of her kin. That the hag who was her mother still lived Cerlyn knew, but it was Firthdun's Oldmother and Loremistress who had taken her almost from her birth hour into the brush about the Forest. There the three had lived, more wretchedly than any animals as to food and shelter, but lived they had.

From the first signs of awakening intelligence in her, Mam Haraska and Widow Larlarn had been her teachers as well as her guardians. Twice they had tried to win deeper into the Forest, but always there had been a barrier set by Irasmus at the Forest's edge to deny them any safety. All the women had was their inbred talent; and that they exercised, sharpening it and sharing it with the child's own awakening powers, small as those were.

Then the two old ones had made their supreme effort—to gain the closed pass and somehow work their way across it—only to be discovered and slain. The young girl had been considered a thing of no account—merely another slave to be added to the workforce. Since that time, it had been her hope to labor within the tower itself and thus learn more—though of what she could not have clearly explained, even to herself.

There was only one of human sort—or human seeming, at least—who was free to come and go as he wished from the dark wizard's stronghold; and he was nearly as great an enemy as the master himself. It was well known that, at his birth, the boy had been hailed as a demon's son and given a Netherworldly naming. It had also been no secret that, through all these years, he had been apprenticed to Irasmus and schooled in shadow magic (though he had never used such magery openly), and that he was doubtless a well-trained assistant for any evil action. Until this day, however, Cerlyn had never seen him close by.

As the girl was marched along by the gobbes, she wondered about one thing. Even given the scantiness of her training, she was aware that any with the true talent could detect the Dark. To this inner sense, Irasmus appeared a monster. She well knew that, could his true self be seen by the eyes of the body as well as the mind, he would wear an even more twisted form and distorted countenance than his hellish minions.

The gobbes—the stench of them alone betrayed their origin in the Black Land. Her own people . . . With lowered

eyes and studiedly blank face, the girl considered the farm
folk among whom she had labored now for many seasons.
Where lay the evil in them?

They were like hollow gourds, she thought, feeling no
pity for their miserable condition but only impatience that
they had slid into it so easily. None of those two-legged
sheep could be hoped for as a helpmate for her! After all,
as Mam Haraska had told her many times over in warning,
they had given their aid to the destruction of her kin, and
their hands had not been clean of blood from that night
after. Not wicked, perhaps, but the valley people had been
weak, which was worse; for that quality in the soul let down
the drawbridge and admitted the enemy into the castle.

Why had Irasmus suddenly appeared in Cerlyn's life?
There was only one answer she could give: because, in spite
of all his power and learning, the mage wanted something
of her.

But why? All she had was a talent that had never been
either truly trained or honed. Her two guardians, certain
that in her veins ran the Old Blood, had called the Wind
once; they had also dreamed in quest of insight. The girl
herself could do neither. However, she was uncomfortably
aware that the wizard might think she could and attempt
to extract the knowledge by his many creatively cruel methods. Far better if she had died under the gobbes' talons back
at the pass with those who had rescued her. It would have
been an agonizing way to depart this life, but it would have
been swift. And Irasmus was a very patient man in his pursuit of a thing wanted.

Cerlyn had known from the start of their mining the hill
that those stones—some of them, at least—had significance.
Yet she had not dared to test what they might be. The
demons were always on watch, and then had come this vile
traitor to his kind, this Fogar and the order that he and he
alone was to handle the stones.

No, there was no reason to weary her mind with guessing what might lie before her. To keep up what courage she

had might make great demands on her, once she entered the tower and was placed at the dubious mercy of its master. She knew certain mental exercises—words not to be uttered aloud—that she had been taught. These were all the weapons she had to defend herself, and she would have to use them as best she could.

Cerlyn went docilely into the tower as Irasmus caught up with her and her guards. The gobbes yanked her painfully to a halt with the chains, and their smell was augmented by a gust of evil nearly as palpable as that stench when the Dark Lord came up beside her.

His hand flicked out, and he caught her chin, tipping back her head so he could scan her face. That study awoke a shame-tainted fear Cerlyn had never felt before, for it was as if not only her face but all her thin, wasted body was bare to his scrutiny.

Irasmus released his hold on her. "Faugh!" he commented, with a contempt she was sure was meant to flay her as much as if he had laid his riding whip about her shoulders. "Filthy slut. Dirt you were born, and dirt you shall die, though how is a matter on which I must think awhile." The wizard turned his head and gabbled an order at his creatures. Pulling the girl along to a well-like opening close to the wall of the tower, with little care whether she would stumble and have to be dragged, they made her descend into its gaping mouth.

Fogar, looking at the pile of waiting stones, flexed his fingers. He longed to draw them across a tuft of grass, even bury them in the dusty soil, in order to rid himself of the sensation that now seemed half ingrained in his skin. There was no chance of doing so, however, with those around him watching.

He advanced to the pile and reluctantly reached forward to pick up the nearest stone. He did not know what he would find when he touched it; but he felt only rough rock and tossed it aside. However, on the second try, the stone fairly stuck to his skin—he could almost believe it was some creature hardly yet awake but quickly rousing to awareness. Accordingly, he started his second pile.

He had added four and discarded as many more when rock apparently no different than any of the others shot into him a sensation as if a small thread of lightning had touched him in warning. To show his reaction to that was, he believed, dangerous. He compromised by laying it with his other choices, near but not quite touching the pile of stones that felt like frozen ooze.

Sassie had gone with Peeper this morning. It was seldom that Hansa's first son visited his mother's chosen refuge, but, each time he did, his small sister became—as far as Falice was concerned—nearly unmanageable. However, Peeper had assured the girl that he would carefully watch over the cubling. He had little choice, really, for Sassie had clung tightly to his leg until he had assured her that she could come with him.

Yet Falice felt an inexplicable need to keep an eye on her charge, and Peeper made no protest as she followed the two of them, Sassie riding his broad shoulder, onto a trail which seemed familiar to the Sasqua but which Falice had never had reason to tread before.

She noted that the trees here appeared to be shorter; that they stood farther apart, so that more sun reached in; and that there was a suggestion of freedom, with vines and brush in place of centuries-grown boles to wall them about. Suddenly the girl realized just where they were bound. From the first, Hansa had impressed upon her that she must never venture in this direction; Hansa's son, however, apparently had no such qualms. Now she was determined to catch up with him and take back her sister in fur.

Oddly enough, the Wind, of which Falice was always aware, seemed to die away, leaving a curious silence. No bird sang; not even an insect chittered. Peeper had stopped and put Sassie down. Now he beckoned impatiently to Falice.

"Come—see what those of the Dark do." The male Sasqua's Wind speech urged her on, and she went forward, to have him pull her hastily down behind a thick bush. There he bent a branch a little back so the girl could look.

20

IT WAS COLD, BUT CERLYN HAD MOSTLY BEEN COLD EVER SINCE she could remember. The cell stank, not only of ancient waste but also of very present evil, for she now lay in the heart of Irasmus's domain.

The girl sat with her back to the wall, knees drawn up and arms wrapped about them so she could conserve what little body heat she had.

There was, of course, no light, and she had not even bothered to try to explore this hole after the gobbes had clipped one end of her chain to a wall ring and had gone out, making gestures toward her she tried to ignore. The creatures had taken the only lantern with them, and now the dark was so thick she felt she could gather it up in her hands and shape it.

She was also hungry, her scant morning ration eaten hours ago; but hunger was nothing new, either. Now, trying to forget the pinching in her stomach, Cerlyn thought para-doxically of past sowings and harvests, and she suddenly recalled the far planting.

At first, all the dunsfolk had thought it some trick of the gobbes, for the demons had always been allowed a certain amount of freedom to make the valley slaves miserable. But

the handful of children who had been chosen arbitrarily
from the slave sheds had returned that night wearied to
utter exhaustion, telling a common tale: they had been out
all day "planting."

Planting—what? None of the youngsters had recognized
any relationship between the large, hard, oval seeds they
had had counted out to them, with threats of what would
happen if each were not put in the proper place, to the seeds
they had, for seasons now, tried to coax into lackluster life.

And the place for that seeding had also been strangely
chosen—in a strip of tillage hard by the Forest, though well
away from any shadow the trees might cast. The children
described how they had each grubbed out a hole with their
hands, placed a seed carefully within, and gone on to dig
another hole. They did not cover any seeds until one of the
gobbes came with a water skin and dribbled into the hole a
trickle of a strange liquid that had a reddish gleam. Then,
said the youngsters, they had gone back to cover the holes
and start another section of the line that paralleled the Forest reaches.

Questioning the small sowers produced no other information, and at last the proceeding had been stolidly accepted as some new trick without a purpose they could
understand of the master's. Yet, as Cerlyn knew, Irasmus
wasted no time on any action that did not in some way
serve a purpose he thought important.

Actions such as bringing her here.

Shivering, the girl thought with resentment of the hope-
sugared promise of Mam Haraska and Widow Larlarn—that
against the Dark moved always the forces of Light. But it
certainly seemed that the three women had been abandoned
by all they had been taught to believe in: the touch of the
Wind—even the woman power of She Who Walks the
Clouds.

They had sworn that a day would come when she could
claim the aid of both powers—and be answered. And what

had come of all such assurances? For her elders, a frightful death; for herself, slavery.

Not even the Great Lamp of the High Lady could send its rays through these walls, and the Wind had long been stilled in the valley. Why dwell on the impossible? Because one could now look for nothing else . . .

Cerlyn leaned her head forward to rest on her folded arms, tightening herself even more. Why should she fight the drowsiness that weighed her down now? It was enough that the wizard and his minions had left her here alone for a while—short though that might be.

She did not sleep at once, but her eyes closed. Then, as she had done for almost every night since she had learned to talk and walk and understand, she sought for the patterns she could see, as though imprinted there, on the inside of her lids. At the same time, her lips silently shaped Names, though the notion that anything might come of such a calling was a delusion no one with firm hold on her five wits could believe.

Three women stood around a waist-high brazier. Now that their heavy cloaks of office had been discarded over a nearby chair, the trio were revealed as nearly alike in height, though differing in age. It was commonly known to all of their world that the learning of the Wise preserved life until the owner of a tired body, having trained another in his or her skills, chose to abandon that earthly vessel. As it happened, however, for many seasons past no girl had come seeking the old knowledge. The number of the mages was dwindling—another indication, perhaps, of the present restlessness and outreaching threat of the Dark.

Two of the Wisewomen, though they stood straight and watched the fire bowl with clear eyes, showed signs of age whose onslaught was controlled by will alone. The third was younger but still past the middle of human life.

It was the eldest of that company who dropped into the low flame, twig by twig from a bundle in her hand, short pieces of dried wood long parted from their parent tree or bush. Sparks caught and held that kindling; then a thin spinning of smoke arose, and all three lowered their heads a fraction to breathe deeply the heavy scent.

All her branchlets gone, the senior mage held out her hands to both of her companions, and they in turn grasped hands so that all were linked. Their eyes were closed now, and each swayed slightly. Then the feeder of the flame spoke aloud.

"If this be of women's power—then let us go!"

No moon shone into the forest this night, and the standing Stone did not show any of its dancing jewels except as the faintest dots of light. But the Wind was rising—first rearing up as might a stallion determined to protect his herd of mares, then suddenly stayed in that defensive posture.

Shadows moved through shadows, though neither human nor Sasqua could have perceived them. The Wind stirred restlessly but kept its distance from those seekers, who stood now before the monolith, studying it as if it held a great puzzle that must be solved. Nebulous forms shifted, as if hands were raised in respectful greeting and petition, as well.

Though those light flecks on the Stone glowed no brighter, they did move until they faintly outlined a woman's body, whose head remained a clouded mask.

"You call upon that which no longer exists." To the distant listening minds, that statement sounded like cold denial.

"There were those who served You to their deaths." The answerer did not seem overawed but—quite the contrary—braced to pursue an argument. "This one who concerns us is of their blood and bone."

"The one of My blood and bone is housed in this, My place, in all safety." That chill iced the first voice yet more thickly. "The mortal maid for whom you speak was not even first blooded in My service."

"And was that her fault, Great One? All things—past,

present, and future—are known to You. Do You say You know nothing of what has happened? This one is the last of the Valley dwellers (save him upon whom Irasmus plays his endless tricks) to come of the kin dun who kept the Inner Shrine when careless—or overconfident—folk forgot. The seed of the talent lies in her, but only the first green shoot of knowing has thrust forth from the dark ground of ignorance. Would You have the Son of Darkness snuff out this girl, the single small spark of Light that remains?"

Silence, except for the fretting of the Wind still held in check.

"This much for you, then." The invisible onlookers saw that veil-obscured face turn, in a near-grudging gesture, to the human maid's bold defender. "It has been said that the people of Styrmir must win their freedom on their own. The girl is bound as much by that geas as all her fellows. If she can face the Night and force a path for the Day, then I shall claim her. But to promise more than that—" Then the shape outlined on the Stone was gone, and, a moment later, *Her* companion shadows had also vanished.

Leagues away, in the chamber of Mage Westra, three women opened their eyes.

The youngest spoke first. "Dreams—this daughter of the valley must be strengthened and guided by dreams, and not those chosen by any man, Light-filled though he may be; this is women's work. To enable any vision to win into that tower needs a battle of wills, as we fully know; thus she may only receive, as does Fogar, jangled fragments. But we have the tutoring of Haraska and Larlarn to build upon— let us see how we acquit ourselves as masons!"

Strangely, on this night the patterns that painted themselves behind Cerlyn's eyelids seemed more sharply focused, firmer; twice the girl caught the meaning of a bit of spell she had never understood before. However, this increased knowledge would place her in even greater peril, were Irasmus to guess it. The dark mage would wring her first dry, then dead, for any particle of power he could use. A fearful prospect—but then, Cerlyn had lived with fear so long that it had become almost a companion.

Companion . . .

Abruptly Cerlyn stiffened. She had been told so often of the Wind and all it bore—was it only a wish that, for an instant just now, she had felt its caress on her skin, smelled the stench of this hole yielding to something else, clean and bracing, to succor body and mind?

"Wind?" Greatly daring, she whispered that Name, but she was not answered. Of course, arousing false hope might be only a further torment devised by the master here.

Talent—even that born of and sworn to the Light—could feed upon hatred. Certainly, Cerlyn's heart was a hot coal of the stuff which, if loosed, could burn this sorcerer's foul den to ashes, as the farmers used to clear a field of choking weeds! But those same husbandmen also had a saying the girl thought well to remember now: "You cannot enter the cow yard without soiling your clogs." To fight Irasmus with his own weapons would be to enter into, and thereby aid, his evil. She must be very cautious, taking more care than she had ever done in her life, as she joined battle with him and his darkness, lest it overshadow what she possessed of the Light—little though that might be.

The girl's resolve made her lift her head and open her eyes on the night that filled her cell. Un-Light might indeed lie about her, but she would not invite it within. She had only herself and her broken bits of talent to call upon, but if that was the way it was, so let it be—on her terms, not his. The ruins of Firthdun might lie beneath the soil its folk once tilled, but she was of that blood still, Cerlyn, and so would she be until the end.

Irasmus's latest captive had not closed her eyes again, for she did not want to invite any more visions that led nowhere useful and left her with nothing of value. Yet now it seemed that the murk about her was broken by shadows.

Cerlyn's first fear of some torture contrived by the Dark Lord was quickly dispelled, but she did know that it was by his will that this barrier rose between her and what reached to meet her with aid.

The chain rattled against the wall as the girl straightened her body, rising to her feet. Her mind stumbled as she sought to recall patterns of power she had long carefully repressed and used only with the two she had once trusted.

"Who are you?"

She spoke the question, then shook her head in frustration and anger, realizing that the sorcerous shield that darkened her sight also deafened her ears and mind.

The shades wavered and flickered, now nearly solid, now mere wisps. However, as Cerlyn watched them, it became evident that, though unable to communicate by the ways she knew, they were fighting—yes, struggling fiercely—to come to her, and that they were of the Light no one talent-born could fail to know.

Suddenly she saw two faces, not connected with the shadows themselves but rather projected by some magical art. One belonged to a girl, perhaps her own age but certainly no daughter of this stricken land.

The face of this stranger bore no marks of privation, fear, or hatred. Instead, there was a kind of ecstasy welling up in those large eyes, as if they beheld some wonder they welcomed with joy.

But—the face beside it! Cerlyn snarled. The traitor, the betrayer of his own kin, the shadow of Irasmus—he whom she had seen all too clearly only a short time ago. This was Fogar Demon-Son, and truly he was worthy of that name—

Or was he?

His face, like the unknown girl's, was also serene, and— But this could not be so! Light did not join hands with Dark. It could not, for then nothing would exist. Still, as Cerlyn looked upon the features of the boy, she did not see the taint she fully expected. And, strangest of all, his countenance—which lay open to her now as though they were, indeed, kin to trust one another—resembled that of the girl, and closely.

She who, even as a shadow here, seemed the very symbol of freedom, might have been a cherished one of Fogar's own blood; however, such happy kinship did not exist—not in the clanless world Cerlyn had known from birth. And, though this vision had stretched her talent sorely thin, the wisewomen's fosterling was sure that she could reach out her hand and touch the cheek nearest her. Somewhere, its owner did have life, and now, at this time, if not this place.

The faces began to waver and ripple; then, with the suddenness of a knife falling to cut a cord, they vanished. Yet in their place for an instant was . . . something else. Cerlyn's hand, still half lifted to reach for the now-vanished girl, flew to her lips to stifle any sound. She recognized the symbol of Her Who Walks the Clouds, and it could only be summoned by one who gave her full allegiance.

Then it was all gone—the Dark's force wall, the Light's shadow play and what it had shown her. Cerlyn swayed back against the rough stone, letting her shaking body be supported by its solidity. She felt as if all of her small power had been drawn from her for that shaping.

As she sank into sleep, however, she was granted one final insight: the certainty that a pattern was being woven here, and that she was to be a part of it—if Irasmus did not dispose of her first.

The tower's master, in a chamber well above Cerlyn's cell, had not attempted to delve into her mind this night, though the tabletop before him was covered with pieces of parchment on which were inked spells, descriptions of rituals, and other arcane formulae. Frustration gnawed him. In all these seasons, he had not been able in any way to penetrate the Forest—there had always been a barrier that had swallowed up every attempt at drawing forth power. And now, since the shocking death of the Forest beast man and the later but equally violent end of Karsh, Irasmus had no mind to send even the gobbes near the place.

Not that he had dispatched the head of his band of horrors to the woods, which strongly suggested the gobbe's death and the subsequent return of his mutilated body to the Valley were in the nature of another warning. The mage thought he had an idea of who might be lurking there among the trees; yet how could the arch-fiend lords he knew of strike any bargain with the Wind?

The wizard needed eyes and ears to enter where all his present skills could not penetrate. Perhaps he had made a good beginning in that direction now. Only time would tell—and time might be far from a friendly ally. He was sure that the mages in the Place of Learning strove to monitor his every act and could not help picking up the energy emanations from some of his sorceries. They were not dullards, save inasmuch as they were content to observe but not to react. Yet might there not come a day, if the Wise felt the threat to be sufficient, when they would take their power in hand and come forth, as they had done once so many generations ago?

Resolutely pushing that thought away, Irasmus reached out and pulled one of the papers to him. It bore no words but only a column of small signs and a sprawling line along the right side that might be compared, with some imagination, to the eastern ridge of the Valley rising toward the Forest. Along the line was set a series of yellow dots, and these had been impressed on the page so deeply that the point of the drawing tool had driven into the surface.

As yet, according to the gobbes who were overseeing this planting, no sign had been given that those of the Forest noted how close the seeders had approached their own territory. This reassurance notwithstanding, Irasmus had raised all the wards that could be erected.

Pushing aside the scrap of map, he stared down at a second strip of notes. On this paper was carefully depicted a plant—one with a huge bulbous root. Its growth followed a fanwise pattern, with other tough stems appearing along the ribs to break ground. Plainly, it both sprouted and spread in a way that made it difficult to control. Good enough—one must never overlook any weapon, no matter how humble or seemingly insignificant.

The Dark Lord's irritation was somewhat soothed by future visions of just what would come of his planting, once its green phalanx truly attacked the Forest. At last he yawned and rose to retire; tomorrow, he would have other and more important matters to deal with.

The sorcerer had slipped into his bed when, in spite of its ample fur robes, he felt a chill. Quickly he made mental rounds of the wards but could find no evidence that any had been breached. Using talent . . . power . . . Drifting into sleep, Irasmus thought of *him* who might (or might not) be approached. He encouraged himself once more with the conviction that That One would look so favorably upon any who unlocked the gate between their worlds that the opener could expect more power flowing to him than he had ever believed it possible to command.

Fogar lay on his pallet. Piling stones was not the easiest of occupations on the muscles, nor did the fact that he must keep the discovery he had made today strictly to himself bring any sleep-coaxing ease to his mind.

Over and over tonight the boy had washed his hands and arms, as well as any other portion of his flesh that had chanced to touch those rocks having the feel of slime, before he could bring himself to touch food; and still he unconsciously rubbed his fingers back and forth across the bedcovering.

The master, he knew, had been hunting those same foul-feeling stones; but what of the two others the apprentice had uncovered during the day's work—those which had seemed energized by the very substance of the Light? He was certain that the dark mage was not aware of their existence, or else they would surely have been detected. Fogar's eyes gleamed in the dark like a tree cat's about to leap onto the back of an unsuspecting prey. He had found a weapon, and he had only to learn when to use it, where—and how.

21

FALICE TRIED TO FIT HERSELF INTO AN ANGLE FROM WHICH SHE could see as much as possible through the rough window Peeper had made for her. Sassie was pressed tightly against her and was being unusually quiet. She seemed as eager as her furless sister to see what lay beyond; yet instinct triumphed over impulse, and the cubling remained carefully hidden.

Some distance from the brush that rimmed the Forest's edge, the valley began. Hansa's fosterling had been shown by the Wind in the Stone enough to recognize that blighted land in all its dreariness. The broad expanses before her were barren, not only of trees but of all other vegetation save a short grass—a rank growth having an unhealthy yellow shade that Falice, used to the lushly fertile Forest land, found very distasteful.

This coarse stuff was being torn from resisting roots by workers who crawled on calloused knees like drought-enfeebled herd beasts. But—

The human girl caught at the small Sasqua as if her discovery might cause Sassie to be snatched from her hands and thrust into that sorry company. For the laborers were *children,* a little older than mere cublings but not yet approaching their time of full youth.

Both males and females toiled in that band, for their worn single garments, ash-brown as the soil being uncovered by their efforts, hardly covered their bodies; and they often had to pause and pull those shifts up, exposing skin as brown and rough as tree bark.

No talking could be heard, nor did they even give signs from one to another that they knew their laboring neighbors. For this, Falice saw a good reason.

These slaves had a driver in control. The girl shivered. His kind she had been shown by virtue of the Stone's window, and nothing existed in all the Forest as monstrously shaped, or mindlessly cruel, as this—thing. Fighting nausea when a vagrant breeze brought a puff of its stink and wondering that even the Wind could bear to touch that carcass, the Forest girl forced herself to look at the creature closely. It walked like a man, but its shoulders were a little hunched so that its long arms hung to a point where talons, each as long as her own fingers, now and then brushed the upturned earth. The skin was a sickly yellow-green and dotted with huge warts. Hair appeared only as an unkempt snarl of locks nearly as thick as choke-vine tendrils and standing stiffly from the all but neckless head. The lower jaw and its portion of the face presented an outline like the muzzle of no natural animal. This was a gobbe, one of the servants of him who had poisoned the valley land.

Its sole clothing was a wide belt, crudely patched in places, to which was strapped a long-bladed knife in a stained sheath. But now the nightmare also went armed with a lash it wielded with vigor, snapping at first one, then another of its charges, while whistling and gibbering to itself. Behind it in the field stood a rude cart, a mere platform on wheels, on which had been piled some lumpy bags.

Now it stamped along that section of the ground where the grass had already been rooted up and the clumps thrown aside. Partway down that march, it stopped suddenly, its beast snout swinging as though it saw easily through the brush and knew it was being watched.

Falice's grasp of Sassie tightened; but the cubling made no move, nor did her brother. The monster had raised one of its dangling paws and was stretching it toward the Forest, its head cocked on one side. It might be gauging a distance—or narrowing the range of its search.

After a few moments, either frustrated in its efforts to locate its would-be prey or postponing the pleasure of pursuit for the time being, it gave a throaty growl. This noise appeared to be a signal, for now, of all the children who had dropped where they stood for a rare space of rest when their overseer's back was turned, two struggled back to their feet and hurried into action, as if they feared at every step that the lash would fall. It took their combined strengths to tumble one of the sacks from the cart, and they had to unite to pull the crude bag back to their labor area.

The gobbe waved the workers back, and they obeyed hastily. Thrusting a talon into a loop of the bag's string, he broke it in two. Out of that sack rolled a smaller one, that the demon lifted to his mouth and used his fangs to tear open.

Falice could not be sure what he held. From this distance, it looked like small stones of a uniform size. The pebbly things also bore a polish, as if they had been fingered for seasons by the silver hands of a river, for the girl could distinguish a faint shine about the heap.

As Irasmus's creature picked the first of these stones from the pile, the Wind returned—not in wild gusts but scarcely forceful enough to make the leaves shiver. Yet what it bore and poured into the minds of the three hidden watchers was a sight so alien to any natural life they knew that they could only watch dumbly as the Breath displayed a living weapon that was meant to strike against their very refuge.

Those things were—*seeds!* Planted and nourished by the liquid the gobbe had begun to sprinkle from the skin bag handed to him by another child slave, they would dig themselves in, putting forth not one root but a nest of them. Out from each of those roots would, in turn, rise spikes of

204 ~ ANDRE NORTON

growth. Under the tutelage of the Wind, Falice learned that the army of plants would creep forward, through the bordering brush, meant first to protect the Valley from any attack by the Forest and then to invade the Green Realm and make that country its own. Let any attempt to cut or tear one of the plants from the earth when it was thoroughly entrenched, and its touch would rust metal, flay skin from the hand that touched it.

The creepers in the soil, those worms and beetles whose small lives had their place in the order of the world, would swiftly die. And any healthy greenery the hell-sprung growth could touch would rot and crumble into nothingness—perhaps even the giants among the Forest trees. *Truly,* thought the girl as she watched in amazement and fear, *such seeds had been garnered from the deepest storehouses of the Dark!*

Emboldened by the enormity of their threat, Falice dared mind-touch the Life Breath. *What do we against such a peril, Wind?*

The answer came straightaway. *Let warning be given; let our furred children know that their minds will be touched, so the years flee and they remember an earlier time; and let this death sowing here and now be stopped!*

It was Peeper who moved first. Throwing back his head, Hansa's son gave a cry such as his human sister had never before heard; then, using a weak spot in the brush which he had apparently noted, he leaped forward.

The gobbe went into a half crouch, spilling the seeds broadcast, its wide mouth suddenly lipless as great fangs appeared. It tried to unsheathe the knife it wore, but Peeper was already on it. His mighty club sounded a loud crack as it met the monster's skull, sending the demon flying backward to strike the cart. The rickety transport crashed to the ground, and the slave driver lay still, a ruin among the ruins.

Thin, shrill cries arose from the children; and they would have fled had not Falice, accompanied by Sassie, emerged through the brush broken by Peeper. Once more the girl called upon the Wind. About the fast-scattering youngsters arose a breeze, far from as strong as it would have been in the Forest, yet enough to quiet the little ones' fears until the girl could reach them herself.

They stood staring at her now, coming slowly together until they were huddled once more in a group, as if they needed the nearness of their own kind. Used as she was to the exuberance of Sassie and the other Sasqua cubs, Falice could feel the terror of the valley children smite her like a blow across the face.

She could never have calmed and collected them without the Life Breath, but now there was a warning in its voice: its powers, for this time, were rapidly being exhausted. The girl and her Sasqua sister circled in behind the half-dozen small bodies as, upon those same ravaged slopes in a time long gone, dogs had skillfully herded sheep.

The starveling waifs retreated before their strange new keepers, heading toward the rim of the Forest. Almost as soon as the two had gotten their charges safely under the trees, they spied Hansa and three of the Forest's other children coming to meet them.

Fogar was listening intently to what Irasmus was saying the next morning as the sorcerer pointed out a design inked on a square of parchment large enough to accommodate a far-traveler's map.

"The stones you *feel*"—the mage paused, and his eyes were very intent on his apprentice, watching for any reaction to that phrase—"must be placed so, the space of two hands apart and in a line marching the guide. This you will do alone, and you will be as quick as possible about it. More other stones will be brought, for it is doubtful"—he glanced at the boy's pile—"that these will be enough to trace the inner path as well. Now—get you to it!"

Despite this final exhortation, Irasmus did not ride off at once but rather sat as Fogar, suppressing his disgust at what he handled, set the first and then the second of the rock discs into place. The result was not unlike the beginning of a walk of stepping-stones. Certainly the sketch from which he worked was plain enough: the discs were to be placed spiral-fashion, curving inward and around several times until they reached a certain point.

Those land grubbers, who had been busy since before dawn clearing this space just outside the tower's courtyard wall, hunkered down unnoticed now and prepared to watch, as if Fogar were on the verge of performing an intricate spell.

However, the gobbes, who had driven them all hither and now prowled about their company on guard, were not so eagerly anticipating the action ahead. The boy was familiar enough with the demons' behavior to realize they were showing signs of uneasiness. They had drawn into a knot of their kind, and the gaze of their bulbous eyes swung from their master to his apprentice and back again. Still, if the creatures felt inclined to dispute this path building, none did so.

Fogar worked with elaborate care. In order to make sure each stone was in its proper place, he measured with a stick, then dug its point into the soil to mark where the next stone must be set. His body might be laboring like any of the folk of duns, but his mind was alert. His sadly fragmentary dreams not far in the past had shown him a portion of the very work in which he now found himself engaged; and within those visions had lain answers he must now force out of hiding. To search so was like walking down a long corridor where many doors lay on either hand. Each was closed, its surface blank of any hint of what lay within, yet still he must go seeking the right one.

Having decided that his somewhat mentally limited pupil could be trusted to do as directed, the mage turned to the gobbes and rasped out some orders in their own harsh tongue. Half the creatures reluctantly approached him, then fanned out to form a line beside the slaves. Grunting what were obviously threats, they kicked the humans to their feet.

Then, driving them back to the remains of the mound being mined, they lashed their charges once again to the same work.

Having made sure that his orders were being carried out, Irasmus wheeled his mount. To Fogar's surprise, the Dark Lord was not heading back to the tower but rather riding, at a pace hardly faster than a walk, eastward toward the Forest. The boy had known for several days now that the wizard was engaged there in another bit of business—one that also demanded a crew of workers with demon overseers to keep them busy. It had, however, puzzled him to learn that all the workers chosen for that mysterious labor had been the youngest and frailest from the slave pens.

Certainly, Fogar was curious, but the master would undoubtedly return the same way he had gone; and it would be best for his apprentice to keep steadily at his own task and have no eye for anything else.

The slimy feel of the stones was a constant irritation. He might be heaving rotting bodies onto a charnel heap. But Irasmus believed Fogar was totally under his control; now was not yet the time to test the tool?—weapon?—that had come into his keeping.

A small flare of excitement—almost as sharp as the flash of energy that had alerted him to the difference in the two Light-charged stones—kindled within him at the thought of them and grew as the morning passed. The feeling was faint but right. Somehow the four gobbes who had been left, undoubtedly to keep watch over him, suddenly wheeled about and started at a shambling trot in the direction of their vanished master.

The valley was not all flat land; in the expanse that began close to the tower and ran to the now-blocked pass, it rose in a series of gentle, low hills, though the Forest's threat could always be seen beyond. However, anyone traveling in the gaps between those hills would be out of sight at ground level.

The laboring youth paused and straightened, rubbing his

hands across the small of his back. He was attempting to cleanse them of the slimy feeling left by the rocks, but he hoped he might be thought to be relieving some stiffness left by repeated stooping and standing again.

Abruptly, air was pierced by a screeching, and the remaining gobbes plunged away to answer what was either a vehement order or a cry for aid. In that same moment, Fogar felt the slightest of touches on his sweat-beaded forehead. It was not even strong enough to stir one of the hairs plastered there, and it was gone again as quickly as it had come, only—he knew. Somewhere, Power stirred, and its farthest-flung reach had found him. Warning? He thought not; rather, an alert.

He had a good portion of the rock spiral finished, using only the evil-tainted rocks. Already the slaves were straggling back from the hill with the morning's harvest of rocks, but none of their baskets were full, and one or two held only a single stone.

As he had done ever since the mage had set him to this task, the boy began to sort the discs. Three of those were besmirched by the Dark, but there was also a single one of the Light-conducting rounds that made his whole body tingle as he laid it carefully aside.

Two of the kitchen slatterns now lugged out a steaming pot, set it lurchingly down, and dropped by it a basket of bread nearly as hard as the rocks. Fogar, though, was apparently deemed worthy of better food, for a greasy basin holding stew and a slightly less-hard half loaf were brought to him where he sat in the nearly finished spiral. He expected that, as usual, the slave would pay him no real attention, but he caught a glance from her half-lidded eyes. They were not as keen and all-seeing as the eyes of the Firthdun girl had been; still, they showed more alertness than was usual among the slaves.

The girl. Fogar thought about her as he swabbed the bread around the bowl. That she lay in the dungeon he was sure. He wondered if she had been fed; however, since Irasmus wanted her enough to bring her in as a special prisoner, it followed that her jailors would keep her alive.

Back he went to his building, if this stone setting could be dignified by such a name. But continued comparison of his spiral with the sketch the master had given him had pried open one of those locked doors in his mind. Yes, he *was* building—a road! He had never seen its like depicted in any of the sorcerer's scrolls, but such paths of power had been described there. From those writings, he also knew that, once the road was built, Irasmus would add an element that would form his own gate, then force it wide if he could.

The boy was considering how he might best act to prevent the success of this dire plan when the Dark Lord came into view. A good distance behind his mount followed the ragtag squadron of gobbes. Fogar sensed that, at that moment, for whatever reason, the monsters wanted to be no closer to their leader.

Their gibbering was not loud, but it sounded excited; and—to judge by the wizard's bleak countenance—something had gone very wrong. It was into the direction from which the hell crew was now approaching that the children and their overseer had gone this morning—but there were no children in this company. Feeling sick, but forcing himself to search for evidence he loathed, Fogar looked as closely as he dared at the talons and fangs of the demons for any telltale stains of blood. Mercifully, there were none. Yet neither were there any children, and, as the boy counted the rabble, the slave driver was missing, too.

The mage had nearly passed the spiral of rocks when he pulled his mount up short. His frown diminished as he took in the serpentine enfoldings, his head moving to trace the pattern from stone to stone. Then the frown returned as a scowl—the spiral lacked three rocks near its very heart.

"Finish!" Irasmus's command was a snarl. "Have this complete before sunset. The Dark may love the darkness, but night may also conceal peril for a worker, and I would not have you come to grief—yet." His voice rose to a shout. "Do it—*now!*"

The sorcerer rode on. The gobbes were left to mill around at the gate of the courtyard, where some of them took out their anger—and, perhaps, fear—by kicking the laborers to hustle them back to their pen.

Fogar continued his task at the same speed he had maintained all day. Three rocks were lacking, yes—but he no longer doubted what he was to do. He smiled tightly as, into those last three places, he carefully set the stones that held within them the fire of the Light.

22

ALL THE STONES WERE IN PLACE BEFORE SUNDOWN, AND THE FINAL three were of Fogar's secret choosing: those that made his flesh tingle with power—surely their thrilling sensation must be power. At the completion of his task, he stood, surveying his work and checking it against the drawing Irasmus had left with him. Yes—what he had done had reproduced that pattern exactly.

Dusk was gathering in, as if the Dark itself were being bidden to this unhallowed work. The boy had the disquieting feeling that, if he turned his head suddenly, he would catch sight of a shadow that was no true shadow scuttling away just at the edge of his vision—or perhaps he "saw" this apparition with other-than-bodily eyes.

Taking great care not to step onto any of the Dark-allied discs, he made his way out of the spiral and became aware, for the first time, that the gobbes—all of them—had emerged from their reeking barracks. From every creature's throat now rose a sequence of guttural tones, the sounds of each matching those of his fellows. The raucous noise was far from singing, farther still from Wind-message touch, yet it was clearly a ritual chant. A—a summoning! As soon as his mind had put this name to the demons' discord, Fogar was certain he was correct.

Others had come to attend whatever would transpire here, as well: human slaves, who stood further away from the spiral path than the gobbes, nearly melting into the earth in this light because of the soil on their skins and clothing. Most of the life remaining in Styrmir, it seemed, was gathering in this place.

Torches flared, restoring clearer sight; then the Dark Lord came walking from his tower. The torchlight formed an aura about him, its brightest point centered on what he bore, almost reverently, in his two hands. He took short, slow steps as if to make sure no unevenness of the ground would disturb his balance and shift, for the slightest fraction, that globe of murkiness that had been for so long the very heart of his chamber.

The dark mage set foot carefully on the first stone on the spiral path. Excitement and triumph surrounded him in an almost-visible cloak. Fogar did not know what was happening to his own mind; but he was sure that he now possessed a heightened awareness to see and feel things he had never perceived before.

On the final stone, Irasmus halted. He had not appeared to note the difference his apprentice's touch had read in the last three discs. Yet behind him swept, like a second cloak, a trailing robe of shadow that had grown thicker with every stone he passed and that now fluttered from side to side as if it were being repulsed. The wizard, however, did not notice that either.

In both hands, he now raised the globe well above his head and deliberately, forcibly, hurled it into the open space at the end of the spiral. Then, raising his wand, he pointed at the sphere.

Both the night and the world came apart—or so Fogar thought. The boy was thrown to his knees by a blast of power that bewildered his wits; then he was—where? His mind could not tell him as consciousness faded.

*   *   *

Cerlyn hunched in a corner of the cell, blinking and blinking again. Sometimes it was hard to know what was real and what was dream—for dreams had crowded thickly upon her of late.

Color had not been known in Styrmir for a long time—no flowers, no blue sky, no bright-winged birds could the girl remember. Yet a rich play of hues was part of her vision, or visions—perhaps one had slid so seamlessly into another that she had not been aware of any separation.

She might still be hedged about by stone walls, but now those barriers were hidden by strips of cloth patterned in tints that fed her color-starved sight. Illuminating those hues shone light born not of any torch or taper but rather from floating bubbles of wondrous rainbow sheen.

Was this beauty some glamourie sent by Irasmus—and was she seeing what was true or only what she hungered to see? She must be wary.

"Cerlyn."

Quickly the girl turned. Who, even in a dream of hers, would call her so? Dream-caught she must be!

She saw very little, at first, of the one who had addressed her, for he sat behind a table so high-heaped with wooden-covered books and rolls of parchment that they towered about him like a barricade (and a most unstable one). But the man himself . . .

Cerlyn met his gaze, and her first fear melted away. This was not her captor playing a cruel trick. The man she saw wore a cloak of shining cloth across which played lines of vivid color that added to his greater bulk. This man had never eaten grass roots, much less gone empty of belly! His hair was dusty brown and thin, and he might have been running his hands through it, for its limp strands were mused. His round face was pale, as if he seldom saw the sun, but his generous mouth was curved upward in a smile the girl found her own lips echoing.

Caution forgotten, she responded, "Master—"

"Do not give me such a title, child!" The stranger raised

large but sensitive-looking hands in a gesture of horror. "My name is Gifford. For my fault of being born with a seeking mind, I am Keeper of the Records in this place. We have no masters here; for all talents are unique, and who can say that one is better than another?"

Treading carefully once more, Cerlyn asked, "Where is this place? It looks not unlike where Master Irasmus spends his days, with all those"—she gestured to the books and scrolls—"evil things."

The archivist shook his head. "Not so! Evil comes from wrong choices." For the first time, he frowned slightly. "You, child, were born with talent you have not been trained to use, so you must add learning." He nodded at the uptowering records. "However, after that, it shall be your choice as to which path you will walk."

The girl wet dry lips with the tip of her tongue. "Irasmus has such—choice—and no good comes from him."

Gifford nodded again. "Irasmus has chosen, yes. Now he delves deeply into Darkness, and he will choose again. But let us speak of you. You are Cerlyn, granddaughter to Haraska, who was daughter in turn to Inssanta, Mistress of the Winds. . . . Oh, I could go on for quite some time naming the generations behind you, but they do not matter. This is here and now; yet you hold the talent, though it lies in your mind and spirit still asleep."

"Haraska—" She choked on her beloved grandmam's name. "The gobbes tore her to pieces by *His* orders. I seek no such end if I can help it."

"You would be safer if you were willing to learn, Cerlyn."

The girl's trust was not so easily captured a second time. "Fogar— The Dark One claims he has talent and has made him study for years, yet we have never witnessed a single spell of his casting. So what good has come of his studies?"

"Child, that young man has his own part in what we all must do, and, when the time comes, he will be ready— though not as Irasmus would have him!"

Suddenly the girl felt a stab of fear. "Will you, indeed, make me safe from—*him?*"

Gifford's smile faded. "That you must discover for yourself. However, this much I can promise: you shall find a task before you, as Fogar will; but, by all the power of the Light, you shall also learn that it brings deliverance and not despair.

"Although"—the lorekeeper rested his plump chin thoughtfully on his hand—"the temptation sometimes arises for an overeager scholar to experiment. I warn you, Cerlyn, casting forth one's line into forbidden waters brings up monsters instead of respectable fish! You must also keep hard hold upon your trust. Nothing in this world is exactly what it seems, for we each view any action according to who— or where—we are.

"But you do not stand alone. Aiieee"—Gifford sang that last word—"we have dealt together in the far past, your breed and mine, for the keeping of the Light! It was into Styrmir that those folk retreated who had been dealt the hardest blows of that war. There, they found the Wind— and the Wind blows fresh and clear when put to the proper purpose; thus the fostering of talent prospered.

"However, as the years pass, those who remember rightly grow fewer and fewer. Folk no longer think of the Wind as a weapon of great fury, the Fist of Death; rather, they conceive of it as a soother, a mere carrier of messages— the Breath of Life.

"Unused, Cerlyn, talent lessens. Thus, when Irasmus struck at Styrmir, he was able to bend the valley born to his purpose: to suck forth their talents and banish their ally, the Wind. The people had grown dull eared to the voice of the Light. They also believed that peace once won is won for all time, and they abandoned their vigilance and thus lost the battle before it had ever begun.

"However, through a few of your people the old strain yet runs true—with or without their awareness. You say that Fogar fails at the tasks Irasmus sets him. Yet that very lack of success is his salvation in two ways: it has prevented him from falling into complete bondage, and it has awakened in him the beginnings of talent. The Dark Lord is aware that the boy has power and keeps that ability locked, as one locks a coffer—but a seal set on talent cannot hold forever."

The mage's expression softened, and again Cerlyn felt the lump rising in her throat as it had when he had talked of Mam Haraska. It had been so long since any had spoken to her with kindness; but she would not cry in front of this stranger—she would *not!* Fiercely she swallowed as Gifford continued.

"Child, you think of your dun kin who were slain, yet you must remember that they were vessels that had weakened. You were saved by chance because, when you were a child, Irasmus could detect no power in you. But now he dares ever greater evil, and against this you must be armored—aye, and armed as well—by learning, which has always been a weapon greater than a sword.

"So let me bid you welcome to Valarian, the Place of Learning. You have already heard your first lecture"—here the lorekeeper laughed, seemingly at his own tendency to let his tongue run on—"and now you must have your first lesson. Come!"

He beckoned with his finger, and, unthinkingly, the girl obeyed. She did not believe that she walked forward in the body; rather, her essence approached her new teacher. As she "arrived" at his worktable, the mage opened a massive book. The novice student saw lines of writing rendered in blue and gold, as freshly colored as if they had just been drawn there. At first, they seemed mere gibberish, but then the archivist ordered her to read the passage aloud. She did so, slowly sounding out each of those sky- and sun-painted words, yet still they made no sense to her.

Only, when she repeated them, Gifford correcting her now and then, she began to feel a throbbing in her ears. This sensation moved into her brain, frightening her at first but then bringing with it a new confidence.

The girl came to the end of the passage, but the lore-keeper did not turn the leaf to continue.

"Your first lesson," he commented. "Let us see how well it has settled into your memory."

Cerlyn discovered, upon closing her eyes and concentrating, that she could clearly reconstruct the whole page in her mind. What was more, in this mental "viewing," the writing was even brighter than it had been to her physical sight!

Gifford nodded, smiling broadly. "So—in you the Old Blood, indeed, runs true." Abruptly his approving expression turned sober. "Now—a warning. The dark mage has leached from your people the strength of their inborn talent. He has also mined the awareness out of the earth, torn it from the fields—even snatched it from the sky. You are now in his power, and if he should guess that you are even more than he suspected—" The lorekeeper paused.

"The Wind should be your armor; however, your weapon of words can allow only a trickle of Its power to force a way through the many guards Irasmus has set. If not for those barriers, you could call upon It, and It would answer. Did they not exist, the land would be clear, and you would be one with It forever.

"Only now, in the Forest, does the Wind range free— but there, also, One rules who may be difficult to convince of your right to treat with It as well."

"Fogar is of the dun kin," she said slowly. "But since he has struck hands with *that one*—does the Wind . . ." Her speech faltered into silence.

"The boy has not yet been corrupted, as you believe, Cerlyn—not yet; although, as I have told you, choices still lie before him. You would ask, does the Great Breath touch him where he now dwells? Let your heart be eased. If he does as little ill as he can—and that with an unwilling spirit—then be sure that the Wind caresses his brow at the day's end as tenderly as a mother sends her child off to its pallet at night.

"And now you must go, or Irasmus may become aware

that you are more than he thinks. Fare you well, daughter of many Wind Callers!" The mage raised a hand, but the gesture he made was not quite the customary one of farewell, and—

Cerlyn lay on the stinking straw of her cell once more. As she moved one leg to ease long-tensed muscles, the chain about her ankle pinched. Iron. What was the old legend? Yes—that that metal provided, in part, a shield against some forms of power. Perhaps, then, she had been chained so that any slight talent she possessed would be damped down— even defeated utterly.

Fogar was moving, but in an unthinking, uncaring daze. Something that had nearly blasted his world to pieces lay behind him—what, he could not remember. He shook his head in an effort to clear it, and memory obliged by stirring dimly. This was the tower, and he was being hustled along by two gobbes. . . .

The spiral he had set into place, Irasmus with his globe, and the rest of the events that had led up to the end of everything—the jagged bits of the memory picture began to fit together once again. Yet, somehow, it all seemed a dream, a vision being forced upon him from somewhere outside himself. Had it really happened?

Irasmus awaited him, seated, as was nearly always his custom, in the thronelike chair. But on the table before him stood no globe; no, that—that was gone. The boy could not tell how much the Dark Lord might have divined of his apprentice's part in the failure of whatever mighty ritual had been attempted.

The demons who had delivered Fogar scuttled away. Then Irasmus spoke with the kind of deadly calm that very great anger will produce in some men.

"What does a workman do with a tool that turns in his hand and sets its blade in his flesh? He recasts it, or—he casts it away."

Fogar still felt as though a fog enwrapped him, entrapping him to be used as his master desired. The suffocating stuff seemed also to touch him now and then, as though with slime-slick fingers. Loathing gagged him.

"You have failed me once—" The sorcerer's voice was deepened by menace. Then he snapped his fingers, and two of the gobbes shambled in from the gloom of the doorway. The creatures shoved Fogar forward until he was jammed against the edge of the table. Then Irasmus began to stare into the youth's eyes. One's very brain could be invaded so, as the apprentice had learned. . . .

Suddenly, in a blessed instant, the sense of the violation of his inmost self ceased. Fogar drew a deep breath and knew that, in some way, the mage had failed.

On the bare tabletop, Irasmus now began to swiftly draw lines with a fingertip he dipped into a pannikin of red fluid. A few of those symbols the boy knew vaguely. However, as he watched the bespelling, unable to tear his eyes away, more and more of his abortive studies returned, now clear and comprehensible, to his mind. He would attempt to fight back—only this was not the time; he needed more—more—

From the surface of the table the red traceries flung themselves forth. The gobbes scrambled back and away, lest they also be snared. The blood-hued netting enwebbed Fogar's legs, body, arms, and neck. But this shroud did not cover him fully. There was yet a space free about his head— his ears—

Faint, very faint, was that sound; still, he heard it—and knew it, too—as he waited for the Dark Lord to complete the binding. However, to the boy's amazement, Irasmus suddenly seemed satisfied, and those torturing cords dissolved, leaving the erstwhile captive weak and wavering.

"Because I still have use for you, you shall continue to serve me." The mage ground out the words as if the admission of his need for another (or—the youth dared to frame the thought—his defeat here?) were a bitter substance he would spit forth. "Be sure, however, that there will come a time of reckoning between us when you shall be of even greater service to me." A clap of his hands brought the demons at a run. "Take him below," Irasmus ordered, "and see him . . . well kept."

23

"HITHER! HITHER!" FALICE SANG, HER VOICE CARRIED AND MAG-
nified by the Wind. They were following her, round-eyed
with wonder, that pack of ragged, near-starved children—
and not only following but showing no signs of fear of
Hansa and the two other Sasqua females who had come
with her.

The human maid caught hands with one of the little
ones, while Sassie accepted gently into a strong leathery paw
the bony, scar-scored fingers of another. To Hansa's daughter the Wind also spoke—beckoning, promising, soothing,
healing—and the young Sasqua sensed It was binding this
humble company into a force that was far more powerful
than Irasmus and his army of demons.

Hansa led the way, one child borne in the crook of each
elbow, and Falice saw small hands venture forth to stroke
the great furred arms that supported them. The other Forest's daughters had likewise taken up the youngest and
weakest of the band. Birds dipped and lilted about them,
making music for a march of triumph, and within her own
mind Falice could feel in the Valley's children an opening, a
budding, a growth, like that of young green things spiring
toward the sun after a years-long drought. The heritage, which

had been denied to those born in the valley since the descent of the nightmare blighting, was at last being bestowed.

So they came to a Forest pool that was open to a sunlit sky. Deer drank there, lifting gracefully sculpted heads to stare at the newcomers. At a signal from their leader, they faded silently back into the enringing trees, leaving the water untroubled—

But not for long! From hunger-pinched bodies, discolored with old bruises as well as fresher stripes and scratches, rags, soil-colored and coated, were stripped away. Sassie, laughing in Wind sound, leaped into the water with a splash. One of the older boys jumped after her without hesitation, and the rest of the children, some with a bit more wariness, followed.

Her hands full of thick leaves, which she crushed together as she came, Falice waded after them. By the time she reached the children, the pulp had acquired a soapy feel and released a fresh, nose-tingling scent. She went to work on first the body and then the matted hair of the nearest girl, watched closely by the Sasqua. Then Hansa and one of the other Sasqua females entered the pool and took their cue from her; and the youngsters (between splashes but during shouts) allowed themselves to be scrubbed from head to foot as they had never been before.

The misery maps of their skins were brown—as much with soil as sun—and lines of grime creased them in places, but the lather of the leaves cleaned every inch. And the former slaves had begun to laugh, then play, some chasing a neighbor to catch and dunk him or her. Such freedom was restoring to them the birthright of all children: innocence and joy.

When the happily tired troop at last emerged from the water, Falice was ready to demonstrate how handsful of noon-warmed grasses could be used to dry small persons. The Sasqua had left; but they soon returned with the nets they had knotted, and those bags were bulging with fruit and edible plants.

The little ones ate so ravenously in the beginning that

Hansa made sure the first portions proffered were of modest size. She then allowed them to concentrate on this or that particular viand that proved the most to their liking.

They were sitting at peace with their world, one of the young humans leaning back against Hansa and smiling up with a berry-stained mouth at the large, kind eyes regarding her. Around them, the Wind sang softly to provide a lullaby for several of the waifs, who had curled up in a contented doze. It was, in fact, lulling them all with its murmurous voice. . . .

Then it screamed.

In an instant, the serene scene was rent, like a curtain of the Forest's vines torn asunder by the wrath of a storm. Power—raw power—had been unleashed, but it had not been directed against the Green Realm—that much Falice knew. This was a backlash from some other outpouring— a disturbance against which the Wind rallied immediately in defense.

The girl could no longer hear the drowsy voices of an untroubled land, for the war cry of the Great Breath drowned out all lesser songs, scaling at last far higher than her talent could follow. She could only open her arms to the two nearest children and hold close their shuddering bodies, hoping that such contact might give them some measure of reassurance, if not safety.

And then the Wind was gone—to do battle? to raise defenses? She could only guess. Even the Sasqua were holding their powerful bodies tense, although, like their human sister, they strove to comfort the children about them. Falice could hear the little ones crying, for, with the Wind's disappearance, all their fears had returned. The child whom Falice held pushed away and actually tried to strike her rescuer's face.

Now there came a sound that even the absence of the all-telling Breath would not have kept from the Forest's myriad ears: the drumming—so deep that the earth about the little company seemed to beat like a giant heart.

Drumming—yes, Falice could envision what caused that:

a forest of huge Sasqua clubs striking the ground in a fierce and fearsome rhythm.

"*Aieeweee—Wind!*" she called, both in her mind and aloud.

Now there was movement across the water, as if that which was approaching must keep a certain distance from them. No, not "that"—*whom*. And Her, Falice knew.

There was the green tunic, clothing the Earth's power bodied forth in womanly form, though the face, as always, was veiled. Such was the awe that vision inspired in her that Falice wanted to bury her face in her hands to hide her eyes, but she could not.

Lady—the little ones. Hansa's mind-speech could still reach Falice.

"It has been said," replied the Earthborn in a voice all present could hear, "that those who claim refuge here are accepted by the Wind. No harm is meant to them. What has happened lies at a distance; still, it has now become a matter for the Forest."

She raised her long-fingered hands and moved them in a pattern the human girl suddenly realized was a summoning.

A second blaze of color expanded out of the air. This new-come figure wavered, as if it held its place only by a high expenditure of energy.

This was a man, but, like the Earthborn, a member of another race. Perhaps he had stepped from another time, as well, for, though he looked like one in middle life, his eyes, which were more visible than the rest of him, held no hint of age.

The Lady in Green spoke first.

"Look you, Archmage." The slightest movement of Her hand indicated the children. "These were they who drudged for your former scholar. And, by him, only a few breaths ago, such power was sought as could have challenged even the Wind—had the Door been opened, as he desired."

"We seek—"

"You 'seek' "—she mimicked his tone—"but do you act?

Oh, you will say you have been honing your weapon—but now full battle comes."

"It was that 'weapon' you make light of that held fast shut the gate!" the chief wizard flashed.

"For this time," conceded the lady. "He of the tower has, perhaps, been halted for a time, but not for good. Irasmus is a far more dangerous opponent than you think. He works magicks, some small and some great (as the one this day), but he is not defeated—nay, nor even more than slightly troubled—by what has happened. I call upon you, Yost, and your company of fellow 'seekers,' to turn your knowledge into power. I summon you to stand against the Dark with every weapon you can raise!"

The figure She addressed flickered and then was gone. A moment later, the Lady Herself followed.

The sense of awe, which had held the onlookers respectfully silent, evaporated also, and the Wind—the soft Wind of the Breath, not the Fist—returned. Under its comforting touch the children's fear dwindled and was gone.

Falice, however, had a question, and it was of Hansa that she asked it. "I am not truly of the Forest, am I, mother one? I am—" she hesitated, swallowed, and then continued as though she must speak a painful truth before her courage failed "—of the same kind as these we have brought this day to safety. One need only look upon us all to know."

"You are of the Wind Stone's holding." Hansa's touch on her fosterling's mind was as tender as any embrace she had given when the girl had been her small furless cubling. "It was at that place I found you with your mother of the body. Her spirit had gone to the Wind, for she had been hard used."

Falice had never felt such depths of wrath as came welling up to fill her at those words. So—chance alone had saved her from the same fate as these little ones. Would that the Dark might feel in its neck the sword of the Light, and that speedily!

The Forest's foster daughter was no warrior, but she

knew at that moment that there was in her the stuff from which weapon wielders—or weapons—were made. Perhaps, she thought with grim pleasure, the Dark Lord had by his own actions shaped her so, to be an agent of his final destruction.

Then Falice's elation vanished as swiftly as it had come. She had the Wind to call upon for war gear, yes—but to realize her wish she must learn more—much more.

How would it sound if earth and sky, like two vast hands, were to come together in one tremendous clap? Much, doubtless, as what Fogar had just heard, who was now on his knees, hands tight over his ears. Within him, pain and terror warred for domination; around him, unconscious, the gobbes lay limply sprawled. Was this a dream— or no? Had he suffered this hell before, then been made to forget?

Irasmus stood on the last stone of the spiral, as motionless as if the life had gone out of him. He was almost hidden by a cloud of dust. As the cloud cleared slightly, the apprentice could see his master's hand unclose and drop the precious wand to shatter on the stone.

The mage turned, his gray face like a thin layer of ash over a barely banked fire, his eyes like burnt-out coals. Perhaps it was only a guess, but Fogar, watching, believed that Irasmus was no longer equipped with normal sight.

"By blood and binding—to me, Demon Son!" Power enough resounded to bring the boy, dazed as he was, to his feet. (Again—what was real and what, dream? Where was the tower—and why did he remember having once before faced the Dark Lord's promise of torment?)

Fogar obeyed, but he felt led to do so by a power he knew was none of his master's. He paused for a breath or two by the last of the stones and held out one hand as if asking aid. As he picked his way among the gobbes, they stirred uneasily, like dead beings roused from the sleep of the grave by a necromancer's call.

Irasmus's dark hollows of eyes remained fixed on him. Were they still organs of sight, the boy wondered, or was Irasmus merely feigning the ability to see what lay before and about him? Or—and this was the worst possibility— had his master, after so many years of ingathering power, developed an inward vision that might see further than physical eyes?

"To my chamber!" the sorcerer commanded. He took a step in his pupil's direction, and his booted heel came down on the broken shards of his wand. He flinched but said nothing, only groping ahead with the hand that had held his rod of power. Fogar did not—dared not—dodge the grip, predatory as the talon of one of the raw-headed rot eaters, that closed on his arm. The two did not now follow the spiral of stones but headed straight for the tower instead. (Only—had the gobbes not taken him there before? Could time twist in this unnatural fashion?)

The Dark Lord appeared to be totally blind, but the youth refused to place any trust in that hope. Thus he must act, and continue to act, as one left bewildered and power-less by the recent cataclysm.

The apprentice guided his master back to that ever-twilit tower room and thence to the vast chair. Irasmus sank back, and the ebbing of tension from his body spoke with mute eloquence of his reaction to that abortive use of power.

"The bottle corked with the head of a drackling"—his voice was studiedly calm, as if he strove to keep it from shaking—"pour from it one measure, no more and no less, into my marked cup."

A cold chill, knifelike as a fang of ice, struck through Fogar. Irasmus had never permitted him to touch this flask, having always ere this reserved its handling to himself. But the boy knew only too well what it contained—a potion that altered, even damaged, the mind. He knew of two gobbes, subcaptains under the late Karsh, who had been forced to drink a draught of this stuff for some act of supposed insubordination. The creatures had emerged from this chamber dull eyed and shuffling, with drops of spittle beading on their warty chins. Ever after, they were capable only of the simplest tasks under supervision. Was the Dark Lord, having learned the truth about the reason for his failure at the spiral, now about to make Fogar quaff the quasi-poison?

Concealing a terror greater than he had ever known before, the boy set about his task. One of the things he had learned early was precise measurement. For this purpose, there was a row of all sizes of cups. These the apprentice had learned to both use and cleanse, washing them in various brews when he had finished, because water did not suffice.

Despite his fear, however, as he searched for the marked cup, his newly awakened inner sense was also viewing the measures in another way. Scraps of knowledge gleaned from dozens of rituals in which he had aided with these tools drew together as they never had before. (Yes, but what of that other memory—the one of Irasmus, still normally sighted, subjecting Fogar to punishment? Should—could—there be two kinds of time?)

Silent, though shouting questions in his mind, the youth did as he was bidden, setting a small cup—hardly larger than two thimbles together—on the table, then filling it to the brim from the bottle Irasmus had requested. He nearly choked as he replaced the stopper, so strong and acrid were the fumes that smote his nostrils from both flask and cup.

"To me, sluggard!" The Dark Lord's voice rose a tone higher in his annoyance. (But which Irasmus did Fogar face? Would the two time streams blend now?)

The boy pushed the cup carefully forward until it rested between the sorcerer's hands, which lay on the edge of the table, unconsciously curved toward each other as if to enclose the globe no longer there. But even this final touch was not to be the end of Fogar's service.

"Now." The mage bent his head once, deeply, as he spoke the word, less (Fogar thought) in acknowledgment of himself than in a seldom-rendered obeisance to the Dark

Powers. "Bring from the fourth shelf the volume bound in scaled skin—the Book of Azhur-ben-M'pal."

The youth now moved toward the chamber's high bookshelves and took down the called-for tome. He had handled this book on numerous occasions, but an infinity of uses would never, he knew, accustom him to the disquieting way in which the volume seemed to fit itself into his hand. Hurriedly, for fear he would drop the thing, he bore it back to Irasmus.

"Now you will display your learning, though you have ever been thick of wit. Look for the Third Saying of Elptus—and do not play the dolt with me, for you have conned that page often enough in the past, though that mutton brain of yours never let you guess the power of what you mouthed."

The youth set the book on the table, where it obliged him further by opening of its own accord precisely to the page the sorcerer had specified. Fogar tensed, then forced himself to relax. Should his master's blindness be only a ruse whereby to test him, an expression that could be interpreted as reluctance to serve could earn him the living-death sentence meted out to the hapless gobbes.

"Read!" Irasmus commanded.

Fogar shaped words whose meaning he had never known. Now, however, they resounded so painfully in his ears that they pierced into his very brain.

"Assua den ulit." It seemed to him that the acid tang of the liquid in the cup leaped up into his nose, then hurled itself down his throat and into his lungs. Were these words, then, so deep-dark-drawn that honest air could not be used to move them into speech? *"Salossa."* He nearly gasped aloud, so agonizingly did that sound stab his brain. (But now he knew the truth, having seen far deeper into arcane knowledge than Irasmus had ever expected him to do. His recollection of an earlier visit to this room had been the false one—*this* was the memory to be kept!)

The Dark Lord's hand moved with extreme care. When his fingers closed about the tiny vessel, he did not raise it to his lips (nor, for which Fogar thanked the Wind, thrust it at *him*) but rather drew it, by minuscule measures, across the table until it occupied the space the murky ball had rested.

"*Revaer,*" the boy finished, then began what appeared to be a new sentence. "*Appolenecter!*" Marginal notes on the page indicated that these syllables formed either a command or a name, and the apprentice uttered them accordingly.

"*Appolenecter!*" he repeated. And, in that moment, he had a flash of intuition about what he was reading. This was a calling; however, it could only be for one of the very minor demons, for the high Lords of Power demanded more pomp and the blood payment of an animal sacrifice (or worse) before they would deign to answer.

A stirring curdled the air, and, between Irasmus's hands, a small rodlike pillar of black smoke, with a dull redness smoldering in its grim heart, arose from the surface of the table.

Moments later, a thing—Fogar could put no more accurate name to it than that, though it made him think of the stone monsters who leered from the corners of the tower—sat there cross-legged. The being was equipped with ash-gray wings that it clapped together in greeting, perhaps, above its round, hairless head. Though as grotesque as the gobbes, it displayed none of the demons' servility, but rather bore itself with easy assurance.

A mouth that ran nearly from one earlobe to the other opened, and the sound that issued was a taunting chuckle. To Fogar's surprise, the words it uttered were in the common speech of the valley. Did the creature do so in order that he, too, would understand any answer it would give—or did it seek thereby to put Irasmus in his place?

"Thought you were a Third-Degree Master, did you?" the gargoyle jeered at the sorcerer. "Able to call up one of the Great Greats? Foolish man! Do you truly believe that, because you have harnessed a people to your will, you can now speak face-to-face with—" the imp touched a horned forehead with a taloned paw in a gesture of evident reverence "—*Zaasbeen?*"

Irasmus's hand balled into a fist. "Silence, nightling, or you will discover that I have claws longer than yours! Perhaps you would care to be pinned here for my pleasure?" Smiling meaningfully and raising the forefingers of both hands, the Dark Lord described in the still-hovering cloud two circles and connected them by a line. The resultant image, which hovered for a few seconds, glowing red, unmistakably suggested a pair of shackles.

The creature was no longer grinning, and, when it spoke again, its voice was sullen. "Truth comes hard to your kind—yet still it exists. You have been challenged, yes, but not seriously enough—"

"Challenged?" Irasmus said so softly that he was half whispering, and it was to himself that he spoke. "Who has challenged me? Those of the order are held by the bones of the Covenant, even as is the Power from the Forest—"

"But with proper help," chirped the small demon, "you seek now to invade that country—to pry at the very door of the Wind! Threaten as you like, rash mortal—the pits are already dug that will entrap your feet, for the talent of the Forest is many times greater than that which you have already encountered."

"I want but one truth from you, misbegotten imp," the Dark Lord ground out between clenched teeth. "Where lies my weakness?"

The fiendling's head turned a fraction, allowing its gaze to flit over Fogar. The boy felt sure it was about to start spouting something that could prove very dangerous to him, and his fear returned. Fortunately, the thing, for reasons of its own, thought better of its impulse. Grinning again, it turned back to Irasmus, and its purple tongue thrust forth at the wizard in a rude gesture.

"Look to—what lies behind you, mortal, for there lie the roots of what will grow into a mighty hedge of menace that will march toward you like those upa plants you sought to seed.

"Oh, by the way"—the imp cocked its head on one side and assumed a politely conversational tone—"have you had any message from Yost lately?" It might have been inquiring about the weather.

A flush rose to stain Irasmus's thin cheeks. "The Covenant binds—" he began.

"So it does," the creature interrupted, "but it binds you, too. Ha! ha! Now let us to business." The thing straightened a long neck and shrugged stone-colored shoulders as if impatient for this interview to be concluded. "You have one request—state it. There is that"—its wide nostrils expanded in distaste—"about this den of yours that does not encourage long visits."

If the small demon had hoped by that taunt to sting Irasmus into a rash reply, it failed. Instead, the mage pushed the cup wordlessly toward his guest. The creature sniffed; then it smirked again.

"Do not treat your toys so carelessly next time, wizard, for we do not have them in abundance." Reaching forward, it closed tiny fingers about the vessel and, tilting the cup forward, spilled the contents onto the tabletop. Both the sense-smiting odor and an oily smoke arose.

The little fiend scooped up the stuff as if it were clay. Rolling this substance between its hands, it set the resultant mass back on the table. With a blow from its fist, it struck the upper end. The lump spun madly about, then took on a spherical shape.

The imp laughed for the last time. "Make the most of this, man, for you shall not get another, no matter whom you cry to. And I wouldn't be too quick, now, to call upon *any* from Beyond, if I were you!" With that, the imp vanished, as swiftly as it had come.

24

EVER SINCE THE SORCERER HAD BEEN LED BACK TO THE TOWER BY his apprentice, the gobbes had jabbered among themselves. In one of their rare cooperative efforts not brought about by Irasmus's whip or words, they drove the slaves back to the pen, even though it was long till night. Then, once the bar was slammed into place at the stockade gate, the creatures gathered in a group, muttering fearfully, their attention fixed on the tower. Within their prison, the human slaves also joined together, the men and boys encircling the women in a vain attempt to convey a promise of protection to those who were wailing for vanished children.

"The Forest beasts—they stole 'em!" The woman who cried out was rocking back and forth in an age-old expression of grief. Her cheeks were streaked with tears, but, though the eyes from which those had fallen were still brimming, they no longer showed the flat dullness set there by her hard and wanhope life. "They have taken my Solvage, my little Lenny—"

As the grieving mother lapsed into sobbing, another of the women spoke. Her lank hair hung about a face touched by a frost of premature age. "The Forest . . ." she said slowly, then halted and began again. "Kin of the duns, have none of you *dreamed?*" She twisted her body about, trying to catch the eyes of everyone assembled there.

"Dreams mean nothing," sneered one of the men.

The woman swung to face him squarely. "So, Numor— you *have* dreamed!"

The farmer scowled, then shrugged. "What mean sleep seeings that come in bits and pieces but can never be drawn together when one wakes? Yes, Alantra"—he raised both hands to fend off an interruption—"I know the old tales that dreams were once speech, and learning, and freedom. But they were brought by the Wind—and does that still blow here, I ask you?"

"But you *have* dreamed," insisted Alantra. "And you, Ganda,"—here she bespoke a third woman—"you were kin, though by a lesser bloodline, to Widow Larlarn."

Ganda seemed to draw in upon herself, hunching her shoulders as if she were being accused of some fault with punishing wrath to follow. Yet Alantra did not have long to wait for her answer. "So little have we become"—Ganda's voice was a whip of scorn—"that there remains but one of the Old Blood—"

"True!" broke in Numor triumphantly, as though Ganda's words had proved his point. "And where lies she now, Alantra? In the very hands of that devil in the tower! Oh, we all heard the talk from old Haraska and Larlarn about the girl's talent. Talent—pah!" He spat the word, then spat in truth. "Any talent we ever had has long since been leached out of us—"

Destin, an older man, interrupted. "You bewail bitterly enough the loss of those who could speak so the Wind would listen. Yet who"—he stabbed out an accusing finger—"is the one with the blood of the Firthdun on his hands? Who was it, Numor, who raised his voice to say, 'Our neighbors prosper while we wither,' and 'Sharing of goods must be equal'?"

The farmer's scowl grew deeper. "You swung a well-sharpened scythe that night also, Destin!"

The older man nodded solemnly. "Yes, I also have my blood debt to be paid. But"—he squared his shoulders, accepting his folly and fate, and the years seemed to weigh less heavily on him for the taking up of that burden—"I shall pay it like a man, as I would advise you to do. If we have signed our death writ by slaying those very folk who might have saved us, then we must either save ourselves or die trying!"

At those words, another mother raised a bleary-eyed face to the speaker and seized a fold of his ragged tabard as though clutching at hope. "But the children"—she looked about her wildly, as if by the very force of her will she could summon a missing small one to her—"must they, will they, too—"

The answer that came was far from the one the beseeching woman was seeking; even more startling was its deliverer.

"Dream," said Antha, the mother who had first mourned. Her quavering voice firmed to a tone of near command as she realized the wisdom of her own words. "Dream, I tell you! For it is in our dreams, broken though they may be, that help lies—for both ourselves and our little ones. Now is the time for us to use what is left of our gifts, for the Dark One has had one of his own spells turn against him. Have we not seen this and felt the power that was loosed, though it did not blot us out? He has sucked us, over the years, yet he had still not might enough to achieve what he would!

"Also"—Antha brushed sodden locks from her tear-trenched face and actually smiled—"the Forest has not moved against us to slay. You, Evlyn—you were close to the master when he and his pack returned. Did they wear any sign of the death of others upon them?"

A murmur of beginning excitement ran through the group.

"The gobbe work driver was not with them," the young man, Evlyn, answered. "No sense can be made of their gabble, but they were angry—and what would fan their wrath higher than to have prey slip through their paws? The children had been sent almost to the verge of the Forest, the closest any of us have ventured since—" he bit his lip, as if he must speak in blood the next words "—that night of madness that set the stain of kin slaying upon us all.

"You, Numor, have said that the Wind does not blow here. That may be so, since we raised our hands against one another; yet does that mean It breathes no more in any place? Whence came It of old, say the stories? From the Forest! Maybe, then, if our little ones reached the Green Country, they have found there a power that will welcome and ward them. At least they are free of this prison!

"Yes." Evlyn, like Destin, now stood up straighter as if reclaiming a role in his clan too long forgotten. "Antha is right. I will say it to all of you. I, too, have dreamed. Broken visions can be pieced together, if the dreamers work one with others, and perhaps each of us has some part of knowledge to be fitted to another. Think you of those scrapwork covers our women made in the duns. None of their cloth bits alone had value, but set edge to edge, they made a thing of use and beauty.

"Surely some of us remember the old dream summonings, however vaguely; so let us throw open our minds and call—now, tonight! The master believes us fully drained, and, besides, he will be busy striving to recover what he has lost. What is more, that ball, through which he could spy out every part of our world, and that wand, with which he could blast us with his dark lightnings, are gone—at least for a time."

Agreeing with these words, those of the scattered homesteads drew together, moving toward one another. Thus, all who were left of Styrmir's people sought sleep that night with every group of kinfolk linked by touch of mind with their own blood; while some of the women also held their arms as if encircling small persons not with them in the body. As they began to shape their quilt, albeit of dreams, they felt like a family huddled beneath such a coverlet, united in comfort shared despite a world grown cold.

This was a night of the full moon. It shone on the Stone which, under its beams, was now afire with more of the rainbow-hued sparks than Falice had ever seen. So, she thought, remembering, she belonged to the Stone; for Hansa had found her here—Hansa, the nurturing one who, when death had striven to take her into its arms, had caught the girl up into her own. Thus the Sasqua female had sustained her life, and was that not what made a mother? Yet—those delicate bones to which Falice had paid proper respect were those of her mother of the body.

Pensively, she went to stand at the head of that hidden resting place. What had she been like, that other life giver? And why—here came a Wind question, blown into her mind—why did the boy who answered Irasmus's orders look like her? Was he kin? Perhaps, then, there were some among the children now sleeping in Sasqua nests who were also of her blood. She knew so little; she would learn more.

Raw force had been unleashed in the world this day. It had been triggered by an act of evil, she knew; however, it was also true that the use of talent draws power, both of Dark and Light. Certainly it had not been Falice's imagination that she had, since that outpouring of might, sensed more purpose in the Wind's song or been urged here this night.

To make use of the Stone was why she had been summoned—she knew that as surely as if the Breath now shouted it aloud. Once again she closed in on the monolith, putting out her hands as if to reach through its surface to touch those visions drawn from another time and place.

The window hole was open, and the girl could see through. She supposed that, as usual, she would have to wait for its choice of scene, for she had never had the power to decide what was to be viewed. Or—did she? Deciding to essay a trial, she concentrated on the face of that male who puzzled her so—the one she could never quite forget.

Falice felt a flash of triumph as she found herself looking at precisely whom she wished to see. There was the young man, but he seemed drained of all energy and appeared to keep to his feet only because several of those warty monsters were giving him rough support as they dragged him down a flight of stairs. The creature to the fore of the group carried something that held light, dim but sufficient to show that the steps ended at an opening.

A maw of blackness gaped beyond and, into that, the horrors threw their captive. Despite the dark, by the power of the monolith Falice was able to see that the prisoner was not alone in this hole. Against the wall huddled a girl who was chained to a bolt in the stone. She was certainly of the same race as the boy and the Forest's foster daughter, though ill kempt and emaciated. However, though her posture bespoke wariness, she did not hunch herself into the slaves' habitual cringe. Far otherwise—her eyes seemed to send out very faint rays of light, and her whole bearing spoke unmistakably to Falice of power.

At last the fierce battery of curses (of several sorts) to which Fogar had been subjected by Irasmus after the imp had shown such scorn had ended. Well aware that the master was far from finished with him, he now lay unmoving, bound by the shackles of a spell, in this dark cell. Cell? There had been a girl, also a captive, and she had been thrust into such a hole as this. . . .

He heard a small rustling sound. Laboriously, he turned his head, though any attempt at action instantly tightened the bonds that had been put upon him—he had been placed under a constraint to act only as the mage directed. But in a small corner of his will that still belonged to him, Fogar thought: *That one may have bound my body, but he can place no manacles on my mind!*

From the direction of the rustling sound now came definite movement, which the boy could sense but not truly see—save for two glowing eyes. Those orbs were unsettling, but they did not belong to an animal, nor to any creature that ran the Dark Paths, of that he was certain. It was, rather, himself who had had the compulsion to set evil upon him.

The youth suddenly found himself moving stiffly, and by no urge of his own. Somehow, in spite of the gloom, he could now see his cell mate—enough, at least, to know where she stood. She had risen to her feet, but she made no effort to elude him as, step by agonized step, he drew ever nearer, fighting the compulsion spell that had invaded his mind, as it intended his body to invade—

No—such an appalling act could *not* be forced upon him! Until this moment, Fogar had felt as helpless to control his own limbs as one of those bird-begones the land grubbers placed in the fields, whipped into antic dance by autumn winds. Now, however, his head came up higher, and he managed—though it took every ounce of his strength—to hold his foot still. The reason Irasmus wished so vile a deed done he could not guess, but Fogar remembered the sorcerer's analogy of the tool that turned in the workman's hand. *Well,* he thought with grim joy, *the master was about to feel the bite of his apprentice's edge in his soft palm, for this was one work that would be—in every sense—undone!*

In some way, Fogar believed, his fellow captive sensed what he had been sent to do—the hellish impulse planted in him by the new tool of murk the little demon had made. He heard a rattle of chain. Was the girl readying herself to met him with the only weapon she had?

Instead of acting, however, she began to speak in words which quickly flowed into a chant:

> "By Wind Ever-Breathing,
> By Law of Orvas,
> Desire of Vagen,
> Ever victorious,
> Judging, holding—"

Fogar knew those Names, though they were used only as blasphemies by most within these walls. What knowledge had this one gained before being taken in Irasmus's net to speak with such assurance—even authority—of the Great Powers? Her words seemed to touch him lightly, like fingertips lifted in an instant, and he echoed, "By the Wind . . ."

All the myriad bits of knowledge he had been able to assemble through the past years, and the many images from dreams—yes, dreams—came crowding into his mind, forming more distinct patterns than he had ever seen before. His tone this time an answer, not a question, the boy repeated again, "The Wind!"

In the body of the valley, the Dark Lord was an ever eating disease, but, at least for this time, his cancerous spread had been halted: he had been balked in one of his longest-laid plans.

"Who are you?" Fogar asked.

Movement again, certain in the uncertain light of the shadows—she had drawn herself up proudly. "I am Cerlyn, daughter to Ethera of Firthdun. Do you not know the ending of our clan, and, after, the torture death of Oldmother Haraska and Widow Larlarn—the last who could claim touch with the Wind? It was they who saved me from the slaughter of our kin, then hid me and taught me. And you"—the girl put out a hand as she said this, not in accusation but invitation to tell his part in the tale—"they name you Demon's Son. But what are you besides what he has called you?"

"I know not, in full," Fogar replied in a low voice. "I only know that that name is not truly mine, for, though Irasmus has tutored me in knowledge of the Dark Path, he never allowed me to understand what I conned. He thinks of me as a tool, a weapon; and he has used me when and where he could as both. It is as if he hones and holds me against a day when, he believes, I will be able to deliver some additional strength for his need.

"This night, he sent my body to try a hideous thing. My flesh and bones moved by his steering, but—maiden, I speak the truth: by some great fortune, that within me—that which was really me—could not be so controlled." The apprentice stumbled to a halt, unsure he could make this Cerlyn understand.

As before, she sang her answer.

"Aiieee—ears wait:
The Life Wind blows—"

"Stop!" Fogar's voice in their tiny cell was nearly a shout. Then, more quietly but no less urgently, "Listen!" he entreated her. "If you can call upon some Power to free you, then summon it now. That one has ways of turning minds inside out like a sower's seed bag, searching for some fact, or memory, or thought he can use. He has made me live in two different times only to disprove a suspicion of treachery! His power may have failed this day, but I cannot believe he would fail to sense that tonight, in the very center of his stronghold, a Power stirs that is his mortal enemy. I warn you, do not attract his attention unless you are sure your talent is much the greater."

Fogar had moved nearer to the girl as he spoke, caught up in his need to convince her of her peril. As he stopped speaking, he realized he was now close enough to touch her. Fearing a return of Irasmus's filthy compulsion, he forced himself to step backward until he felt the dank wall of the cell against his shoulders. From this position, he concluded, "If you can cause the Wind to come to your aid, I beseech you—do so at once. Irasmus has many wards, and he will be tightening them all as swiftly as he can."

"I am no Caller." For the first time, Cerlyn's voice was uncertain. "What came was by the sending of another."

"Then summon him—or her!" Fogar urged.

"I have no such power," she replied bleakly. "Whence

the Wind comes and why, I do not know; only, this night, it moved to save us."

The youth was thankful for her use of the word "us"; perhaps he had won the trust of this Wind-kissed girl. He must not try to ally with her here—to do so would alert Irasmus in an instant. Yet fear for her safety still drove him to try to warn her. "Then you must do all you can to play the slow-witted land grubber—"

Once more an assured motion in the shifting shadows, but this time a negative one—Cerlyn shook her head. "The time is long past for such feigning," she replied. "Irasmus already suspects I have the talent. What he tried to force you to do tonight is proof."

"How so?" asked Fogar in bewilderment. "In what manner would my—attack—on you have struck against your gift?"

"You have not lived among the people," Cerlyn explained, "and the Dark One has seen to it that you know but little of us and our ways. There is a long-held belief that, if a woman who holds any talent is ravished, she is thereafter no longer a fit vessel for power." The girl laughed suddenly. "*You* have never had bodily knowledge of another, either—such information would have been current coin. Thus," she concluded, her mood once more grim, "Irasmus planned to draw from your action strength twofold."

As before, Fogar felt oddly heartened by this stranger's concern for his welfare, and he was seeking the words to tell her so (for he also felt strangely tongue-tied in her presence) when the door of the cell opened, and the gobbes were back. Their leader, its lantern lighting its face from below to a harvest scare-gourd, shambled in and seized the boy's arm. As he was jerked away, he caught a clear glimpse of his fellow captive—enough to see that, though she was clad in rags and her skin was mottled with dirt, her head was held high. He did not—dared not—look back as they hustled him from the cell.

* * *

Falice leaned her head against the Stone, grateful for its support. She could hardly believe she had been able to make contact—even though they did not realize it—with those two, much less that her thrust of power, weak as it had been, had helped give Fogar the strength to withstand the abominable urge implanted by Irasmus. She knew she could never have stopped the boy had his own will chimed with that of his master. However, it seemed that, despite the youth's years-long submersion in the Dark, the Light in his heart yet burned clear, like a candle in the murk of that benighted tower. He, Falice felt sure, could help himself; but Cerlyn—who would hear the Wind more clearly—she was, indeed, one to be saved but Falice have aid. Yet how was such a rescue to be accomplished, and when?

The Forest's fosterling closed her eyes and tried to think, only to realize she was so weak she must cling to the Stone. At last, as the first gray suggestion of dawn lightened the sky, she slipped down its length to lie on the ground. Though she tried to fight off sleep, her eyes closed; and, beneath the monolith, whose myriad twinkling lights kept a night of miniature stars above her, Falice lay alone in the growing light, deeply asleep in the glade.

25

CERLYN WAS IN A PLACE SHE HAD COME TO KNOW WELL—AS WELL, in fact, as if she had lived there most of her life. However, she faced the one who had summoned her there with a frown and a less-than-respectful tone. "You call me, and I come, as a child set to learn. But, teacher, can you answer this question? Irasmus strove to play some high-magic trick, and it turned on him. How and why?"

"The Dark Lord's sorcery did not 'turn.' Say, rather, it *was* turned—on him," Gifford replied calmly. "The Lady of the Forest no longer strives to suppress Her power, for She has in Her service a maiden through whom she can speak—and summon a Power we both know. That girl is kin-linked to both you and Fogar. She may not have had access to all this"—a wave of his hand indicated the shelves of stored wisdom in his chamber—" but she has had the favor and aid of one of the very Oldest Ones. It was Her Wind-calling that helped break the compulsion laid upon Irasmus's apprentice to dishonor you by force."

"But," Cerlyn said in surprise, "there were only two of us in that cell, and he was tightly held by his master. . . ."

The lorekeeper was shaking his head before she faltered to a halt. " 'Master' no longer, Cerlyn. What Fogar holds—

though partly unaware of it as yet—would place him on the level of any of our scholars, even if he does not choose in the end to come to Valarian. This is the truth! The boy has been forced to read those forbidden tomes Irasmus stole from us, yes; and what was taken has led to dark doings and dealings alike.

"However, as I have said"—Gifford paused and raised a finger in the classic gesture of teachers everywhere—"no knowledge is evil in and of itself but only according to how it is used. The warrior and the healer both have an edge on their tools, but would you wish all blades dull because one is used to bring death? I tell you, girl, that when the moment comes, Fogar will be equipped far better for that encounter than he could now ever guess, and that he whom Irasmus has named 'demon's son' will make *that one* wish he were confronting *only* fiends!"

"What moment?" Cerlyn asked irritably. "Where—and when? I am tired of being given only snippets of information!"

"The hour we cannot foresee, for the Dark Lord has bought a breathing space by trading once more with the under realm. Only"—Gifford's usual smile here widened to the grin of one relishing a fine jest—"his bargain was not struck with the One he sought. Thus, for what he has pur-chased—as well as from whom—he shall pay the price.

"We are divided from the Dark, Cerlyn, by a wall pierced by crevices—and sometimes even windows and gates—none of which are made fast but can be used by either side under certain conditions. Years ago, Irasmus made, as he believed, a pact with one of the Dwellers in the Dark, and thereafter set himself up as a worthy agent for that being. However"—once more came a teacherly motion as Gifford held out his hand, palm down and fingers straight—"think of this as a bridge of rope that must be walked, with yourself wearing a pack to weigh you down. As you advance one way, the bridge dips—" he tilted his fingertips down and his wrist up "—but when you do that, the opposite end rises. It is thus with more powers than the pull of the earth: when one exerts force on an object in front of him, that whereon he has just turned his back may be lifting itself to overthrow him.

"There are certainly those of the Shadow Lands who harbor vast hatred for us of the Light and for all we are, do, and would achieve. Generations ago, a war was fought against them, and at its ending was forged the Covenant. Unfortunately, when the years pass, bringing no challenge, men forget, and they come to believe that peace and prosperity are rights rather than privileges hard won that must be vigilantly warded. Then one such as Irasmus arises and begins to pick at the seals of their safety. Power, to him, is as a great jar of wine with whose heady draughts he would ever wax more drunken." The lorekeeper paused, then shook his head and made a dismissive motion with his hand, a gesture Cerlyn had come to know as one of self-deprecation for a tendency to run on or digress.

"To return to that Dark-warding wall: on its other side are creatures who are likewise impatient. However, those of the dark who possess the mightiest talents remember only too well what happened before their exile. Here in the Place of Learning, we have delved into the annals of that age, and we now know the nature of the Being with whom the dark mage sought to make contact but who prudently remains beyond his reach; and since we have discovered whom he would invoke, we have been making ready. That entity, though, is not one of the Great Powers, as your would-be master thought—he calls potent names in his rituals, but those who answer him bear other titles." The girl's teacher bent his head for a moment over fingers interlaced on the tabletop. Possibly he was doing no more than collecting his thoughts for the summing up of her lesson, but perhaps he was raising a silent plea to the powers of Light for his aid—and hers. Drawing a deep breath, Gifford resumed.

"Now—listen well, Cerlyn, for we are come very near to the end of this play with Irasmus. From the beginning, your line has served the Light, and great heroines and heroes were numbered among them in the days before the Covenant. I cannot promise you a triumph to equal theirs, for defeat can be the prize for one small error. But, even as Fogar now dreams of what must be done, so I shall tell you that which will prepare you.

"Child, you have been marked by Irasmus as a gift to be handed beyond the Wall into Darkness and thus secure favor for him. I shall give you certain words, but the finding of the proper time to use them—and the courage to do so—will rest upon you alone; for each warrior must choose not only the manner of her weapons but the moment in the war at which to wield them."

Her chain rattled against the wall as Cerlyn sat up and opened her eyes. Fogar was gone—she had watched the sorcerer's hellhounds drag him out—but there was no breaking the bonds that held her. In her mind, however, those three names the mage had repeated to her so slowly and intently fairly burned, and she knew she would never forget them.

But something else had come here while she had lain entranced. The new presence was, without doubt, a force of the Light, and the very air of this noisome box smelled the fresher for its arrival. It seemed to Cerlyn that the Wind was still there, either having remained after it had freed Fogar of the ugly compulsion laid upon him, or returning. Now, there was also a pale glow suspended in the air above her at what would be head height if she were standing. Rising to her feet, she stepped before it.

The light came from no torch or lamp; instead, it looked like the gray of early dawn shining through a small window. Remembering Gifford's talk of the piercings in the Wall of the Dark into which, at times, the Light might enter, she moved closer to the opening and saw—*through.*

Before her was another face—the apprentice's again? No, this countenance was that of a girl probably of her own age; yet the resemblance of the stranger to Fogar was very strong.

Cerlyn wondered if her dreaming had touched her mind so deeply that, waking, she would see his image in any who were tied to him—no, she corrected herself—to them both by blood.

Obviously the girl on the other side of that window could see her in return, and it was she who spoke first.

"You are Cerlyn, of what was once the dun of Firth."

"Yes." Cerlyn was still bemused. "But you—you have the look of him the valley folk name Demon Son—Fogar—"

"Why should I not?" the other returned, almost proudly. "Long ago, Mam Hansa had learned from Wind Song that two babes were born to my mother on the night that saw most of our kin slain. Irasmus took only one; my mother fled to the forest, where she bore me, then died. I am Falice, and I am a Wind Caller, as is the birthright of our blood.

"However, that is of little moment now. The Dark Lord is putting forth his power once again—and this time, kin sister, you are to be his offering to the Under Ones. The Wind has sung it, and always the Wind knows. Yet this I now swear to you: the Forest will move, at long last. The Great Breath gathers itself to deliver a blast against the forces of the Dark; and, when the bonds that restrain it are broken, we, its children, shall come forth to do its desire. You and my brother kin will not stand alone in the final hour!"

The light which had painted that speaking portrait on the gloom winked out, as though the spot were, indeed, a window that had been abruptly curtained, and Cerlyn could no longer feel the touch of the Wind. Yes, what the vision visitor had said was true—at least as far as the part of her story that Fogar might have a twin. Grandmam Haraska had once let fall the revelation that Fogar's mother had been heavy with twins but, after Irasmus had snatched the child first to appear, she had been aided to escape by the women who were huddled beyond the firelight and so out of the sorcerer's view. That brave life bearer might well have sought the Forest as a refuge.

Cerlyn sank down into the sour straw, feeling suddenly weak, for the buoying energy of this latest vision had vanished with the going of the light. Now, she supposed, all that remained was to wait for the dark mage to move; for it was by his actions that all within the range of his much-desired mastery would either be freed, or— But she refused to follow that fearful thought, which was a temptation to despair, born of the Dark to drain her confidence and, thus, her strength.

The gobbes had again thrust Fogar into Irasmus's chamber. Once more, the wizard had his hands curved about the globe the imp had fashioned—though this new sphere was smaller and more sullenly murky than the first—and he did not look up as the demons shambled out, leaving their charge behind. The apprentice could not be sure, even now, how keen was his master's sight, for his eyes still bore that shuttered appearance they had shown since the explosion at the spiral. The boy, for his part, was scarcely anxious to attract the mage's attention, remembering what he—or that shadow of the shadow lord in the other-time place—had warned him about tools which twice failed. In Irasmus's view, Fogar thought grimly, he could certainly be deemed such a worthless—and dangerous—thing.

Hunching before the table, the sorcerer had bent his head to bring his eyes very close to the cloud-cored ball. Moisture trickled from beneath the outer edges of his lids, as though he were putting his physical sight to a tremendous strain. It looked very likely to the youth that the would-be power-summoner still suffered from some degree of blindness. Yet the Dark Lord's injury, whatever it might be, apparently meant nothing to him as he stared into that sphere, for he plainly perceived therein something that was both a cause for fury—and for fear.

Then he began to draw on the wood, inches from where the globe rested, a series of runes. Fogar was too far away to recognize any of them, but he somehow knew that Irasmus, concentrating all the talent he possessed, was reaching further than he ever had before, both down into himself and into—The Place Not Named. He next commenced muttering to himself, or perhaps only his lips moved, for no sound reached the youth.

The actions of the mage absorbed Fogar's attention fully at first, but gradually he became aware of power rising within himself. The gobbes had left him neither chained nor bound, and he suddenly recalled that they had seemed almost reluctant to touch him when they had dragged him from Cerlyn's cell. Thus his hands were free, and now the tips of his fingers began to tingle, the itch rising up his palms to his wrists. He recognized it as the same feeling that had reached him from some of the stones during those hours he had labored to build the spiral. This sensation was not that born of the loathsome aura of those Dark-hearted discs he had handled but was, instead, a warm, invigorating flow of force—not strong, yet steady. The apprentice was sure it was not caused by his master's activities but that, quite the contrary, it ran counter to them.

Suddenly Irasmus jerked up his head, and his still-crooked forefinger froze, leaving a rune partway sketched. The darkness in the globe had thickened, but not enough to conceal the lines of red that had begun to form at its top and spread downward, evenly spaced, until they covered the upper half of the sphere with a glowing web.

Now the wizard did look at Fogar, though his captive could not see even a suggestion of true eyes in the sockets turned toward him but only the emptiness of twin pits. His lips shaped a snarl, and the hand, which had rested nearest the globe, arose from the table, in the swift motion of one who hurled an object, straight at his student. The luminescent lines broke from the ball to cleave to Irasmus's gray flesh, clinging so only for a moment, then spinning out through the air toward Fogar.

The youth had no idea of proper defense. He could only raise both hands in front of him. It was at that moment, however, that the tingling faded, and he tasted defeat before he had ever had a chance to essay his strength. The blood-colored strands enlarged as they sped, assuming the likeness of a net. He tried to shift his feet, to turn, to run, only to find himself fast rooted until those filaments lashed themselves about him, their ends weaving over and around. When they touched their intended victim, he could no longer see them but only feel the bonds they now laid upon him.

Irasmus's predatory smile looked well sated. "You will keep, dirt spawn. You hold yet within yourself that which I would learn; however, if I do not—why, who would be a more fit offering to the Great Dark One than his chosen son?"

Abruptly, as if Fogar had ceased to exist, the mage turned back to study the sphere and to trace occult symbols around it.

The boy made no attempt, as yet, to struggle against the invisible netting that held him. He was becoming more convinced by the moment that he had not been brought to this chamber solely by the whim of his master but rather by the workings of some other Power for whom he had a mission to perform. A high, distant drone hummed in his head—speech? The sound of an animal? No—a summons to those with ears to hear. Fogar struggled to listen as he never had before.

He did not even have to close his eyes to see two faces he had often glimpsed, though indistinctly, in the broken dreams that had so frustrated him. Now, however, those countenances were not misty and ill defined. Their eyes, in especial, were bright, so bright they transfixed his own with their beams. . . .

Memory showed Fogar mind pictures of pages of Irasmus's arcane texts he had once conned without understanding. The boy began to comprehend exactly what purpose drove his master now; and he perceived, as well, that through him two others were reading and learning in turn.

Of them, however, he had no fear; for now he also knew this: he had been born with a gift that could always distinguish the Light from the Dark.

As those pages fluttered by his inner sight, he, too, read—and understood. His body grew taut as he was made inexorably aware of the battle that must come soon—and the world-altering power of such a clash.

At this realization, Fogar began to breathe in short gasps. Irasmus's ball-spun bonds were drawing tighter as if they would squeeze the life from him even as they forced him to yield up the modest knowledge he possessed.

The boy ran a tongue tip over fear-dried lips. He could not speak aloud, for the web that cocooned him would not permit speech. However, he might—

No words Fogar had ever learned could explain the instinct that led him to attempt what he now tried, but he read in the two intent faces before him an urging, a virtual commanding, that he do this thing. Then those twin watchers were gone. In their place was left the mind picture of a mighty tree, wide boled, thick leaved; and within him sounded, silent except to his own ears and every cell of his body, the singing of the Wind among its branches.

The youth was now a part of that vast growth, for the Breath opened the way for him. Watching below those swaying branches—for his awareness radiated into them from the trunk of the tree like spokes from a central hub—he saw movement, a passing cavalcade of the inhabitants of the Green Realm.

To its fore strode the great Forest beasts, marching nearly as one; behind them followed other creatures, even beings no thicker than shadows; and all were heading in one direction. At the head of the company, far more diminutive than those she led, danced a girl. She was girdled with trailing vines and crowned by a circlet of flowers, and about her played a glow of green light the color of new leaves.

Only for an instant was Fogar able to hold that unity with the Forest, that vision of its children and their—guardian? goddess? That moment, however, was long enough for him to understand that he would not fight alone when the Dark and the Light crossed swords, for, though he did not know the ones he had just beheld, he would swear they were allies.

"Sooo—" The apprentice was brought rudely back to the reality of the wizard's chamber and his own immobility therein by Irasmus's drawing out of that word. The master's tone held not only satisfaction but triumph. "So shall it be!"

He arose from his chair, stretching as might any man who has sat overlong; then he laughed openly and patted the tabletop not far from the globe (though not, the boy observed, quite touching the thing). His mouth gaped in an undignified yawn, which he strove to stifle with one hand; with the other on the table, either to support or guide himself, he came to stand in front of his prisoner.

"Demon's Son!" Irasmus laughed again. "Well did I name you! I trust your illustrious father will find you a suitable gift." His predatory smile was back—and hungry once more.

Fogar nearly reeled, for, again, it was as if those cords that seemed to have melded themselves to his flesh were closing on his heart. Yet the Power that held him would not let him fall.

"Young fool, you might have been among the great, had not the seeds of the Old Knowledge been brought to flower within you. Yet I must say you make a tidy package, and here you shall await your—delivery—at the meeting arranged."

With this final threat, Irasmus left the room, walking with such care that the boy was now sure the sorcerer had suffered some impairment to his sight. The intended present from the lesser Dark Lord to the Greater, tied with a most unusual ribbon, was left where he had first been bound.

However, though the master might believe so, he was not this time abandoning a helpless prisoner. Deliberately, Fogar closed his eyes. He did not try to summon from memory those dream faces but instead concentrated with all the energy he could bring to bear on that vision of the Wind-tossed tree. It was—must be—a guide. Even as he had blended his awareness with that of the Forest patriarch, so had the Wind once merged with all the life of this land, its very Breath. So it would be again! he thought with the forcefulness of a vow. What aid he, captive as he was in this web of sorcery, might bring to the fulfillment of that oath, Fogar did not know, yet swear he did.

Holding that image of the Wind-made-visible, the Breath-stirred tree, as clearly in his mind as he could, the youth began to trace the lacing of those invisible bonds and try to loosen them. As he did so, that droning hum that had heralded the vision thrummed once more in his ears, growing steadily deeper and stronger, until he knew that he would never again be without its song.

It was done. Gifford let his head fall forward to rest between his hands. As far as those in the Place of Learning could reach, it was done.

"The boy is more than we believed." Yost sounded almost awed. "Irasmus shaped him—or strove to—but the strength of spirit that was his birthright would not let him yield to the Dark." Then, feeling like a tactician shifting his skill at strategy from a field where victory seemed sure to one on which battle was yet to be joined (and where, what was more, the very identity of the enemy was in doubt), the archmage addressed the other matter that had long perplexed the scholars. "Loremaster, perhaps He whom the dark mage strives to summon is not any of Those we guessed; for the Light has revealed that none within the First Hierarchy of the Dark have been on the move."

"Whether that be truth or not," the archivist replied in a voice ragged with fatigue, "our hell-bent one will use the door-opening spell. The burden of battle will rest most with those two of the Old Blood who are his captives and upon her whom the Wind Wakener has chosen. To us is left only the watching. We can interfere no further, for by the Covenant these three are in the right: they strive to defend what is their Spirit-given own."

Overcome by exhaustion, the archivist slumped forward, his head dropping onto the crossed arms which rested on his ever-overflowing desk, and was asleep. His superior, nearly as weary, did not rise from his chair. This would be the reckoning; for the mortals upon whom they had gifted powers now stood at the crossroads of destiny and would have to set foot down either the Path of Light or the Path of Darkness.

However, thought Yost as his own eyelids began to droop, even if the Light prevailed in the coming conflict, the mages themselves would have a heavy price to pay for the lapse in vigilance that had allowed evil to creep in among them. It had fed at their board, lain in their beds, and—worst of all—taken their learning, which was intended to heal, and turned it to the hurt of the world. The old innocence had been violated beyond return or repair, and Valarian, so long wrapped in the soft robe of peace, must now resume its war gear and mount stronger wards and guards. Such suspicion would be torment to live with, a bird of ill omen croaking from the battlements at all hours of the day and night. The archmage breathed a sigh from his heart for all that had been lost as he slipped into sleep.

26

FALICE STOOD BEFORE THE STONE. THE TIME, TO JUDGE BY THE slant of what little sunlight could reach this glade, was at least midday, and she had slept only a short while after her vicarious visit to the tower. Yet she felt neither fatigue nor—oddly enough—either hunger or thirst. It was rather as if, during that brief rest, she had been fed in body and spirit and thereby renewed—no, more than renewed, reborn in some strange way.

As the Forest girl had arisen from her nest at the base of the monolith, she had unconsciously closed her fingers around and brought up a straight stick. This object was not brittle or brown like a dead branch but supple as a living tree limb; and it bore a green cast on its surface. As Falice turned it wonderingly to and fro in the light, she noticed that it seemed to drink in the rays that touched it, becoming a more intense green, like a young plant thirsting for the golden rain of the sun. When an especially bright shaft of sunlight struck the branch, so vivid was the answering flare of color that she seemed to hold a spindle of green fire. The wand was a gift—yes, she was sure of that—but from whom? She might never know, but she was certain of something else: this was a symbol of the power of the Light, as well as a weapon she must be prepared to use against the Dark.

Huge furred forms were squatting on their heels with the patience of those other Forest giants, the trees, about her. The glade could hold only a few of the creatures' massive bodies, and the company stretched back and away behind the curtains of the branches. The human girl was seeing gathered here more Sasqua than she had ever dreamed existed. As she stood, holding the branch radiating its green glow, their clubs struck the ground until the earth throbbed like a mighty heart, and the Wind arose to whistle around the Stone, passing in its path across her shoulders to form an invisible cloak.

Falice could think of but one reason for such an assembly, and she asked the Breath to carry her question to her foster sisters and brothers: "Does the Evil Lord move?"

It was Hansa, appearing almost immediately before her, who answered with Wind touch.

"He moves, yes, because fear drives him. He does not wish to lose all he has gathered, so he will strive to draw more strength to himself—from the lightless land. We are the Forest Born, and it has been given to us to bear the Wind through those walls and wards the Dark One has set. But it is you, my heart's cubling, who are to lead; for you are of the valley, and his barriers were not reared to repel your kind. Following you, we shall feed our gifts to the strengthening of your talent—you, who now hold a thing of power that will open the path for us all.

"And these"—the Forest's daughter waved a generous hand, and small pale faces, belonging to the children who had been rescued, popped up here and there, looking like sudden mushrooms sprouting from the dark loam of Sasqua fur about them—"these little ones shall seek out their kin. They, too, are now the children of the Wind, and they can carry much of its power back to their own people, breathing its life into what talent remains among them."

Thus they went forth, slipping between the trees Sasqua

fashion, in no straight line. It was well into the afternoon
when they reached that torn-up stretch of tillage where the
youngsters had labored to seed the hell-rooted plants. Even
in so short a time, one noisome knob of stalk had appeared,
but this was promptly crushed by club blows.

Out into the dead valley of Styrmir strode Falice. She
felt resistance for a moment, as if she had come up against
an invisible wall. Like a warrior hacking his way through
the press of the enemy, the girl used the branch wand she
carried to slash the air up, down, and across, calling the
Wind with confidence as she did so. From the blighted land
about them came the faintest of answers, which grew in
strength as those from the Forest moved forward.

Now the youngsters, their bodies wreathed with vines
and flowers, raced ahead of her, their goal the distant staked
walls which contained the slave huts. Movement already
showed among the hovels, as the valley folk hastened forth
to meet their children and—a blessing even more unlooked
for—the Wind, and to be refreshed and replenished, even
as the drought-cracked countryside around them swallowed
thirstily what it had so long been denied. Of the gobbes
there was no sign, and the people were taking advantage of
their overseers' absence to arm themselves, albeit crudely,
with the same tools they had been forced to use in labor.

The tower, however, still stood, a black curse shouted
into a sky which was, for the first time in the living memory
of many thereunder, beginning to clear. Around the fortress
wheeled the wizard's pet carrion birds, screeching loudly.
A sudden commotion below made them break their circling
pattern to string out behind the band of demons that now
emerged in tight formation from the gate. The creatures
prodded along two prisoners in their midst, but even from
a distance Falice could see that the pair held their heads
high as they were driven and seemed to wear their chains
as threads to be broken. At the head of this macabre march
rode Irasmus on his rawboned mount, cherishing close to
his breast that second murky globe.

The Forest's fosterling quickened pace, and her furred brothers pounded behind her. She knew what the sorcerer was planning to do now: he intended to spend blood from his captives to tempt the appetite of the Great Dark One he wished to summon. And his choice for that abominable ritual was the very ground of the MidWinter Feasting where, so long ago, those of Firthdun had been slain by their own kin.

None of the troop from the tower either turned head or appeared in any other way to note the coming of the Forest army. Nor did the Wind now blow before Falice and her foster folk but rather ensphered them, bearing them forward within itself like reflections on a bubble and evidently thus offering concealment.

Fogar could hardly hold back, match his pace to that of the Dark Lord's company. No one in his right mind would hasten toward such a dire destiny as would likely be his; yet he found it hard to restrain the excitement rising ever higher within him—the knowledge that they marched toward what might well be the last struggle against Irasmus's evil, at least for himself and his companion in misfortune.

Every so often, the boy glanced quickly toward her, then away again. Her bearing intrigued him, and not merely because it embodied a calm and courageous acceptance of her own fate. Cerlyn held her hands, wrists trailing chains looped inward, cupped at the height of her waist. Just as the mage nursed his seeing-stone against him, she might also be bearing some treasure, but if so, it was not to be seen by him.

Something else was curious, too. Twice, it seemed as if an insect buzzed within his ears and must be sent on its way with a shake of his head; then, for a second or two, a message that had been striving to find its way to him was made nearly plain.

The apprentice found he could also sense, more clearly than ever before, the temper of the gobbes about him. The monsters were not forgetful of their charges—indeed, they crowded in far more tightly than was necessary to make sure of those two—but they were so absorbed in some concern of their own that they were in constant communication among themselves on a level the boy could neither hear nor guess. Their movements were restless, as well. Watching them carefully, he became aware that their attention was fixed upon the Forest, though that realm remained as much an unbroken wall as ever.

The place toward which the sorcerer and his slaves were now bound had been avoided for as long as Fogar could remember, although, in a peculiar way, it was his own because he had been born there. Their destination was that ill-fated site where Irasmus had claimed him, still wet from the womb, as a "demon's son," and where those of his own blood had been overrun by their formerly friendly neighbors in an attack that had equaled the worst frenzy of the gobbes. The youth often wondered what had set the valley folk against their own kind. Had it been more of the master's dealings with the Dark? Whatever the cause, outside the tower, at least, that spot, whose soil had drunk the blood of kin slain by kin, was by far the most evil-soaked area within the boundaries of Styrmir. What better location, Fogar thought grimly, for another gory slaying?

Without warning, that inner excitement he had been feeling came to a head in a real thrust of pain, as though some message which must not go unheeded was about to be delivered. So sudden was its onset that he swayed, then fell, dragging Cerlyn down with him. Seemingly by chance, the girl's hands, which she still held cupped, brushed his cheek, and he jerked his head to one side, in time to see a pale lump in the soil at his feet. Before he hit the ground, he strained with all his might to twist one arm under him and was quickly rewarded by a sharp prod against his skin. His fingers scrabbled vainly for a moment as he felt his hands caught up short by the wrist chain; then he had it—something smooth and solid. Luckily, the object was small enough for him to hide in his palm as their guards, the pattern of their sullen tramping interrupted by the misstep of their captives, stumped over to get them once more on their feet. The head slave driver raised his weapon while he pulled their chains taut once more, but in the end he contented himself with a snarled warning.

Irasmus paid no heed to the slight commotion behind him; his focus was turned deep within his own mind as he studied each phase of the ritual he must perform, and he could not afford to spare attention elsewhere. His sorry horse plodded on, heavy footed, and its rider did not look over his shoulder; yet still Fogar dared not glance down at what he had in his grip.

He did know he held a stone, a smooth rock that issued the same tingling alert to his nerves as had emanated from the last three rocks he had set in the spiral. This—he was so certain that he could have shouted it aloud—was of the Light! What good so small a fragment might do for his cause and Cerlyn's in the battle to be he did not know. Only, as he continued to hold it, he could hear—not with his ears but with a sense for which he had no name—a breeze, such as might ruffle playfully the meadow grass.

By touch alone, not yet able to risk a look at his prize, the boy tried to identify this find. Like the much-larger discs from which he had built the spiral, it was nearly flat, but its outline was oval rather than round. And the longer he continued to clutch it tightly, the stronger grew the sensation of—of life, sparking and sparkling through it. Fogar would not have been surprised had the rock suddenly split open and sent forth a green shoot to reach for the sun. This feeling of imminent rebirth expanded outward from the rock until he perceived that the whole valley was being freed, to cringe no more beneath the iron mace of the Winter King but rise and kiss the flowering scepter of the Spring Queen (would She truly come again?). The youth had, he now knew with a leap of the heart, a weapon. Of its nature and use he was still ignorant, but he would learn—yes, he would learn!

In the irregular circle to which Irasmus led them, what vegetation contrived to grow looked unhealthy; all bushes and plants Fogar could see were wizened and shrunken. Considering that the soil had been watered with blood, the boy thought, it was a wonder that anything natural could rise in such a place. What should have clawed their way up were growths of the Dark.

His examination of what might well be the place of his death, as it was of his birth, was interrupted when the gobbe nearest him seized him roughly by his arm, with a pull that almost overset him once more. The creature then freed his ankles, while another monster, he was pleased to see, did the same for his companion. As the rusty loops fell heavily to the ground, a thought flashed through Fogar's mind. The demons used iron, it was true, forging ugly weapons for themselves and shackles for their slaves; yet what did all the old tales say? Iron and magic did not mix. Even the blades of ancient heroes, though wrought by gods, had been fashioned of other metal.

However, though the dark mage had supplied his soldiery with that metal for daily use, the gobbes now tossed not only their prisoners' chains from them but also cast down their axes and such other weapons as they normally bore. Only Fogar and Cerlyn were left touching iron—their wrist chains, which had not been loosed—as the demons scuttled away.

With ill grace, the creatures heeded the orders that now issued from their master. They chopped and pulled at the plants which had dared to root at the old feasting site until they had cleared a space fully the size of the Dark Lord's tower room. However, the apprentice noted that they kept well to the outside of this "chamber" area, though they sometimes bent their bodies at strange angles to seize upon some vagrant tuft of vegetation that lay within the circle.

Irasmus did not seem over anxious about the quality of their work. He still hunched in his saddle cradling the sphere, head bent, as if he could, in fact, only see clearly if

that seeing-stone was able to pick up what lay around him—
or below.

The afternoon was well gone. The Wind was no longer
urging forward those from the Forest but rather slowing
their advance, as if the time of meeting with the wizard's
army was not yet. However, Falice was now close enough
to clearly see the two captives. The cupping gesture of the
girl's hands kept her watchful—certainly their position signified Cerlyn carried something, yet nothing was visible—to
physical eyes, at any rate. But to the inward sight—? The
Forest's daughter cast forth a questing tendril of Wind—and
then she "saw"!

Even as the mage husbanded his globe, so did the valley
maid hold what was assuredly a goblet, though so faint was
the outline Falice could discern that perhaps not even the
power of the Wind could bring that cup into full visibility.
However, the force that flowed back along her inquiring
thread was a surge of power that held in it a lift of the heart
such as the Stone imparted to her at times. This was not
born of the Breath, but it was of the Light; and each power
was aware of the other.

Something was closed in one of Fogar's hands, as well;
yet his burden must have substance, for his fingers were
curled about it in a screen against prying eyes. Again the
Forest girl probed, but this time she was answered by a
familiar energy song. The boy held a stone, which, small as
it must be, was as awake—and ready for action—as its great
counterpart in the glade. Yet, vital as seemed the strength
of both objects, Falice could not foresee the use of either as
a weapon. To her Wind-enhanced sight, the chalice Cerlyn
cupped showed empty, while the stone Fogar kept was
small enough to be curtained by a closed hand.

However, that ball thing which Irasmus fairly wor-
shipped, lifting it directly before his sharp, sour features,
was now close enough for the Forest maiden to see plainly,
identify—and know for a peril of the most potent. The Wind

tightened about her for an instant, shaping phantom armor against the conflict to come and also sharing this knowledge: the Dark Lord held a key, and he was now seeking a gate to be unlocked.

A sudden movement of the sorcerer's hand sent the gobbes to seize the prisoners and push them forward into the circle. Then the monsters took positions around that ring just within its boundary, facing the two who had been forced on into its very heart.

Falice tried to advance with the Sasqua, but it would seem that the Wind would deny them, for they could not lift feet far enough to move forward. Once more the girl wielded her wand, as she had done to dissolve that other barrier, but the branch merely swung through the air and did not open a way for the Forest force. Yet surely they were here for a reason!

Irasmus now climbed awkwardly down from his saddle and passed into the circle. He began a measured pacing around its circumference, just a little inward from the gobbes, who stirred and showed their fangs. The creatures were afraid—Falice did not need the Wind to translate those grimaces. A thick, musky scent was also rising from them, yet their fear went unnoticed—or ignored—by their master.

Returning at the same stately pace to the center of the ring, the mage now turned to face outward. With one hand gripping the globe, he fronted the deepening dusk beyond. Twilight was falling—or perhaps the forerunner of the Nether Night—but it was gathering fast.

For the first time, a sound arose other than the whispering of the Wind: the sorcerer had commenced a chant. He had also begun to move, swinging the sphere, still tight in his hold, first toward Cerlyn and then to empty space, and repeating the same gestures with Fogar. Again, the Forest girl needed no Breath-borne explanation: this was a preparation for the offering.

Falice signaled with her wand, and this time the Wind did not stay the Forest folk. They marched. The ponderous strides of the Sasqua woke a ringing echo from the earth, yet none of those within the circle appeared to hear their advance, for not one turned to witness their coming.

Fogar had been exerting a steady pull on the end of the chain which bound the wrist of his stone-holding hand. The iron links were loosening—he was certain now. He dared to tug a little more. Yes, the bond no longer bit into his flesh! Carefully, he slid a finger around the metal loops to keep them from falling away. He was tense, his every sense alert. Gone was the time for recalling dream memories and striving to learn from a patchwork pieced of their facts. He now knew what was going to happen, and, if the Light was with him, he held a weapon allied to it.

"Arshabentoth, Mighty One, Eater of Souls—come to your feasting!" Irasmus's voice rang out. Above his head he elevated the globe, no color swirling through it any longer; it held only a solid clot of darkness.

Outside the ring, true night had closed in. Under its cover, those from the Forest posted themselves about the outer rim of the clearing at the ready.

And, though they might not be seen, others were forming another circle beyond the Sasqua. Hope-starved men, women who had lost the gift of tears—all strained forward, reaching, calling without words, not to the evil Irasmus would summon but to its opposite. The people of Styrmir, reclaiming a fraction of their old life were gathering.

Though most of the valley had been blanketed by night, a glow of light remained within the circle. Falice could not be sure of the source of that pale gray luminescence, but the rising stench was enough to let every being present know what must also be approaching—there!

"Arshabentoth!" Irasmus repeated his entreaty. His voice sounded hoarse, as if to speak that Name even a second time put a strain on his throat.

Fogar let the last segment of useless chain clank to the ground, hearing an echo of the sound from where Cerlyn stood. She, too, was free. Perhaps, if the two of them could not fight, they would be able to flee—

But in front of Irasmus, in that wide space that had been left vacant and from whose boundary even the gobbes had been quick to edge away, the pale light brightened. No longer the hue of a haunt's grave robe, it was now shot with fiery lines of red that looped up and over the intended sacrifices and bound them in a cage of force.

And then That Which had been summoned . . . came.

27

"ARSHABENTOTH!"

Irasmus staggered forward a step or so toward the form slowly materializing in the center of the circle. It was—

Cerlyn stared at the thing, unable to summon any words to describe what she saw there (or did she see it? Could a human mind truly perceive such a shape?). Still, ill-defined as it was, it broadcast waves of evil as powerful as if they defied the very Wind at its worst fury.

The monstrosity towered as tall as one of the Forest people now. Its body, however, was still evolving and apparently not to any definite pattern of development, for its appendages changed constantly, one type of supposed hand or foot melting into another, then yet a third. Evidently, either the creature could not control its physical form while entering this new dimension, or else it was, in some fashion, trying on various shapings to test their effects.

This Being was of the Dark; that could not be denied. But there was something else about it which was—*wrong*. Gifford's young scholar refused to allow what she saw before her to distract her from remembering past lessons about such entities. Knowing whom Irasmus planned to invoke when he had amassed sufficient power, her teacher had searched old records and even combed legends for information on the Great Dark One's appearance. The loremaster had not expected such a manifestation as this, and even Cerlyn, after what he had told her, had been awaiting something quite different.

The girl had learned that, in the days before the Covenant, when such Underdwellers had been free to come and go without open challenge, most of the High Ones of the Dark had assumed near-human guise when on her world's level. She recalled all too clearly the descriptions of that dark master, who would answer to the name Irasmus had just spoken—and it bore no likeness to this.

More stirring in that central place, but human movement this time. The Mage, his globe now held before his face as if he used it to aid eyes that had indeed been deprived of a measure of sight, stood very close to his female prisoner— so near that she could see a spasm of feeling akin to pain twist his thin features. He raised the seeing-stone yet closer to his eyes as he called once more: "Arshabentoth!"

"Your longed-for Lord seems to have altered somewhat." The girl was startled to hear those words from Fogar. She had never truly believed that, when the end came, he could stand forth like this and speak almost as dryly as Gifford correcting her for some error of lesson recitation.

Irasmus did not appear to hear him at first, but, a moment later, he spun to face Fogar, the ball whirling in his hands.

"This—slug—is the first dainty I offer you, Mighty One," he said expansively, in a mockery of merchant's patter, "and this is the second." Releasing the globe with one hand, he reached out as if to grasp the chains that no longer bound the girl and so hurl her forward, but his fingers passed through empty space. Cerlyn, sensing that her moment in this conflict was near, raised the all-but-invisible bowl to lip level.

I—am—summoned—

As with the Wind's touch, the Dark Thing's message

entered its listeners' minds more powerfully than words spoken aloud.

"Eater of souls—feast upon this, my bounty!" Irasmus's gesturing hand struck the girl's shoulder, almost sending her off balance and into those appendages the creature seemed to have at last decided would be arms, with huge talons sprouting from what were, by its present whim, hands.

"This one is not He whom you call." Fogar offered an insolent comment again. As he spoke, he slid an arm about Cerlyn's waist, steadying her against him, and she felt a sudden shock of energy at his touch.

The would-be master held the ball so close to his face that it rubbed the tip of his nose. His features twisted in rage—which was fast becoming fear.

The two in the circle were dimly aware that the gobbes on watch were moving in closer to their leader and his prisoners. No longer silent, the horrors were gabbling as if to attract the attention of the newcomer.

"I did not summon you!" The wizard might be amazed at the result of his dabbling in hell spells, but his sinewy body straightened, and he seemed to be getting his fear under control.

Fogar and Cerlyn were not the only ones to feel a sudden nearly irresistible pull—one that actually drew them closer to Irasmus; all others present were similarly drawn. The Forest folk howled and pounded their clubs against the earth, as if by clamor and drumming they could break what seemed to them an unseen bind-vine. Falice described a circle in the air with her wand, pointing its tip directly toward the man who still faced the under one with confidence.

"*Ayyheee!*" Her voice fitted into Wind's, and quickly enough so that the ragged mob of land grubbers, who had begun to run toward their master, slowed at once. Under the calming touch of the Breath, the valley people stood fast again, and their anger raised a barrier to his efforts to draw energy from their awakening talents.

The gibbering of the gobbes fought the song of the Wind until the thing before the sorcerer held up a hand as though hushing—children?

"Irasmus!" It was the Nether Being who spoke—and not merely spoke, but nearly whooped with laughter. "So you still believe you can call up one of the Dread Lords? Stupid, you are, as well as blind! He whom you would have stand before you is no longer concerned with this world. Why should He be, when He holds half a hundred such poor pickings in His hand?" The creature thrust forth a taloned paw in cup shape, then lifted it to its maw, showing how its own master—and, doubtless, itself as well—could scoop up all before it, suck the life juice out of them, and toss their husks away.

"Vastor!" The wizard still stood tall and defiant. "We have dealt together before. Only look upon these I have to offer now"—he indicated his two captives—"are they not far sweeter morsels, truly fit to your tooth?"

The Being snorted, a sound Cerlyn thought was meant either for mirth—or mockery.

"Last time you set my table," it replied, "the 'morsels' were two merchants with no talent—a meager meal, indeed, and hardly an even exchange for what you asked from me." The Thing turned its head a fraction to regard the gobbes. Most of those creatures had fallen to their knees and were holding out misshapen hands toward Vastor. As the great ghoul's eyes swept over them, they raised a long, low wail.

Again the newcomer laughed. "It would seem that my dear offspring find but scant good in your service, little man. And if you cannot persuade my get to serve you as you wish, how dared you believe that one of the Great Dark Lords would come at a crook of your finger?

"You would give me *these*"—a flick of talon acknowledged the offering of Fogar and the girl, who now stood together, his arm still about her waist. "You would need to have one of the Great Ones of the Light pinioned here to bring Him whom you just invoked! Well, perhaps for a brief time, they can serve me—if you *will* bargain again—"

The fearful moaning of the gobbes arose higher; it was plain that such a transaction was one they wanted none of. Their sire made a warning gesture, and their voices fell silent. Now Vastor's burning gaze began to survey his two tidbits more closely, critically.

Cerlyn felt Fogar's inner excitement. What, she wondered, would he do if that Thing, so much greater than the gobbes, *did* accept the proffered sacrifice? Suddenly she mind-spoke, clearly and loudly, at a range only the Wind could give her.

"Our weapons, together—" She shifted position a little. What "weapon" her companion might actually bear she could not guess, but she was aware that he had come here armed in some fashion.

Cerlyn balanced that bowl of green which was and yet was not on her two hands, well within the boy's reach. In turn, his right hand moved, lifting into the weird light of the cup a smoothed round of rock on which blazed a coating of colored sparks. Bringing the stone down swiftly, he thrust one end into her bowl.

At the same instant, in from beyond the circle shot a swift spear of green light, more vivid and visible than the hue of the girl's half-unseen cuplet. Once more Falice cried aloud, *"Ayyheee!"*—

—to have her call met and melt into a similar invocation, then mingle with the sudden Wind that whipped up from that meeting of bowl and rock.

Irasmus backed away, half turning his back upon the monster that had come to his summoning. His eyes were mere slits, as if he must strain to the utmost to see.

"Take them!" he almost shrieked. "Are they not ripe with talent you can savor?"

His servants, meanwhile, had edged away from the two captives, some of them crawling almost on their bellies in an effort to wind around the three and reach the dimensional opening before their fearsome father. One of the demons screeched aloud a command or battle cry in his own tongue and, catching up a length of the prisoners' discarded chains from the ground, swung it like a lash.

Beyond the edge of the unlight cast by the Great Ghoul, and behind the Forest people and Falice, the valley folk, who had once bent beneath other lashes wielded by the gobbes, began to circle. Their wheeling movement drew and strengthened the Wind. However, its full force did not reach those within the circle. What they felt was a breeze, not a blast.

The sorcerer's features were twisted into a mask nearly as monstrous as the face of any of his servant fiends.

He shouted: "Blood and power—blood and power! Yours—for the taking!"

"Mine?" The ghoul's disbelief was evident. "But you did not summon me. You impudently—and imprudently— sought to raise one of the Great Old Ones! If you cannot control your own spells, how can I know this is not a trap?"

Moisture—red moisture—had gathered in the corners of the mage's eyes, and bloody droplets now trickled down his skull-tight cheeks. To all who beheld him, his struggle was plain to read.

"You wish more of my little ones?" Vastor gestured with a casual paw at the groveling gobbes. From close to the ground, where those miniatures of his awesome self were abasing themselves, rose a piteous whine, as the creatures protested his disposal of their persons.

Irasmus held out his hand, on which the black-hearted ball still rested at eye level. That taunting question from a being so much less than the One he had summoned awoke in him a rage great enough that his body shook with the effort to contain its force. His mouth opened, and he stuttered out a Word that rang like a thunderclap through the close air.

Falice was keeping a careful eye upon the demons. Most of them lay still now, their warty hands pressed over their outsized ears. Their sire, however, remained calm enough, viewing the Dark Lord's performance with the air of one enjoying a show in which he had no part. The wizard spluttered and started to shake as he called up from their depths all the power he had gathered and guarded so jealously— the talent he had leached from those he considered helpless.

Now Falice could, with the aid of the Wind, see the two sacrifices standing shoulder to shoulder. Fogar grasped one end of the sparkling stone as he might a dagger; and, though its moon shape was awkward, he had no difficulty in aiming it toward the sorcerer. Cerlyn still held the half-seen cup; but, even as the Forest girl watched, the apprentice's fellow prisoner suddenly clapped her hands together, and the phantom bowl vanished, to be marked now only by specks of green light that floated out over the gobbes.

Whether or not those sparks had any power in themselves, they appeared to move with purpose toward the cowering ghoul brood. Three of the creatures tried to throw themselves backward, and there was a rise and fall of the relentless Sasqua clubs. At this skirmish, the Wind began to whirl in near-shrieking gusts about the circle. Under the goad of that Voice they feared even more than they once had their master's, the demons drew together, crouched, and made a rush at the three standing before their true lord, Vastor. Their crook-fingered claws could close on neither Fogar nor Cerlyn but only slash the air impotently.

Then they aimed for Irasmus. Struggling to see more clearly, he held the globe as a man benighted might raise a lantern; but the first of the rabble he had called out of the Dark years ago were upon him.

Vastor stood watching, fairly licking his thick lips. Irasmus had offered him a banquet, and here was a most appealing appetizer, which his children—who had always had the lamentable habit of playing with food—must not be allowed to damage. The ghoul squalled forth a single word: "Bring!"

And bring the mage they did, "serving" their false master for the last time. The sheer weight of their foul bodies carried him off his feet and bore him to Vastor, who put out a casual hand and clutched him by the throat. The gobbes' sire gave a vigorous shake, and the wizard went limp. The dusky sphere spun out of his hand, but it did not go far; for those light flecks from Cerlyn's cup, aided by a second shaft of green radiance that shot toward the ball from behind the group, caught, held, and crushed that window on hell all in a moment.

Taking advantage of the confusion, the demons had worked their way around behind their true lord and there seemed to regain courage once more. The stench of evil was chokingly heavy.

Still grasping the lax body of Irasmus, which looked somehow shrunken as if much of the life force had gone out of it in its owner's last desperate dredging-up of his power, the Great Ghoul now began a leisurely inspection of Fogar and Cerlyn. He swung his first trophy to and fro as he did idly, as a child might swing a puppet, but his calculating attention was fully focused on the two young people. A purplish tongue emerged from his massive jaws, long as a snake, and its tip wriggled as a true serpent would test for scent.

"This presumptuous one"—the monster again shook the limp body of the sorcerer—"had the truth of the matter, in part. You are a fit sacrifice, though perhaps not strong enough in the power to tempt the Great One this offal wished to woo. No, you are more to my strength—"

Abruptly Vastor's eyes narrowed to slits, and he started in such astonishment that he nearly dropped his trophy. The demon had to shake his head from side to side to make sure he really saw what he thought he did.

Over the cleared earth of the circle came flitting a newcomer, a third human to stand with the other two. As if the Wind itself had borne her here to stand beside Cerlyn and Fogar, the girl moved with feet hardly touching the ground. The perfume of her garment of vines interwoven with flowers cut across the charnel reek of the Nether Ones like a breath of spring. Now Fogar stood flanked by the two maidens, one of the valley and the other of the Forest, and something inside him said that this was right and proper. Kin the trio were, and as kin they should—and would—stand against their common enemy.

Irasmus chose that moment to wriggle feebly; and Vastor, with careless force, threw the mage behind him. The slack-muscled body did not touch the ground but simply vanished, as if it had fallen through a—door?

The ghoul parted his lips hungrily again. "Three of you—more sweets for the feasting." He raised a paw to reach out for Cerlyn, who stood the closest. "Perhaps that sniveling fool was not so wrong, after all. A master is needed here, and—" the thing jerked its head in the direction the sorcerer had vanished "—the gate has been well opened."

The gobbes were on their feet again, massing at their sire's back and screeching a phrase in their own tongue over and over again like a slogan to underscore his speech.

Fogar swung Cerlyn closer and a little behind him. One could not stifle all fear of the Dark—one could only hope to stand firmly against it. His right arm went back and, with all the precision he could manage, he hurled that piece of star-studded stone.

His aim was good—the missile struck against Vastor's wide chest. The rock did no visible damage and left no sign of any wound, but the Dark One gave forth a great roar. However, he did not spring to attack, as Fogar had expected, but rather retreated a step.

Meanwhile, Falice had brought her branch to the fore, and she now sent it whistling through the air in a whiplike slash. Cerlyn, watching that flashing arc of green, sensed that that wand was slicing into strips some unseen ward. However, the onlookers were able to watch the Forest girl's actions for only a moment—because the Wind returned.

Yes, it came—this time not to shield, not to save, but as

a battle weapon, once more well-nigh the Fist of Death it had been before its binding by the Covenant. Odors of rock, tree, earth—all the myriad scents of daily life filled the surrounding air. Hansa's foster daughter dropped her wand at last. She had opened the way, and the Light must meet the Dark, as was always destined to be.

The Dark, in its turn, was rising; coils of oily vapor already hid the gobbes. Vastor had retreated to the place where he had first appeared and was half crouching there, snarling. As the greasy fog wreathed about him, at his feet, where Fogar's stone had come to rest, silver flame sprouted up in licking tongues.

Not even the roar of the Wind could drown out the ghoul's single cry of frustrated evil rage. The creature blazed in the heart of that white light for an instant like a lightning-struck tree, and then he was gone.

The Wind swirled around the circle, and now the three who were cloaked by it could hear sounds like an army of voices raised in a song of triumph—such music as lightened even the true night, which was all that lay now about the beings gathered here. The door Irasmus had opened was closed, locked—perhaps even destroyed forever.

The remnants of the people of Styrmir came forward with dancing steps, weaving in and out among the Forest's folk—neither fear nor awe stayed them in their desire to reach the trio who still stood in the circle's core, now linked by hands as well as minds. For that which the valley dwellers had abandoned in the past had not forsaken them, or at least not those three. Ears never opened to the mysteries and marvels of the Speech of the World knew, in that moment, the Hearing to which their forefathers and mothers had had the right. And yet, though they had advanced so eagerly, they still did not quite dare to approach Fogar, Cerlyn, or Falice.

Were their labors ended? Fogar wondered. But, even as he framed the question, the Wind gave him the answer: a new era and world must be born here, in this very place where he had been ruthlessly seized from his mother's womb.

Then he heard speech which was not borne by the Breath but rather framed by human lips. "I, too, entered life on that night, brother," said Falice, as her hand touched his shoulder. The all-holding memory of the Wind confirmed her words. She was, indeed, blood of his blood; closer kin none could know.

"Lord—" This was another voice, timid but managing to speak. One of the men of Styrmir took a small step forward. "What is your will, you of the Light?"

It was Cerlyn who answered then. "Take again your land, clan kin, for this awakened earth shall bear fruit once more, as of old. Rebuild what was torn and destroyed. Let in the Light, and never fail to remember that you yourselves are the lamps in its shrine; therefore, keep the shrine in repair and the lamps well trimmed. Forgetting was the sin of our people, and we must remain ever alert and ready to maintain and defend what we have come to hold anew."

While the girl from the Valley had been speaking, the daughter of the Forest had drawn away from those other two. The light of the moon, which had just emerged from a shadowing bank of cloud, seemed to wrap itself about her as a cloak, and then the Wind also drew in upon her.

"Sister—" Fogar extended a hand warmly in her direction, but Falice eluded him.

"Kin I am, yet not of the duns," she replied sadly, "for my path is laid by the Wind, and I must follow it." She gazed intently upon him while she spoke, as though she would etch into memory every line of his face, so like hers and yet unlike, shaped by a life she sensed she would never know. She felt the wetness of tears on her own cheeks as she did so, shed for that blood binding her heart had leaped to acknowledge and that, no sooner than found, was about to be lost.

"Walk well with the Wind," she managed to say, speaking now to both her brother and Cerlyn, "for it has broken all barriers this night, and henceforth we shall no longer be Valley and Forest, but one body given life by its Breath."

"Please—stay—" Cerlyn made the last plea. But Falice dared not allow herself another moment in this place, lest her strength waver as she went forth to the fate decreed for her by the Great Powers.

Then, as she had come to join them, borne by the Wind and bearing the power of her talent, so did she leave. Even the kin in fur, whom she had led, could only sense the swiftness of her passing. The wand had fallen from her grasp, for she suspected—her belief growing stronger every moment— what destiny awaited her; and that being so, she needed no weapon beyond her own self. What work was set for her, she was not yet sure, though perhaps her future would prove as demanding as this confrontation had been.

Falice did not even appear to be running any longer— the Wind bore her, softly cradled, at a speed that outran any living thing from either Valley or Forest. The moonlight showed her the Green Realm ahead, and its trees parted in answer to the force that carried her.

Then a tall white glow rose before her: the Stone. Those sparks that played across its surface grew larger as the girl entered the glade; and now they whirled more riotously than she had ever seen them move, in a glory of light that outshone even the moon above.

She had been gently lowered to stand just in front of the glittering pillar, facing the window hole. Like the rest of the monolith, that opening was brightly lit, yet it was not now, she felt, for her use as a viewing place. The light that filled it was green, and it spilled forth and ran down over the flashing rock face to form what was at first the mere outline of a figure and then the full impression of a woman's form.

Out from the surface that Being stepped. Her features were hidden, as always, by a veil of mist, but Her arms were opened wide. Even as Falice had, years before, embraced the Stone itself, so was she wafted forward into that hold which matched body to body. The two made one melted, melded, and reformed. Once more the Green Lady stood in the Forest; now, however, She wore a face.

Falice-Theeossa was filled with such power and purpose as she had not known even when she entered the battle with Vastor. Her arms were still outheld to enring the Forest Guardian, but that One had chosen. The girl's hands dropped down to smooth her slender body, and she saw that the soft greenish radiance of the Ever-Living seemed to cling to her more closely than moss could clothe the trunk of a tree.

So—this was to be her path. She who had been born and fostered here was truly of the Forest now, and her future would be to serve, watch, and ward, upheld by a Spirit which seemed too potent to be housed in any frail mortal form. But she was yet, in a way, human, and thus kin to those of the dun of Firth she had never known. So the Power of the Forest was wedded to that of the valley, and all the land would be one. Still a single tear was wet on her cheek, for with any gain, no matter how great, there was always a matching loss; and she now could never again be the innocent maid who had run free through this realm, for she had bound to it forever.

The mages in the Place of Learning had assembled before the seeing panel.

"They are more than we thought." Gifford broke the silence first.

"They are the roots from which new growth will rise," said one of the women.

"The honors of battle are theirs," commented Fanquer, with the envy of an old soldier for a rousing conflict missed. "We did little enough."

"In the sense of giving aid, perhaps not." Yost sounded soul weary, as if wrung dry of all energy. "But it was *we* who loosed the Shadow. So, brothers and sisters, look well into your hearts, for we, too, must guard against complacency and overmuch trust. There will be a new Covenant—"

Then the archmage's speech was drowned out by another Voice, raised in a song at once otherworldly and thoroughly earthly. Those assembled felt the Wind enter into the age-old hall, touching the hangings and setting each a-quiver as it passed. Once more the scholars listened to the near-forgotten voices of life, hailing the return of the Light and the hearing that bound all things together.

Yost raised his hand as if in salute. "So be it," he said, and his tone now held peace, "so be it. We, too, have slept—but at last we wake."

In Styrmir, the moonlight continued, bright almost as the coming dawn of a new day. Only Irasmus's tower stained that brilliance with darkness, rising like a finger of menace pointing skyward.

Even as the Sasqua silently withdrew to the Forest and Her who waited for them there, so the people of the valley followed Fogar and Cerlyn back into their long-barren heartland.

As the group neared the sorcerer's stronghold, the Wind wrapped itself about that fortress and, like a giant hand, closed into a fist to crush what it held. The outline of the tower blurred; stones thundered to the ground, falling with enough force to bring those who watched to their knees.

Only Fogar and Cerlyn remained standing, the two steadying each other with their arms, and looked their last upon the site of their imprisonment—and meeting. As the echoes of that mighty crash died away, they turned to face their own path: the place where Firthdun had once stood. After a little while, the rest of the people rose, to take likewise the old, remembered roads through the land where they would root again.